Red Hot

Also by Dana Dratch

Confessions of a Red Herring

Seeing Red

Red Hot

DANA DRATCH

KENSINGTON BOOKS
www.kensingtonbooks.com

KENSINGTON BOOKS are published by

Kensington Publishing Corp.
119 West 40th Street
New York, NY 10018

All Kensington titles, imprints, and distributed lines are available at special quantity discounts for bulk purchases for sales promotion, premiums, fund-raising, educational, or institutional use.

Special book excerpts or customized printings can also be created to fit specific needs. For details, write or phone the office of the Kensington Sales Manager: Attn.: Sales Department. Kensington Publishing Corp., 119 West 40th Street, New York, NY 10018. Phone: 1-800-221-2647.

Kensington and the K logo Reg. U.S. Pat. & TM Off.

First Printing: June 2020
ISBN-13: 978-1-4967-1660-6
ISBN-10: 1-4967-1660-4

ISBN-13: 978-1-4967-1661-3 (ebook)
ISBN-10: 1-4967-1661-2 (ebook)

10 9 8 7 6 5 4 3 2 1

For my family

CHAPTER 1

Like most of the weirdness in my life, the entire adventure started with an innocent phone call.

Or not so innocent, as the case may be.

"Cissy!" My sister Annie's voice exulted through the speaker. "I'm so glad I caught you. I need a teensy little favor."

For anyone who doesn't know it, my sister is Anastasia Vlodnachek. *The* Anastasia Vlodnachek. Or, as the world, the gossip columns, and *People* magazine have dubbed her, "the supermodel Anastasia."

This girl wants for nothing. Looks, brains, charm, money, sense of humor—she's got it all. Along with a heart the size of the Lincoln Memorial.

She's exactly what I want to be if I ever grow up: gorgeous, graceful, and cool. Like our mother without the bitter aftertaste.

So when it comes to sisterly favors, Annie is usually on the granting end. Which is why I smelled a rat.

"What have you heard?" I blurted.

"No idea what you're talking about. But I'm hoping you can help me with something. A little project."

I looked over at the cold coffee by my laptop and realized it was the only thing I'd consumed today.

I squinted at the screen. Three thirty-five. How did that even happen?

The trifecta was when I realized I was still wearing the pink T-shirt and striped pajama bottoms I'd slept in. I'd been so intent on making the deadline for my latest freelance story, that's all I'd done.

My younger brother, Nick, had taken off before daybreak to run deliveries to a couple of clients in Annapolis—with our pup, Lucy, riding shotgun. After that, he'd dropped her off for a doggie playdate down the block and was spending the rest of the day baking at the bed-and-breakfast across the street.

We Vlodnacheks have never been afraid of hard work. Or long hours.

And thanks to plenty of both, plus an innate talent for schmoozing clients, Nick's fledgling bakery was growing like crazy. Even after one of his competitors tried to scuttle it by bribing a crooked health inspector to shut down his (admittedly unlicensed) kitchen. Which was actually in my house.

Did I mention Nick was living with me temporarily? Long story.

The short version: Cheating partner in his first business (an Arizona emu farm). Followed by a quickie trip to Vegas. Followed by an even quicker engagement, breakup, and broken heart.

But Nick doesn't stay down for long. His new venture—called Baba's Bakery, after our Russian grandmother—was doing great. As was his social life. And thanks to our British ex-pat neighbor Ian Sterling, who runs a bed-and-breakfast across the street—and relies on Nick's treats for teas, desserts, and events—my brother's business has a temporary new home in a very proper, very legal English kitchen.

At least, until he gets mine up to code. A project that would be starting any day now, judging by the yards of painter's tape and multiple visits by dueling contractors. The only detail they all agreed on was the time frame. Since Nick was just making a few small changes to add some equipment, we were looking at a week, tops.

But with Nick and Lucy out of the house today, I'd had no real incentive to change out of my pajamas. So apparently I hadn't.

"What's the favor?" I asked Annie, opting for the "rip the Band-Aid off" approach.

"I need an escort."

"I'm the wrong gender, and I look lousy in a tux. But Nick might be available. Angelina Jolie took her brother to the Oscars."

"She also kissed him on the mouth, and people are still talking about it. Besides, it's not for an event. It's for a trip. I have to fly to Miami. You remember my South Beach condo?"

Boy, did I! My sister has a string of homes across the globe. But the Miami penthouse is my all-time favorite. Not only does it look—big surprise—like something out of a magazine, but the neighborhood is Party Central.

There were four of us kids—now adults—scattered to the winds.

My uber-successful older brother Peter was a lawyer and a partner in a Manhattan firm—and married to my glamorous sister-in-law, Zara. Annie, thanks to her own modeling agency and some hefty endorsement deals, was a citizen of the world with a collection of pricy homes in even pricier locales. Our youngest brother, Nick, was even more footloose. He'd dropped out of college and, most recently, lived on a ranch in Arizona. But a few months ago, he'd migrated back to our home turf of metro D.C. and was bunking with me temporarily.

Our mother, she of the tart tongue and designer threads, resided in a tony part of the District. And Baba, our dad's mom, still lived in the same small, immaculate Baltimore apartment where he'd grown up.

Still, when the need arose—or especially a food-centric holiday—somehow we always found enough room under one roof to coexist almost peacefully. For twenty-four hours, at least.

"Well, the homeowners association board's scheduled some sort of super-secret emergency election," Annie explained. "I was hoping you might come with."

"Can't you vote by mail? Like with stocks?"

"Normally, that's exactly what I'd do. But there's something weird about this. The annual election's supposed to be in December. Because that's when more of us are actually there. Now they've suddenly scheduled a special election in July with practically zero notice. Who does that? This time of year, a lot of the residents are away. And I can't get a straight answer from anyone on why they need this vote."

"You think something's fishy?" I asked, suddenly curious.

"It's probably nothing," my sister admitted, sighing. "But if you came along, it would at least be fun. Road trip!"

Annie flew back and forth to Miami all the time. Now the owner of her own mega-successful modeling firm, she did a lot of business there. Hence the condo. And with brains to spare, she was more than capable of sorting the election mystery mishigas on her own. So why the sudden invite?

"What did Nick tell you?" I asked, taking a swig of my now tepid coffee.

"The word 'workaholic' may have been mentioned."

From the outside, it looked like I'd planted roots, too. I'd been a reporter for the *Washington Tribune*, one of the area's two daily newspapers, for more than a decade. And two years ago, I'd purchased my snug little home—a tiny bungalow in the Northern Virginia bedroom community of Fordham. Close enough to the Beltway to be convenient. Far enough out that I could almost afford it.

But Nick wasn't the only one of us still searching for a niche. After ten happy years as a reporter, I'd allowed myself to be lured away to an executive spot with a public relations firm, enticed by the prospect of a salary that I could actually live on.

That had lasted all of three months. One of my two bosses had been a megalomaniac who drank too much, used people, and had his hand in the till. The other one went to prison.

As career moves go, not my best decision.

So now I was freelancing. I loved setting my own hours and choosing my own assignments. But I missed perks like health insurance, a retirement plan, and a steady income.

My best friend, and former editor at the *Tribune*, Trip Cabot, regularly encouraged me to come back to the newsroom. And there'd been several offers.

But I was enjoying my new-found freedom. And skinny bank balance or not, I wasn't all that anxious to give it up.

"Hey, it's not easy maintaining a steady income when you're freelancing," I said to Annie.

"Exactly," she replied. "But 'freelance' means you can literally work from anywhere. From what I'm hearing, you're long overdue for a little fun. And so am I. So trade the home office for a poolside chaise with a view of the beach. Just for a week. Two weeks, tops. You won't hate it, I promise. Besides, I wasn't kidding about the election. I really could use your help. Something's up. And before I vote one way or the other, I'd like to know what's going on."

I couldn't. Not really. Not if I wanted to keep my name in front of editors, keep landing assignments, and keep my bills paid. But I was sorely tempted.

I glanced toward my kitchen—and the virtual rainbow of contrasting tape from Nick's competing contractors. In the home renovation shows, this was about the time the homeowners were gently bundled off to a hotel—to reappear only for the stunning reveal. When the place had been carefully cleaned and all renovation glitches were firmly in the rearview mirror.

Which, right now, seemed like a really good idea.

"OK, you've got yourself a houseguest."

Six little words. Who knew they'd spark so much trouble?

CHAPTER 2

By the time Nick and Lucy rolled in that evening, I'd showered, changed, and was packing a suitcase. Or, more accurately, a battered duffel bag.

What can I say? The idea of a week of fun and sun had inspired me.

"Can I take this to mean you said yes?" Nick inquired, grinning as he lounged against the bedroom doorframe.

"Annie needs my help," I said, as I tried to decide between two white T-shirts. Opting for expediency, I shoved them both into the bag. "And far be it from me to say no to a family member in need."

"Good to know. Because I have a little news. And I need a favor."

"Hey, the more the merrier. At this point, I don't care if I have to sleep on an air mattress on the floor. But you know Annie—I'm sure she's got room for all of us. How soon can you get packed?"

"Not that. I mean the kitchen. Your kitchen. I finally hired a guy, and he can start tomorrow."

"Nick! That's great! Congratulations!"

"Not a huge deal. All I had to do was talk with every

renovator in town and throw wads of money at the one I wanted. Big honking fistfuls."

"No lie." I'd seen the estimates. He wasn't exaggerating. "So what's the favor?"

"Well, my guy is gonna have the whole thing done inside a week. But while he's working, that kitchen's pretty much a no-fly zone. And it's kind of Lucy's main hangout spot."

Lucy may have started life as a stray in the back alleys of Las Vegas, but she'd quickly acclimated to the comforts of suburban life. And my sunny, yellow kitchen was her favorite room in the house.

Mine too, if I'm honest.

Every morning, Lucy skipped out the back door, down the steps, and into her private backyard to romp in the grass, chase butterflies, and sniff flowers. Her water bowl lived just under the kitchen table. When we ate there—which was just about all the time—she shared the food and the hospitality from her favorite spot on the floor (within reach of whoever might slip her a few extra nibbles). And she loved nestling under the table when Nick was baking—a definite no-no, according to our new mandate from the county health department.

I'd realized early on that Nick's construction plans were going to upend our lives for a few days. But, for some reason, I'd never considered the impact on Lucy.

I glanced up. The pup was stretched out, sphinx-like, at my brother's feet, sporting a pair of sunglasses.

"Admit it, she belongs in Miami," he said.

"Are those for real?"

"Doggles. The latest in canine eye protection. Sun, sand, or surf, the little dog is ready to party, South Beach style."

"She's better prepared than I am. Are you sure you can manage without her for a week?"

"Nope," he said, stroking her velvety russet head, as

Lucy flipped over exposing a round, white tummy. "But it's gonna be too dangerous for her here. Between the dust and the noise and the power tools and the open doors."

"Your basic doggie danger zone."

"Times ten. And I can't take her to Ian's. I spend all my time in the kitchen, and she's not allowed in there. Besides, the guy is already loaning me work space."

I mentally bit my tongue. Ian Sterling was not my favorite person at the moment. I loved that he was helping Nick. But I still didn't trust him.

Ian was magnetic, I'll give him that. Tall and athletic, with dark hair, blue eyes that changed color with his mood, and the quiet self-assurance of someone who knew how to handle almost any situation. I admit the man made my heart beat a little faster.

And that was before we shared an electric kiss during a lightning storm.

That was also before I found a listening device in my home phone. And learned that Ian Sterling had planted it. I understood his reasons. But I'd also resolved to keep my distance.

Once burned.

"I thought about boarding her," Nick continued. "But she's never been away from home that long, and I think she'd be scared. Or feel like we'd abandoned her. She's really still a puppy. Dr. Scott says she's not even fully grown yet."

"Look, no sweat. Annie loves her. I love her. And you're right—she's going to have a blast in Miami."

Besides, Lucy adored car rides. Road-tripping with her would be a breeze. The pup's standard auto trip agenda: Spend the first five minutes sniffing the back seat for stray french fries, spend the next five minutes staring out the window, then curl into a ball and sleep for the rest of the trip.

I should be so lucky.

"I've already packed a bag with a few of her favorite toys, a spare leash, and some food," Nick said. "And her vitamins. And I threw in a set of booties."

"Booties?" I was hoping the word meant something different for dogs. I couldn't see Lucy prancing around in high-heeled ankle boots. Canine fashionista or not.

"It's Florida in July," he said. "You can fry eggs on the sidewalk. And paw pads are sensitive. These things are like heavy socks with traction. If you lose one or she chews it, you can get replacements at PetGo. But they're not cheap."

"What about you? How are you going to make do without a kitchen for a week?"

"Between fast food, takeout, and delivery pizza, I'll be fine. Besides, I can always fire up the grill. Or use Ian's stove if I get desperate. Which I won't. The last thing I want to do after a long day in a hot kitchen is cook."

I felt the same way every night. And I didn't even work in a kitchen.

"Then it's official," I said, bending to pat Lucy's downy flank, as she leaned in and licked my knees. "The Vlodnachek girls are going to Miami!"

CHAPTER 3

"Uh, I think you're going in the wrong direction," I said to the guy who was driving our ride-share. Or, more accurately, to the back of his head.

"No, ma'am, this is the right way to the address they gave me. Shortest route, too. Ain't gonna carry you to the Washington Monument and back. Honest. And that's not just because you're a local."

When he pulled into the entrance to a small private airport, I knew something wasn't right.

"We're supposed to be meeting my sister at a rental car counter at Reagan National," I said, noticing that stress had sent my voice up half an octave. "She's flying in and getting a car to drive us to Miami."

No use explaining that we couldn't use my car unless my supermodel sister wanted to be ferried around town in an ancient station wagon with a couple of nasty expletives carved into the paint, courtesy of a psycho-killer I helped catch. And once worked for.

Long story.

"Lady, this is the address they gave me. Really."

"But it's the wrong airport. She's gonna be at the Hertz counter. And we're, well, wherever this is."

I looked past the driver out the windshield to see a sleek private jet behind an even sleeker blonde. And she was waving at us.

Annie!

The driver pulled up parallel to the jet as I rolled down the back window. Lucy, napping on the seat beside me, raised a drowsy head.

"Change of plans," my sister said. "We're hitching a ride."

"You do realize that when most people say 'hitching a ride,' they mean standing on the side of a highway with their thumbs out?"

"And that's exactly how we'll tell the story to Mom," Annie said, grinning, as she opened the back door. Lucy hopped over me and out onto the tarmac.

"Come on," she said, grabbing the pup's leash. "I want you to meet Esteban. This is his jet."

I climbed out of the car and turned to reach for my duffel and Lucy's two neat bags. Because, while she still may be a puppy according to my brother, the little dog doesn't travel light.

"Don't worry about that," the driver called, opening the other back door. "I got these. All part of the service."

"Thank you," I said, digging through my purse for cash.

"That's taken care of too," he said softly. "Even the tip. And your friend's a good tipper," he added, nodding at Annie, who was chatting animatedly with a tall, good-looking guy, as Lucy sniffed his shoes.

"She's my sister," I said, both proud and dumbfounded.

"Wow, you sure don't look alike." If I had a dollar for every time I'd heard that, I could buy Esteban's jet.

"Really?" I said. "Most people can't tell us apart."

Chapter 4

Turns out flying in a private jet is pretty much like flying commercial. Except instead of charging five dollars for a soda, a nice lady handed me a glass of champagne. For free. In a real glass.

And rather than my usual straightjacket-sized seat that smelled vaguely of air freshener and old socks, I had an entire cushy mini-sofa. No screaming babies, chair-kicking tweens or seatmates exercising their right to bare hairy toe knuckles.

So basically nothing like commercial.

Once we were in the air, Esteban busied himself on his laptop. If he'd had a phone on his shoulder, he would have looked right at home in any newsroom.

"New boyfriend?" I mouthed silently to Annie.

She shook her bouncy blond mane.

"So tell me about this condo thing," I said, as she settled in next to me on the sofa. "What's going on?"

"Super weird. We haven't had a homeowners' association for very long. Before that, the builder and their management company took care of everything. And they were wonderful. But then the residents started making a fuss about costs getting out of hand and how they wanted more control and that we needed a homeowners' association. The next thing you know, we had one. And Leslie McQueen—she's a star in the local real estate community—became the interim president. Between you and me, I think she was the one behind the push for an association in the first place. She really wanted the president's job. Plus, I think the residents figured that since she works in real estate, she'd have the know-how."

It was a familiar story. And HOAs could be a minefield, at least in some areas. You paid a set fee every month for the assurance that someone would step in if a neighbor painted their house bubblegum pink, let the grass get too high, or opened a neighborhood bar in their garage.

For my money, I figured the world had bigger problems.

"So who called the special election?" I asked, as Janet, our flight attendant, refilled our glasses.

Beside me, Lucy, worn out from sniffing every inch of the jet (and finding nary a french fry), was curled into a ball, dozing peacefully.

"She's adorable," Janet said, admiring our snoozing stowaway. "Let me know if she needs anything."

"Thank you!" Annie and I said in unison.

We clinked glasses.

"No one knows," Annie said, after Janet headed back to the galley. "Or if they do, they're not telling. That's what's so weird."

"So who's running for election?" I asked.

"No one I've ever heard of. No one that anyone's ever heard of, as far as I can tell. I have the list of names on the ballot, and I'll show it to you when we get to the condo. But honestly, Leslie's name was the only one I even recognized."

"Could Leslie McQueen have done it? Called for the election, I mean?"

"Why would she want to? Leslie's already president. She'd keep the position automatically until January if it wasn't for the special election. And from what I've seen, she doesn't want to give up that title anytime soon."

"OK, it sounds like there's a story here," I said, taking a sip from my glass.

I looked out the little window and saw big, puffy clouds off in the distance. It seemed surreal that I was even here. By all rights, I should be at my own laptop in my dining-room-turned-home-office. Finishing stories, cultivating sources, and pitching editors for assignments. Instead, I was sipping bubbly on a private jet sailing through the clouds.

I wondered what my kitchen looked like right about now. I pictured a muscled goon-squad armed with sledge-hammers—and took a longer swig from the glass.

Annie paused, thinking. "I don't want to prejudice you one way or the other," she said finally. "I need someone to look at this with unbiased eyes."

"But?" I asked teasingly.

"The place hasn't been the same since the HOA took over. And I think they're cutting some corners. At least, that's what I hear. They hired a management company for the day-to-day stuff. It's not like Leslie's calling carpenters and plumbers and locksmiths herself. But I get the feeling that she's super involved."

"Micromanaging?"

"It's just the sense I got from a couple of the neighbors I talked with the last time I was there. And that was about a month ago."

"What did they say exactly?"

"Well, Mrs. Plunkett downstairs? She needed her locks changed. She found a couple of things missing after the last time her pet sitter left. Two leftover bottles of prescription meds and some cash. It wasn't much. I think she was more skeeved out than anything else. But after two weeks of phoning every other day, still nothing. And she was afraid to leave home for fear the guy would come back for more. So she finally called a locksmith herself. And paid for it herself. The next day, the HOA cited her for 'unauthorized modifications.' They fined that poor woman five hundred dollars and forced her to pay to change the locks a second time with an approved vendor. When Mrs. Plunkett tried to appeal to the board, Leslie called her personally and threatened to hit her with more fines, take her to collections, and ruin her credit if she didn't pay up immediately."

"That's awful," I said.

"That's Leslie McQueen. But it gets better. When a new resident, Josh Roundtree, wanted his big-screen TV mounted on the wall? The crew showed up in less than twenty-four hours. Didn't charge him a penny."

"Let me guess. Josh is friends with Leslie?"

"I think she'd like to be." Lowering her voice to just above a whisper, she added, "Josh is a hunk-and-a-half. But Leslie's also the agent who sold him his unit."

"As president of the HOA, does Leslie get a salary?" I asked, probing the old "follow the money" angle.

"Not a cent," Annie said, shaking her head for emphasis. "The position is strictly voluntary. And if you do it right, it's at least a part-time job."

"See, that's the bit I don't get. Who takes on a second job that doesn't pay a dime?"

Says the girl who was working a first job that didn't pay all that much either.

Annie giggled.

"What?" I asked.

"We chatted about that once," my sister said. "When they were first forming the HOA, Leslie told me she didn't want the position. But they simply needed someone with her organizational skills. And she just didn't feel right saying no. She felt it was her civic duty."

"And . . ."

"Well, it was a load of hogwash, obviously. I knew she was up to something. I just didn't know what. I still don't. And the election's only a week away."

"Don't worry," I said, poking her arm like I did when we were kids. "Between the two of us, we'll nose around and figure out what's really going on."

Chapter 5

Standing in front of Annie's condo building, with my beat-up duffel bag slung over one shoulder and Lucy's leash in my other hand, I felt like a country rube visiting the big city. I couldn't help looking up. The building, known simply as Oceanside, did not disappoint.

Built only a few years ago in the Art Deco style, the whitewashed tower stretched into the cerulean sky.

"See that?" I said to Lucy, pointing. "We're going to live here this week. What do you think of that?"

She looked dubious. And I didn't blame her.

As residents bustled in and out, sporting a variety of attire from Brooks Brothers to Tommy Bahama, I was beginning to feel like the brown shoe at a black-tie ball. Even the seventy-plus retiree who toddled in wearing white knee socks with even whiter knees looked like he'd dropped a mint on his electric-green Hawaiian shirt/Bermuda shorts/straw hat combo.

"Let's get settled in; then we can regroup," Annie said. "I'm thinking first the pool, then lunch. What do you say?"

"Sounds good to me," I said.

"Oh, and here's your key," my sister said, handing me a

black fob with a key card and a golden key dangling from the ring. "The key is for our place. The fob gets you into everything in the building—the pool, the workout room, the sun decks—you name it. And I have an account for resident services, like dry cleaning, laundry, the in-house cafés and the spa, so just swipe the card and they'll put everything on my tab. The theme for this trip is 'rest and recharge.' "

Did I say she was great, or what?

Right after I pulled on my swimsuit, my cell phone rang. Nick.

"How's the little dog? She's not getting car sick, is she?"

"I'm fine, thanks. How are you?"

"Sorry, it's been one of those days. I don't have long to talk. I've got a batch of custard tarts in the oven. And they go from totally liquid to crispy critters in no time flat."

"Lucy's fine. We're already here. Some friend of Annie's let us hitch a ride on his jet. So you're gonna have to make a lot more tarts if you want to maintain the little dog's current standard of living."

I looked up and saw Lucy staring out the glass doors to the terrace. Head cocked to one side, she appeared perplexed.

Earlier, Annie had opened the doors, picked up her lead, and invited her gently out onto the balcony. But Lucy wasn't having it. She had thrown back her head and howled until my sister finally gave up and closed the doors.

The penthouse was ten stories up, and I was beginning to suspect Lucy was not fond of heights.

"Damn, you girls are living large," Nick said. "Oh, I don't want to panic you or anything, but you might have an electrical problem."

"What?!"

"The contractor found some kind of glitch when he came over to prep the site this morning. It looks like the wiring's outdated, and he's not sure it's gonna be able to handle the load from the new appliances."

"That's not possible!" I screeched. I looked out the glass doors at the tranquil blue ocean and took a slow, deep breath.

"I had the wiring checked before I bought the house two years ago," I continued, trying to channel my sister's natural calm. "Trust me, it's totally up-to-date. The couple who sold me the place had it professionally rewired. Plus we have the capacity to add more appliances. And I've got the stack of paperwork to prove it."

I did, too. Faced with the prospect of making the biggest purchase of my life, I'd hired an inspector who'd literally crawled over every inch of the house. And I'd followed him through most of it, taking notes. The only bit I skipped: the roof.

Lucy's not the only one in the family who gets queasy around heights.

"Well, I hope you're right because the alternative sounds kinda pricy," Nick said. "And messy. Anyway, we don't have to worry about it yet. Right now, he's only running some tests. Depending on what he finds, that could set us back a day or two. I just wanted to give you a heads-up."

I heard a buzzer going off in the background.

"OK, that's the oven timer. Got to go now. Time and tarts wait for no man." And with that, he hung up.

CHAPTER 6

The funny thing about relaxing on vacation: It's not as easy as it looks.

I'd done laps in the pool, drained a can of soda, and read the same two pages in my book three times.

I looked at my watch: We'd only been at the pool twenty minutes.

My mind kept wandering back to my comfortable—though possibly outdated and dangerous—kitchen. What if the place couldn't be brought up to code? What if Nick's new business crashed and burned because of me? Heck, what if my faulty wiring burned down the whole neighborhood?

I glanced over at Annie, reclining serenely in a lounge chair with a fashion magazine. Under her big fuchsia sun hat, her shiny hair spread out like a fan, she didn't even appear to be sweating.

What they don't tell you about south Florida: In July, the air feels like the inside of a blast furnace. That was one of the reasons we'd opted to leave Lucy in the cool comfort of the air-conditioned penthouse. And I'd only checked the locks on that patio door three times, thank you very much.

"I'm going to get another Coke," I said to Annie, tugging on the oversized T-shirt I'd brought as a cover-up. "Do you want anything?"

"Ooh, I'll take a Sprite," she said, grinning. "And a bag of those barbecue potato chips. I know it's a lame excuse, but in this heat, you have to replace salt. I'm thinking we can grab a light lunch here. Then, for dinner we can hit that seafood shack on the beach I told you about. Total hole-in-the-wall, but the best fried fish you've ever tasted. And I honestly have dreams about their hushpuppies."

Oceanside's upscale dining area was just off the pool. But over to one side, they also had a lounge-slash-snack bar. From sodas and umbrella drinks to snack food to more upscale fare, if you resided at Oceanside, it was yours for the asking.

If I lived here, I'd never use the kitchen again. Of course, given the news Nick had shared, I might not anyway.

As I walked toward the restaurant, I caught motion out of the corner of my eye. I turned just in time to see the back of a woman exiting the pool area. Billowing white pool cover-up, deep tan, and sky-high espadrilles.

She reminded me of someone. Odd.

"Could I have a Coke, a Sprite, and two bags of barbecue chips?" I asked the bartender.

Next to me at the bar, the guy with the electric-green shirt was swapping stories with a pal.

"I'm tellin' ya, Ernie, it's weird," he said. "The stuff was moved. He even reported it to the cops. They took a statement and everything."

My ears perked up. Another break-in?

"Nah, I think he just had a visit from his old buddy Jack Daniel's," his friend said, using the universal hand gesture for downing a shot. "Few of those, and I'm convinced my old lady is Ann-Margret."

"Well, she does have some nice gams," the first one admitted.

"Did you say there was a break-in?" I asked.

"Alleged break in," Ernie announced. "I'm Ernie Doyle. This is Stan Cohen."

"I'm Alex Vlodnachek. I'm here for the week with my sister, Annie."

"Ooooh, the penthouse," Stan said. "Very nice."

"Have you seen the sister?" Ernie said. "She's very nice, too." He gave me an avuncular wink.

"Nothing to worry about—we're not having a crime wave," he continued, palming a handful of roasted peanuts from the bowl between them. "Just a neighbor of ours might have had a little too much of the old firewater, if you know what I mean."

"Hey, Larry swears . . ." Stan started.

Ernie waved a plump paw dismissively and popped a peanut into his mouth. "The guy's fresh off a divorce. And half the time I run into him, he smells like a distillery."

"So what's his story?" I said, pulling up a bar stool next to Stan.

"Guy's name is Larry," Stan said. "He lives on two."

"One of the cheaper units," Ernie said. "Just a one bedroom. And the view is crap. Too low to see anything, and it faces the street."

"Hey, I live on two and I can see plenty," Stan said. "Plus, if there's a fire, I can jump."

"If you jumped the curb in a golf cart, you'd break a hip," Ernie said.

"The break-in?" I prompted.

"That's the weird part," Stan continued. "Yesterday evening, I come home, and the cops are buzzing around Larry's apartment. Door's wide-open, and I can see one of 'em's taking a statement from him. Another one is prowling the halls. Wants to know if I've seen anything."

"Not with those cataracts," Ernie jibed.

"Hey, my vision's twenty-twenty—and so's my hearing," Stan countered. "Anyway, I'd been up in Lauderdale visiting a lady friend. So naturally, I wanna know what happened. You know, for security and all."

"Naturally," I agreed.

"And the cop says Larry swears somebody broke in. He calls up and reports it. And the cops come out. In the meantime, Larry's had a look around—you know, to give 'em a list of what's missing. But that's the really weird part."

"What is?" I asked.

"Nothing was missing. They just shuffled stuff around."

"Bull," Ernie stated flatly, scarfing another peanut.

"What if there really was something missing?" Stan theorized. "Something he didn't want to report."

"Only thing missing from that home is booze. And you don't need Nero Wolfe to figure out where it went."

"Like what?" I asked Stan, ignoring his friend.

"I don't know. An unlicensed gun. Drugs. Some of that really nasty porno. Viagra."

"Little blue pills are legal, Stan," Ernie said, dropping another peanut into his mouth and washing it down with a sip of amber liquid from his highball glass.

"Yeah, but a young guy like Larry wouldn't want to admit he needs 'em," Stan countered.

"Maybe the burglar got spooked and left before taking anything," I said.

"That too," Stan said, nodding.

"Any other break-ins recently?" I asked, remembering Annie's story about Mrs. Plunkett. From what she'd said, that would have been at least six weeks ago.

"Well, now that you mention it, there was that business with Ethel," Ernie said. "But she was pretty sure it was that kid she had walking her dog."

"Made off with two different kinds of pain pills and fifty bucks in cash," Stan said, slapping the bar. "But no sign of a break-in. That's how come she figured it was probably the kid. He had a key."

"So in one case, there's evidence of an actual break-in, but nothing's missing," I said. "And in another, money and meds are gone, but no break-in."

Stan nodded vigorously.

"Do the police think the two incidents are related?" I asked, as the bartender put two cans of soda and two bags of chips in front of me. I handed him my key ring.

He turned, deftly swiped the key card and returned it to me, all in one fluid motion.

"I don't think so," Stan said. "Ethel never reported it. She wasn't a hundred percent sure it was the kid, so she didn't want to accuse him. And with Larry, I think the cops agreed with him." He cocked a thumb at Ernie.

"Probably because Larry's cologne of choice smelled suspiciously like bourbon," Ernie said. "Look, don't get me wrong. This place is great. Food and drink all day long, right here in the building. And a smorgasbord of joints to eat and drink in the neighborhood. All in walking distance. And as long as you can pay the tab, nobody ever says no. So you gotta learn to say no to yourself. Heck, I gained back my freshman ten when I first moved in. And right now, Larry's having a little trouble in the no department."

"So what have you heard about the election?" I asked.

Hey, as long as I had them talking, might as well prime the pump.

"Never heard of any a' these clowns," Ernie said.

Stan nodded. "I was all set to vote for Leslie McQueen, until the thing with Ethel. Now I might just sit this one out."

"You can't do that, Stan," Ernie said. "You have to vote."

"Yeah, yeah, I know," he said, waving off his friend. "But what if I vote for the wrong one?"

"I got news for you, buddy," Ernie said, shaking his head sadly as he shoveled another handful of nuts from the bowl. "They're all the wrong one."

CHAPTER 7

A nnie was right about the seafood shack. It was fantastic. And it was, oddly enough, an actual shack. The
place didn't even have a name. Or regular hours. One of
the owners was married to a fisherman. Whenever they had
enough from a catch, the shack would open for business.
And once they put the word out, people flocked from all
over the city.

The shack was surrounded by a half dozen scarred
wooden picnic tables, overflowing with families. We opted
to eat our dinner off of paper plates right on the beach.
There was a light breeze from the ocean, and the sun was
just setting. It was glorious.

We kept Lucy out of the hushpuppies because of the
onion bits. But she loved the fish. And we made sure the
morsels we gave her were free of bones.

I even clicked a few photos of Lucy frolicking in front
of the place—and gently accepting nibbles of fillet—so
that Nick could see we were taking good care of her.

That night, as I was getting ready for bed, my phone
rang. Reflexively, I checked the number. Trip.

"So what's it like being a lady of leisure?" my best friend asked.

"Well, I sipped champagne on a private jet, spent the afternoon lounging poolside, had a picnic dinner on the beach, and met an eligible gentleman who offered to show me around town."

I left out the fact that the gentleman in question was over seventy.

"Bored out of your gourd, then," Trip concluded.

"Except for the dinner, yeah," I said. "And I'm worried about what's going on at home."

"Yes, I hear that black mold can be nasty stuff."

"Black mold? Nick said it was old wiring." I felt the bile rising in my gut. Or maybe it was one of the hushpuppies. Between the two of us, Annie and I had pretty much cleaned out the shack.

"I'm sure it's nothing," Trip said. "Hey, for what it's worth, you scored yourself a freelance gig."

Before I'd left town, I'd pitched a feature—"South Beach in the Summer"—to my former newspaper's travel editor. The general gist: Anyone can visit during the cooler months of tourist season. But in sizzling summer it's more affordable and less crowded. And, since I had family connections there, I promised the piece would include "tons of insider tips" from the locals.

No sense admitting that my family connections consisted of one jet-setting sister who spent more time in Manhattan than Miami.

"One slight change," Trip said. "Instead of the money angle, they want dogs."

"I think you cut out there for a minute. It sounded like you actually said 'dogs.'"

One of these days, I had to invest in a better phone.

"Exactly," he confirmed. "Travel desk says the money angle's been done to death. Look, I was in the story meeting, and I knew you needed an assignment. When they started to shoot it down, I had to think on my feet. But I was going on three hours' sleep. You'd mentioned you guys were taking Lucy, so I suggested 'a dog-friendly guide to South Beach.' They loved the idea. And if you can get some good pics to go with it, they're willing to double your space and your fee."

"Well, Lucy *is* very photogenic."

"And the check would keep you both in kibble for quite a while."

"I'm going to have to eat kibble because apparently my kitchen is a death trap. Even without me in it. What did you really hear from Nick?"

"When's the last time you talked with him?" Trip asked.

"Answering a question with a question. Somebody's been to editor school."

"Editor college, if you please. And I have the bags under my eyes to prove it."

"Nick called this morning, right after we got here," I said.

I heard Trip yawn. "Talk to him, Red. Really, I'm sure everything's fine."

"What's up with the three hours' sleep? Is everything OK?"

"Tom is schmoozing some hotel bigwigs from California."

Tom, Trip's partner of just over a year, was the head chef and part owner of Polaris, one of D.C.'s hottest restaurants. And his hours were brutal.

"Could mean mucho business for the restaurant," he continued. "So I had to put on a suit and be at my witty best until all hours. Seriously, I didn't think they'd ever call it a night. Then it was back in here first thing this morning for the editorial meeting. At this rate, I'm going to have to start putting more coffee in my coffee."

CHAPTER 8

The next morning, I stumbled out of bed, heading for the coffeemaker that lives on the counter in my cozy kitchen. Lucy, curled up on the other side of the bed, shifted, stretched, and rolled toward my pillow.

The minute my feet hit the floor I realized something was different. For one thing, the décor was nicer than my place. The bed, low and stylish. Beneath it, a round area rug, made from big loopy white yarn that resembled a puli, cushioned my feet from the slick, blond hardwood floor. And sunlight streamed through a wall of windows I didn't have in my own bedroom.

That's when it hit me. Miami. The trip had been so quick and painless, it didn't even seem possible.

Waking up in the penthouse was like being back in the jet. I could make eye contact with the seagulls cruising past the windows. Off in the distance, the ocean was deep blue and inviting.

At home, I'd let Lucy out the back door and plug in the coffeemaker. But ten floors up, that wasn't an option. And if I was going to have to go down the hall, into the elevator, and through the very public lobby, I was going to have to make myself presentable in a hurry.

A few minutes later, the bathroom mirror revealed that, while I liked Miami just fine, it definitely did not like me. Thanks to almost ninety-seven percent humidity, my naturally wavy strawberry-blond hair resembled a bad home perm. And despite never leaving the house with anything less than SPF 45, my nose and forehead were bright red.

I looked like Bozo.

Yesterday, Annie and I may not have looked like sisters. But today we didn't even look like the same species.

An ugly thought popped into my brain before I could squelch it: Thank goodness Ian Sterling can't see me like this.

Wait, what?

I brushed my hair madly, adding water and mousse as needed and formed an acceptable ponytail. It didn't necessarily look good. But I could pass for a human who'd recently been for a swim.

A lot more sunblock, topped off with some strategically placed concealer, a little mascara and some lip gloss and I was good to go.

I dashed into my room, grabbed my purse, and unzipped Lucy's suitcase. The Doggles were gone.

I'd also tucked all four of her booties under the chair last night. This morning, there were only two.

I grabbed a couple of bags for her pooper-scooper and prayed the thing was still out on the balcony, where we'd parked it last night.

One more little secret Nick had neglected to share: He'd packed a brand-new one in Lucy's luggage. Along with a hundred-count box of bags.

I'm guessing that when he suggested bringing Lucy on our trip, he wanted to stack the deck in her favor. And there's nothing like handing someone a box of poop bags to give them second thoughts.

I looked down. The pup was staring up at me with an urgent look. "I know this isn't our usual morning routine. But it'll be fun. I promise."

Her tail wagged slowly.

When we trotted through the living room, my sister was sitting on the sofa with a mug of tea, reading her tablet. Clad in a cream-colored T-shirt that skimmed her hips and black yoga pants, topped off by a smooth, bouncy ponytail that was none the worse for the weather, she could have been doing an ad for hair products. Or electronics. Or tea.

Her face lit up when she saw us. And urgent or not, Lucy scampered over and jumped into her lap. Which just made her smile wider.

"So how'd you sleep?" she asked me, as she stroked the pup's downy flank.

"I think I was out before my head hit the pillow."

"It's the sea air," Annie said. "I always sleep better here."

Lucy jumped down from the sofa and ran pell-mell for the front door. Then she looked back at us. Presumably to see if we had noticed.

"There's an early-bird Pilates class in the exercise studio," Annie chirped. "It starts in ten minutes. Want to come with?"

"I'm gonna get Lucy out for her morning constitutional," I said, spying the scooper on the deck. Without the Doggles or the booties, at least I was one-for-three.

But it was still early, so it should be fairly cool. If worse came to worst, I could always carry her to a grassy spot.

"How about we meet up here at eight and go for breakfast? There's a little outdoor café around the corner—Diamond Jack's. They do these amazing lemon ricotta pancakes. And everybody brings their dog, so the little one will get treated like a queen."

Pancakes, no exercise class, *and* fodder for my travel feature? Even with the prospect of manning a pooper-scooper, this day was getting better and better.

Now all I needed was a tall cup of coffee. And the truth about what was really going on at home in my kitchen.

CHAPTER 9

When we got to the elevators, Lucy balked.

But the desperation in those soft eyes told me she'd never make it down nine flights of stairs. Time for drastic measures.

I carefully picked her up and stepped quickly into the elevator. Once we were moving I deposited her gently on the floor. Like an unexploded grenade.

Those doggie vitamins Nick gave her must be working. Lucy was getting big. Now in her canine adolescence, her legs were longer. And she'd gotten a lot faster. Which was why I'd never take her off-leash—especially in a place she didn't know.

When the door opened on two, Stan Cohen got in. "Hey, good morning! Nice pooch. She yours?"

"My brother's, actually. But he's got a home renovation project going. So I'm watching her for the week."

"Well, you might want to steer clear of the Wicked Witch of the West."

"Leslie McQueen?" I asked.

Stan nodded. "Don't know what she has against dogs. But I think she'd ban 'em from the building if she could. As it is, she just tries to fine 'em out of existence. Come to think of it, I bet that's why she got so ticked off at poor Ethel. She's got this little white furry thing." He held his hands about a foot-and-a-half apart.

"Are there many dogs in the building?" I asked.

"Not a lot, but a few. And I've noticed that a lot of 'em are keeping a low profile lately. Taking the stairs or the service elevator. Staying well away from the building when they go outside. That kind of thing."

The elevator bell sounded, and the door opened to the lobby. Lucy rushed through it—tugging me by the leash.

"Thanks for the tip," I called behind me.

"Any time," Stan said, waving.

Outside, I don't know who was happier to see that big patch of lawn across from the building's portico—me or Lucy. Let's just say we were both relieved.

Newly refreshed, Lucy sniffed her way from one end of the perfectly manicured horseshoe-shaped lawn to the other. When a grasshopper jumped, it startled her and she took off at a trot.

Near the curb, I reined her in, reached down, and touched the concrete. Still cool. Perfect.

I looked over at Lucy. "We're going to take a nice long walk and see all kinds of interesting things. Along the way, maybe you can tell me what happened to those booties. And the sunglasses."

She looked away quickly. The sure sign of a guilty conscience.

CHAPTER 10

As we walked South Beach in the cool of the morning, I ruminated over what I'd learned so far about Oceanside and its curious election.

No one seemed to know who'd called the election. And no one seemed to know any of the candidates—except for Leslie McQueen. So I definitely needed more information on both angles.

Leslie seemed to be big on fines. At least, for some of the residents. And she didn't like dogs. A definite strike against her in my book. I looked over at Lucy, who was busily sniffing a patch of scraggily dandelions near the curb.

How could anyone not like dogs?

Suddenly, Lucy's oversized ears shot straight up. She turned her head and looked at me. And if I didn't know better, I'd have sworn the expression on her face was shock. Pure shock.

I'd long ago become convinced she could read my mind. Or maybe just smell my emotions. Either way, the pup was wired.

"Just trying to figure out some of my fellow humans," I explained. "Sometimes they make zero sense."

She appeared to give that some thought. Then she licked a dandelion and resumed sauntering down the walkway—with me bringing up the rear.

I was also curious about one more detail that was probably irrelevant: Why had Leslie McQueen wanted to be president of the HOA in the first place?

From what Annie had said, it seemed as if Leslie had created the position for herself. First, by pushing for an association. Then by swanning in to lead it. Why? What was she getting out of it?

She'd claimed a sense of civic duty. But if she was truly that high-minded, she wouldn't be playing favorites with the rules and strong-arming retirees out of their money and due process.

In my early days at the newspaper, a really smart editor told me that everybody does things for a reason. Figure out the reason, and you're halfway to the story. But without the reason, the story won't make sense.

I had to admit, this story made no sense at all. At least, not to me.

I pulled Annie's ballot out of my purse. Four names, plus Leslie. The names didn't mean anything to me. But they wouldn't.

Other than Annie, Ernie, Stan, and Ethel Plunkett (who I hadn't even met), I didn't know anybody in the building. And the place was large enough that even the residents probably didn't know more than a few of their neighbors.

I definitely needed to learn more about the other candidates. And it wouldn't hurt to pick up a little more information on Leslie McQueen, too.

Because at this point, I had nada.

Chapter 11

I considered our walk an hour well spent. Lucy and I got some quality outdoor time together touring the neighborhood. We even found a coffee bar with a walk-up window—which yielded a large mocha latte for me, and a big dish of water for Lucy—plus two bone-shaped treats after the barista pronounced her "winsome."

While I was no closer to figuring out what was going on with the election at Oceanside, at least I understood the problem a little better. And the players.

So I chalked that up as progress.

As we strolled into the lobby, I noticed a cluster of women chatting near the elevators. All three were in tennis whites and carrying racquets. Since they weren't sweating yet, I concluded they were on their way out to the courts.

I jabbed the call button and stroked Lucy's back. Keep the little dog calm, and she might not notice we were getting on an elevator.

Not my best idea. But it beat taking her and the scooper up nine flights of stairs.

"I'm sorry, I don't think I know you—are you sure you're

in the right place?" A fiftyish petite brunette with a deep tan inserted herself between me and the first elevator door.

Lucy looked at the woman, then at me. As if she was watching a tennis match of her own.

"Yes, I'm sure," I said with a smile.

I didn't know who she was. But I was pretty sure I didn't want to talk to her.

"I don't think so," she continued, thrusting her face even closer and giving me a hard squint. "Animals aren't permitted in the elevators. If this was really your building, you'd know that. Are you a dog walker? Or a renter?"

I felt like saying, *Lady, I'm the one who's going to shove you out of the way with a slightly used pooper-scooper when that elevator finally arrives because I've got a nervous dog and a breakfast date with pancakes.*

But I didn't. This was Annie's home, and I was her guest. So I decided to try a little tact. Preferably as little as possible.

"I'm sorry, I didn't catch your name?" I replied. *Or your badge number.*

"I'm Leslie McQueen. I'm president of the homeowners' association."

OK, that explained a lot.

"I'm Alex Vlodnachek. I'm visiting my sister in the penthouse."

"Anastasia can't possibly be your sister," she said, looking me up and down.

"Well, according to our parents, she is. But we only have their word for it," I added lightly.

McQueen's expression was a thundercloud. But what fascinated me was her hair. A nimbus of carefully curled, obviously dyed blackish-brown that came to her shoulders, it didn't move. I'm guessing in this heat, that took at least a full can of hairspray. Maybe two.

"Well, I hope she's not letting you stay there unaccompanied. That's strictly forbidden. And guests are limited to seven consecutive days, as per our state hospitality statutes."

Her eyes narrowed as she studied me. "And I'm very sorry your 'sister' didn't inform you," McQueen said, using big air quotes, "but dogs are not allowed in the elevators. Animals must be confined to the stairs. That's not just our rule, but a county health department regulation. And if there are any little accidents along the way, be sure to clean them right up," she said, smiling. "We don't want to have to issue any citations."

"I'd love to stay and chat, but I have breakfast plans," I said, stepping back and to the left—closer to the elevator door.

But Leslie McQueen wasn't having it. She put her arm across the door frame, blocking my path.

"I'm sorry, but I just don't see how you could actually be related. For the security of the building, I'm going to have to verify your status. I need to see some identification."

My status was steamed. I so wanted to tell her exactly where to put that tennis racquet. Or hey, just to be helpful, do it for her.

"Well, hello, Leslie," a chipper voice called out from behind me, as the elevator bell finally dinged. "I see you've met my sister Alex. She'll be staying with me for the foreseeable future. And this is my brother's dog, Lucy. I'm sure I told you about my brother. He's a partner in a Manhattan law firm."

My sister wasn't exactly lying. She did have a brother who was a Manhattan attorney. And a brother who resided with Lucy. They just weren't the same person.

But I'm guessing lawyers were a lot scarier to Leslie than bakers. Extra carbs or no.

But my sister was on a roll. "If we're lucky, my brother will be joining us soon, as well. I'm so glad you all have had a chance to meet, but we really must get going. We have breakfast reservations."

With that, Annie bounced into the elevator and Lucy and I followed.

As the doors closed, Leslie McQueen looked totally deflated. Except for her hair.

CHAPTER 12

"How do you put up with that?" I asked Annie, as we rolled back toward the building, stuffed to the gills with eggs, pancakes, bacon, and sparkling cider. The lemon ricotta pancakes were delicious. Even Lucy had one with her bacon and eggs. Without syrup, of course. The winsome pup has to watch her figure.

I was able to snap a couple of extra pics for my South Beach story. Including one of Annie in her wide-brimmed hat and big sunglasses, chatting with some people enjoying mimosas at the next table, while Lucy listened intently.

"I'm never here," my sister replied. "So that helps. But, honestly, it wasn't always like this. In the beginning the atmosphere was great. The building was new and luxe. Everyone was so happy to be here. And they were so friendly. Even right after they formed the HOA, things didn't change that much. At least, not that I noticed. But the last few months? This is awful. It's not the same place."

"Maybe that's why someone challenged Leslie for president," I suggested. "I sure would like to know a little more about these guys," I said, using the ballot as a fan. Not even eleven o'clock and it was already steamy.

"Well, then you're in luck," Annie said, grimacing. "We've been invited to a candidates mixer this evening in Leslie's apartment. She's calling it 'Cocktails and Candidates.'"

"Oh geez," I said. The name conjured visions of the cutesy names for every rubber-chicken dinner I'd covered during election season. My favorite: a pancake breakfast dubbed "Eggs and Issues."

No matter what they called them, no one ever ate the food. Candidates were too busy pressing the flesh. Constituents were trying to extract promises from the candidates. And reporters were just trying to get straight answers from anyone who might actually know something.

I was lucky to finish a glass of juice.

"I know," Annie said, wincing. "The Evite arrived a couple of days ago. And I wasn't planning to go. But it would be a good opportunity to meet everyone and maybe learn a little something."

"You really think she's going to let me in the door?" I asked. "Especially after this morning?"

"She has to. She's courting my support in the election."

That made sense. Leslie McQueen might not be a name-brand, but everyone had heard of Anastasia. Women were desperate to learn her beauty secrets. Guys just wanted her phone number.

And having her endorsement would lock up the single-male voting block for Leslie. They'd cast their ballots for Lucrezia Borgia herself if they thought it might give them a shot with my sister.

"The thing about dogs taking the stairs?" I asked. "Is that true? I mean, about it being a local health department rule?"

I had my own beef with the health department back home. First, a crooked health inspector took a bribe to ban Nick from using my kitchen for his bakery until we'd installed a laundry list of pricey upgrades. Now I was in renovation limbo. And despite leaving a flurry of phone messages, I wasn't getting any return calls from Nick.

"You know, I have no idea," Annie said. "Since I never had a dog, it never came up. Come to think of it, I haven't noticed any lately. But I didn't realize that until you mentioned it. To be honest, when I hit town, I always have a pile of flyers from the association in my mailbox. Announcements, notices, rule changes. I just toss them into recycling."

Service dogs were allowed everywhere—that much I knew for a fact. So Leslie McQueen couldn't ban all dogs. I also had a sneaking suspicion that her edict might have been bluster. Or wishful thinking.

Election or no election, travel story or no travel story—Lucy's health and comfort came first. So when we got back to the penthouse, I knew exactly what I had to do next.

CHAPTER 13

I'd been on hold with the county for twenty minutes—and transferred three times—when call-waiting buzzed. I checked the number.

Nick!

The county could wait. I wanted to hear what was going on at home.

"So how's the little dog liking the big city?" he asked.

"Your little dog is a big dog now," I said. "She's eating at fine restaurants, charming the locals, and hobnobbing with supermodels and politicians."

"My girl's a star," he said. "Seriously, is she taking her vitamins and wearing her booties?"

"Yes, on the vitamins. We're having mixed success on the booties."

No lie. It took both Annie and me fifteen minutes to find Lucy's missing shoes (stuffed under a couch cushion), and another five to get them on her.

Once we did, she proceeded to high-step one leg at a time in slow motion, like something out of a horror movie. And the only way I could get her into the elevator was to carry her.

Ever lithe and leggy, Lucy had grown taller and stronger over the past few months. She had to weigh at least forty pounds, easy.

At this rate, I was going to have to take up weight training. Or join Annie for that next early morning exercise class.

"OK, Lucy's fine. Annie sends her love and, it goes without saying, all of us wish you were here. Now what the blazes is going on in that kitchen?"

"Everything's fine. Nothing to worry about. The contractor just had to run a few more tests, that's all."

"Black mold?"

"Odds are it's not. He just needs to be sure. Before they start."

"They haven't even started yet?"

"He says a couple of preliminary tests are totally routine with an older home. You have to find out what's behind the walls. And we're still mostly on schedule. I mean, it might add an extra day or two, tops. But as soon as we get the results back on the wiring and the, uh, other stuff, we're good to go. And he says it's probably safe to sleep there."

"Probably?" I'd been sleeping there for over two years. And, at various times, so had most of my family. What had I done to us?

"Look, I'm sure it's all fine. We just haven't gotten the official OK yet. Ian would have let me stay at the inn, but they're booked solid."

I had a feeling I knew exactly where this was going. "So where are you staying?"

"Trip and Tom's guest room," Nick said. "Just for a couple of days. Until we get the all-clear. And I brought them a big batch of brioche rolls. You know, as a way of saying thank you."

That explained how Trip knew about my mold problem before I did. And why he didn't want to be the one to tell me.

Once again, Trip had galloped to the rescue. Only instead of a white horse, his ride was a shiny red Corvette convertible.

In Fordham, Virginia, just outside D.C., I have the smallest house—a snug hundred-year-old bungalow—in a pretty neighborhood with rolling lawns and plenty of trees. And, up until now, I'd felt lucky to have it.

Trip and Tom lived in Trip's townhouse in the heart of historic Georgetown. Most of the time, my neighborhood smells like freshly mown grass, mulch, and—occasionally—new paint. Trip's smells like money.

So Lucy wasn't the only one who was getting a taste of the good life this week. The question was, when those test results came back, would any of us want to go home?

CHAPTER 14

"Leslie has a corner unit on eight," Annie said, as we rode down in the elevator. "I've never been there myself, but I hear it's quite the place."

I tugged at my dress. Annie had kitted me out in a Kelly green paisley vintage sheath from her closet. She finished off the minidress with a pair of matching strappy sandals and a tiny beaded bag that dangled from my shoulder on a fine gold chain.

I suspected the purse cost more than I made in a month.

She'd even helped me with my hair. And thanks to the perfect combination of her skill and products, I had red, silky waves that fell just past my shoulders. My own hair. Only, somehow, better.

I felt glamorous. Even standing shoulder to shoulder with a supermodel.

Too bad Ian Sterling couldn't see me now.

Wait, where did that come from?

I'd wanted to bring Lucy to the party. Preferably sporting a dressy lace collar, like the one she'd worn to a friend's recent wedding. When Ian's father, Cecil Harkins, married long-time love Daisy Campbell in the backyard of the B&B, the pup had been their ring bearer. Sensing she was part of something important, Lucy's tail had never stopped wagging. And that was before she'd discovered the bacon in Nick's pocket.

But this time, my sister felt that bringing Lucy might be pushing it. And this was Annie's turf.

So the pup had the run of the penthouse living area. After we'd puppy-proofed it thoroughly. And I'd hidden her booties.

Those Doggles were still missing.

Before we could knock twice, a uniformed cater waiter opened the door and ushered us in, while a second one immediately offered champagne from a silver tray.

To keep a position she claimed she'd never wanted, Leslie had spared no expense. Several uniformed waiters circled constantly with trays. I'd done that same job recently for an event. So they had my sympathies. I hoped Leslie McQueen tipped better than my former employer. But I doubted it.

There was a buffet table of nibbles set up at one end of the expansive living room. And the entire place was decked out in campaign chic—yards of red, white, and blue bunting set off with clusters of red, white, and blue balloons.

As I took my glass, I glanced around. The cocktail party was in full swing. And I didn't know a soul.

The layout was vaguely familiar, though. Like an echo of Annie's place, on a smaller scale. Glass doors to the deck made the most of the ocean views on two sides. The furnishings and knickknacks were fragile and pricey. As if they'd been purchased from an exclusive boutique and arranged "just so" by an interior designer. The result looked expensive. But impersonal. Cold.

Annie's place was very minimalist. She was never there and didn't want to waste time dusting tchotchkes when she was. And if anybody knew her way around boutiques and design, it was my sister. But her place was open, bright, and cheery. Welcoming.

This one? I couldn't wait to leave.

Maybe it was the company. As if on cue, Leslie swooped over to greet us. Clad in a red silk dress with short butterfly sleeves, matching pumps, and lots of inky black mascara, our hostess would have fit right in at "Eggs and Issues."

She actually attempted an air kiss with Annie, who promptly pulled back and looked down to adjust the tiny purse on her own shoulder.

"So glad you could make it—both of you," she added in a booming stage voice. "So, Anastasia, can I take this to mean you're firmly in Camp Leslie?"

Worst summer camp ever.

"I'm so glad you invited us," Annie said brightly. "I can't wait to learn more about the candidates. And I have to say, Leslie, you have a beautiful home."

My sister, the master of the conversation pivot.

"Why, thank you!" Leslie gushed. "That means a lot coming from you. You know I hired a decorator at first. But in the end, I had to redo it all myself."

Yeah, right.

"Well, we were going to have speeches, but none of my erstwhile opponents have arrived just yet. But when they finally do, we'll each take a few minutes to talk about the issues that are truly important to us. In the meantime, I'm sure you know most of the people here. Just enjoy yourselves."

And with that, she was gone.

What issues? It was a condo building. Keep the lights on, the pool clean, and the elevators running. What's to discuss? It's not like one of them was going to draw up a trade pact with France or negotiate peace in the Middle East.

From what (admittedly little) I knew about presiding

over an HOA, it was a thankless job. Someone was always dissatisfied. Residents were constantly suing or being sued. And people called to complain at all hours of the day and night.

Yet this woman was spending oodles of cash to snag the dubious honor. It was like campaigning for a suicide mission.

My spidey sense was definitely tingling.

"Look, there's Ethel Plunkett," my sister said, gesturing with her glass.

I looked over and saw a well-kept older blonde chatting animatedly with Stan.

"I'd love to dish the dirt with her," I admitted.

"Now's your chance," Annie said, and I followed her lead.

"Ethel, I want you to meet my sister, Alex. She's staying with me for a while. And she brought the family dog. Alex, this is my neighbor, Mrs. Plunkett."

"Call me Ethel," she said. "And it's nice to see a friendly face. After that kerfuffle with Mrs. Pickles, I'm getting the cold shoulder around here."

"Well, I'm glad you're here," my sister said. "And I want to learn more about these other candidates. When are they supposed to arrive?"

"They were supposed to be here forty minutes ago, but apparently none of 'em has a watch," Stan said.

"What do you know about them?" I asked Ethel.

"Not a blessed thing, dear. I hadn't even heard of them until their names showed up on the ballot. The only thing I can think is they must all be fairly recent additions. I mean, it is a fairly new building after all. Either that, or I'm getting forgetful."

"You're sharp as a tack," Stan said earnestly.

"Kelsey on five said she ran into one of them, Mike

Smith, when she was getting her mail," Ethel said. "Practically mowed her down. Insisted he needed to go first because he was in such an all-fired hurry."

Annie shook her head. "Well, that's not very promising."

"Looks like he's not in any big hurry tonight," Stan said, checking his watch again.

"Who's Kelsey?" I asked.

"See that kid in the orange at Leslie's elbow?" he asked, pointing. "That's Kelsey."

I spied a plump woman in a coral toga-style evening gown. "Friend of Leslie's?" I asked.

"What the online kids call BFFs," Stan said, nodding.

Consider the source. That little reporting mandate had saved my job more than once. That second-hand Michael Smith story might be true. Then again, it might not.

Stan elbowed me in the side. "She's giving away T-shirts that say 'Leslie McQueen for President.' Big bin of them by the door. Calls 'em party favors."

"Well, I for one could always use another dust rag," Ethel said. "Or something to clean up after Mrs. Pickles. Too bad they don't have McQueen's face on them."

"Ethel, you are awful," my sister said, giggling.

"So what's the deal with dogs on the elevators?" I asked. "I tried to bring Lucy up from a walk, and I got a lecture on public health and hygiene."

Ethel shook her head. "I never knew it, but apparently the county prohibits them. After Leslie took over, she insisted we follow all the state and local regulations to the letter. She says if we don't, lenders won't be able to make loans on these places, and our property values will plummet. I'm glad I only live on two. As it is, I have to take a breather when I make it to the landing. And that stairwell is some kind of hot."

"No air vents," Stan agreed, nodding.

"Did you ever check with the county?" I asked, remembering my twenty minutes on hold this afternoon, before Nick had clicked in. I'd called back and left a message, but so far nothing.

"What do you mean, dear?" Ethel asked.

"Sometimes laws are open to interpretation," I said. "I was just wondering about the county's current reading of the rule book. There could be some wiggle room."

"She thinks the dame might be lying," Stan translated.

"That too," I said, taking a sip from my glass.

"You mean I might have been schlepping Mrs. Pickles up and down those hot cement stairs for nothing?" Ethel's voice rose in intensity.

A couple nearby turned and looked at us.

"Ixnay on the volume," Stan prompted, gently patting her arm.

"I swear, if I find out that woman has been lying to us," Ethel hissed, "I'm going to wring her scrawny chicken neck."

I spent the rest of the evening making small talk and eavesdropping. Typical reporter skills, but I didn't use them as much now that I was freelancing.

I'd gotten rusty. But then subtlety never was my strong suit.

Dad claims I come by it naturally. He always said, "If Russians were subtle, the world wouldn't have Fabergé eggs."

From what I could tell, most of the crowd was here to drink, nosh, and gossip. The election was almost an afterthought. Which was just as well because, more than ninety minutes in, the other four candidates still hadn't shown.

"Look, there's Anastasia!" I heard one woman titter, as my sister and I walked past.

"What's she doing here?" her male companion asked.

"She lives in the penthouse," chimed in a third woman in a pale pink suit.

"Did you hear about the duchess?" asked her friend in a flowing black midi dress.

"Which one?"

"The one who lives here," Midi Dress replied. "She's summering in one of the corner units. She's American— with a Southern accent. But she married a European duke."

Heading back across the room five minutes later, I overheard one fifty-something executive type in a blue blazer and gray slacks talking to a buddy in a gray pinstripe suit, as both of them parked next to the buffet.

"Hey, look, there's Anastasia. And you'll never guess what I heard tonight. She's going to be in *Penthouse*!"

"Damn, man, that issue will break the Internet."

OK, so anything I learned tonight, I definitely had to double fact-check. And take with a grain of salt. Still, I couldn't wait to tell Annie.

"That's nothing," my sister said, grinning. "It's usually that I'm getting married, have secretly gotten married, am checking into rehab, or am bravely battling a deadly disease. Or that I'm pregnant. Half the time, I think it's Mom starting that last one. Wishful thinking."

She wasn't wrong.

"She's just started plotting to get me married off," I confessed.

"Sure, for now," my sister said, nodding. "Just wait."

With four grown kids and not a grandchild in sight, I almost felt sorry for my mother. Or would have if I didn't actually know her.

I looked across the room and spotted Ernie Doyle with a seventy-plus redhead in a short black sequined dress: Mrs. Ernie.

Stan was right. She did have good legs.

Annie and I split up to work the room. I hated the idea, but we could cover way more ground that way. And from what everyone was saying, the other candidates would be here any minute.

I sauntered over to the buffet table, where a couple of women were debating the merits of one-piece swimsuits versus bikinis.

"So how do you know Leslie?" I asked, as I lifted one of the little puff pastries onto a cocktail napkin.

"I'm a secretary at SecureHome Title. Leslie uses our company a lot. And Becca's a freelance photographer."

"Videographer, too," Becca added. A tiny diamond stud on the side of her nose glimmered in a now-you-see-it-now-you-don't trick of the light. "These days, everybody wants to tour the house online before they trek through in person. Leslie's a steady client."

A freelancer myself, I loved steady clients. And relied on them to keep the bills paid. But I was surprised that a secretary and a freelancer could get a mortgage at Ocean-side. I couldn't have gotten a mortgage on my own snug home if I'd been freelancing at the time.

For some reason, lenders read the word "self-employed" as "unemployed."

"I'm Alex. So how long have you guys lived here?"

"I'm Rose. And we don't live here. We were just invited to the party."

"And the hot tub!" Becca said.

"Leslie's a pretty big deal at her agency, so this is really cool," Rose said. "I didn't even think she remembered my name. But when I logged in this week, there was a cute lit-tle invitation. To her own home. Plus, I mean, who says no to the chance to dress up and drink champagne in a posh condo? So here we are!"

"Leslie even said we could use the hot tub later," Becca said, slapping her purse. "We brought our suits!"

"Cool!" I said. "So, do you know any of the candidates? Besides Leslie, I mean?"

"No, I don't know anything about the election," Rose admitted.

"I hear one of the guys is a real jerk, though," Becca said. "He stole an elevator from some mom with an armful of groceries while she was trying to find her house keys. Just left her standing in the lobby like a pack mule, while he rushed in and took off."

"That's just mean," Rose said.

"That's exactly what Leslie said when she told me about it!" Becca recounted.

"Do you remember his name?" I asked.

"Kyle something," Becca said. "Kyle Brown—that's it! Man, if I lived here, he would definitely not get my vote."

"I just spent fifteen minutes talking with a guy, only to find out he doesn't even live here," Annie said when we met up on the balcony.

"But he has a connection to Leslie," I stated.

"He's a house painter, and she throws him a lot of work, apparently."

"That seems to be a theme. I just talked with a secretary from her favorite title company, a freelance videographer she hires regularly, and the woman who runs the cleaning service Leslie uses before walk-throughs."

"This is bizarre," Annie said, turning to look out at the ocean.

"What's weird is that everyone seems to have heard some nasty story about one of Leslie's opponents. But I'm getting the feeling that Leslie herself is likely the original source for all of them."

"Manuel Garcia reported one of his neighbors for dumping too many boxes in the trash room," Annie said, snapping her fingers. "And Bill Johnson had someone's dog hauled off to the pound."

"I heard Kyle Brown swiped an elevator from a woman when her arms were full of grocery bags. And we already know the ditty about Mike Smith pushing poor Kelsey out of the way in the mail room."

"A smear campaign?" Annie asked.

"It's just a stupid HOA," I said softly. "Who cares who wins? But you know what else is weird?"

Annie tossed her blond mane. "What?"

"This is Leslie's party. But I haven't seen the guest of honor in a good fifteen minutes."

"I'd bet she's touching up her makeup," my sister said. "Next up—campaign speeches."

"Oh goody. Then what say we grab another glass of champagne? The only thing I have to drive tonight is an elevator. That's assuming the evil Kyle Brown doesn't poach it from me."

Unfortunately, my sister was right. Fifteen minutes later, Leslie stepped onto a little stool in front of the ocean backdrop. She'd traded the pumps for flats and added a boxy navy-blue blazer with padded shoulders over the red silk dress.

More presidential?

She clinked a spoon against the side of her glass.

"Neighbors, friends, and soon-to-be friends," she effused, as the general party noise tapered into silence. "It appears that my opponents are not going to grace us with their presence. Perhaps they're just too busy to take a few minutes to speak with you. With us."

At this, there was a general rumble of dismay. Leslie might not have been a real pol, but her timing was first-rate. Ditto her sense of drama.

"Or, just maybe, they know they can't win," she finished with an impish smile.

At that, her buddy Kelsey started the applause and the rest of the room quickly joined. It's amazing what a few cases of champagne will buy you.

As the clapping gained momentum, Kelsey pumped one fist in the air and let out an enthusiastic "Woo, woo!"

Annie and I looked at each other in disbelief.

So where were the other four candidates, and why weren't they here? My money was on their not getting an invite in the first place.

It was also possible that they didn't want to give Leslie the home-field advantage. Maybe they'd host their own meet-and-greets elsewhere. Or perhaps, like me, they didn't believe in over-the-top campaigning for an HOA post.

"But we don't want to count this as a win yet," Leslie intoned somberly as her voice rose. "Because. I. Don't. Take. You. For. Granted," she said, punching every word against a scattering of "spontaneous" applause.

She paused to let the clapping stop. "You know me," she said almost conversationally. "You see me every day. This building is my home. I love this place. I know what it is now. And I know what it can be. I understand the spirit of this unique and beautiful community. I'm Leslie McQueen, and I want to be your HOA president!" she shouted, triumphantly thrusting her left fist into the air.

The room broke into thunderous applause. Kelsey pumped her fist and "woo-wooed" again—joined by Leslie's two tennis friends from this morning.

Annie and I clapped politely. I looked around and noticed that Stan and Ethel were nowhere to be seen. Given that the evening was turning into a Leslie McQueen love-fest, produced, directed by, and starring Leslie McQueen, that was probably for the best.

CHAPTER 15

"She salted the crowd," I said, as we stood in the hall-way just outside Annie's penthouse.

"Is that what they call it in politics?" she asked, fishing the keys from her evening bag.

"I don't know about politics. But it's an old trick that carnys, con men, and fly-by-night auctions use to control a crowd or create a bidding war. Big corporations do it too, for press announcements or in-house symposiums. You load the crowd with friendly faces. In this case, a bunch of nice people who feel like they owe Leslie big-time and were touched to get an invite to her home. And you plant a couple of shills—like Kelsey and the tennis team—whose job it is to applaud in the right places and get the crowd fired up."

"What's the purpose?" she said, putting the key in the door.

"Right now, almost everyone who was in that room believes that Leslie's a shoo-in to win the election. Some people will vote for her because they want to say they backed a winner. Or they want to curry favor, in case they need something later. Then you have people like Stan. He hates

Leslie. But it looks like she's going to win in a landslide. And the other candidates are practically invisible."

"Or have the reputation of being jerks," Annie added, jiggling the key.

"Exactly. So he's just planning not to vote."

"That's awful," she said. "And totally diabolical."

"What still bugs me is why? Why do all of this? And where were those four other guys tonight? One or two sending their regrets I can understand. But all four of them?"

"That *was* weird," my sister agreed, still fiddling with the lock.

"What's wrong?" I asked.

"For some reason, it's really sticking," she said. "I mean, sometimes when it's really humid, I have a little trouble, and I have to wiggle it a bit. But this is truly stuck."

She gave it a sharp twist. "Ah, there we go."

I heard the bolt slide, and she pushed open the door.

"Lucy's going to wonder what kept us so long," I said, sailing into the living room. "Come to think of it, so do I."

"Hey, Lucy-girl, your second- and third-favorite Vlodnacheks are home!" Annie said, giggling.

"Third and fourth," I corrected. "You forgot about Baba."

"I would never forget about Baba," Annie said. "But she's in a category all her own. Like a super Vlodnachek."

Ian may have looked like a man who could handle anything. But Baba really could. And had.

That I was alive and causing trouble was a testament to her nose for danger and her skill with a cast-iron frying pan. And one would-be murderer probably still had the goose egg to prove it.

Ironically, the only thing she couldn't do with that frying pan was cook. Not that I cared. Baba was my hero.

"Got that right. Hey, I don't see Lucy in here," I said, my head whipping left and right.

I walked into my room, half expecting to see her asleep on my bed. Exhausted after hiding her booties again.

"You closed that door," Annie said. "She couldn't have gotten in there."

"She does that at home sometimes."

I never understood it. But somehow the pup had learned how to work doorknobs. She didn't do it all the time. I'm guessing just when there was something she really wanted on the other side of the door. So the levers in Annie's condo would be a piece of cake. That's why I was always so careful to lock the outside doors.

"Hang on," my sister said. "I'll check my room."

Annie came flying back out, her face a cloud of distress. "She's not there."

"The balcony door is still locked." It had been the first thing I checked. And Lucy couldn't manipulate locks. Especially these.

We spent the next five minutes looking behind and under every piece of furniture in the penthouse. By then, we were disheveled and frantic.

"Does anyone have a key to this place?" I asked in desperation.

I wanted to believe some dog-friendly acquaintance had just taken Lucy for a walk. It beat the alternative.

Annie shook her head vigorously. "Just my Miami assistant. And she's pregnant and on bed rest. Leslie was pushing for a key. She said the management service needed it in case of emergencies. I told her if there was an emergency, they could call me, and I'd have someone let them in. The truth is, if it was a real emergency, I'd let them break down the door."

"Where *is* she?"

I wanted to cry, but I couldn't afford the luxury. That sweet, innocent creature was alone and lost in a strange place. And it was all my fault. I should have stayed home, and let Annie go to the party. What was I thinking?

"We know she's not here in the apartment," Annie said matter-of-factly. "If she somehow got out, where would she go?"

"Not far," I said. "She hates the elevators."

"Could she have tried to follow us? You know, by smell?"

"Lucy likes to smell things. But she's not a scent hound. At least, not that I know of."

Found eating out of a back-alley garbage can and brought home by Nick's ex-fiancée Gabby, Lucy's family tree remained a mystery. The only thing we could say for certain: She was a dog.

And I'd never seen another exactly like her. An adorable puppy, who was turning into a beautiful russet-colored adult, she was truly one of a kind.

"So let's lock the door and walk the halls," Annie suggested. "Can she do stairs?"

"I don't know," I said. "She's kind of afraid of heights."

"We'll find her," my sister said. "She's wearing her tags, and she's microchipped. Even if she got out of the building, they'll know she's not a stray. And if we have to, we'll call all the shelters."

I had a sick feeling in the pit of my stomach. My arms and legs felt limp. How would I tell Nick? He'd trusted me. And I'd let him down.

"What if we get up a search party?" I said. "There are still a few dog lovers in the building. I bet Stan and Ethel would help."

"That's a great idea!" Annie said.

A sudden buzzing startled us both. My phone. I looked at the screen, and my heart sank.

"It's Nick. What do I say? How do I tell him what I've done?"

"You didn't do anything. She got out. Dogs do that."

"'I didn't do anything' is right. I didn't do enough to protect her."

"We'll find her," Annie said, reaching for her own phone. "Tell him the truth. And the search party's a good idea. I'll start calling people."

"So, how's my baby girl?" Nick's voice boomed through the handset. "Can you put her on the phone?"

"Nick, she got out. I don't know how. Both doors were locked. But we're gathering a search party, and we'll call you back as soon as we find her."

"She's at Diamond Jack's."

"What?"

"The manager just called. My number's on her tag. She showed up there about two minutes ago. He remembered her from this morning, because she polished off a full breakfast, and sampled one of his specialty lemon ricotta pancakes. And apparently she liked it, because she came back this evening for more. Hopped up on a chair and sat there politely waiting to be served."

"They found her and called Nick!" I shouted to Annie, across the apartment. "She's at Diamond Jack's."

Annie grinned. "What did I tell you about those pancakes?"

Relief flooded my body as I sagged against the sofa. I felt something wet on my cheek and realized I was crying.

"Nick, I'm so sorry. I still don't understand how she got out."

"The little dog's a regular Houdini," he said, laughing. "That's why I named her Lucy. She's a crazy redhead, and she's always up to something."

CHAPTER 16

The next morning—in keeping with my new vacation mode—I slept late. Annie handled Lucy's early morning walk. And brought us back coffee and doughnuts. So if Lucy escaped again, we'd have another new place to look for her.

After our high-carb splurge, I decided to do a little more digging into the other four HOA candidates. I knew precious little about any of them. And neither did anyone else I'd spoken with so far.

I had borrowed one of Annie's big sun hats. I planned to take Lucy for her second stroll of the morning, then drop her off at the condo and do a little research poolside. After an hour, I figured I'd pop upstairs, refresh the sunblock, collect Lucy and escort her on another tour of the neighborhood. Annie and I reasoned that if we took her for more regular jaunts, maybe the pup wouldn't feel the need to strike out on her own.

We still couldn't figure out how she'd managed that one.

I coaxed the pup into all four booties with promises of walks and treats. Then I clipped on her leash, and we were good to go.

But when we reached the elevators and I pressed the button, nothing happened.

I jabbed it again. Nada.

I pushed it down and held it—still nothing.

I looked down at Lucy. The pup looked up at me.

"How do you feel about getting a little extra cardio today?" I asked her.

She appeared to give it some thought.

After what Ethel and Stan had said about the stairs, I wasn't exactly eager for the experience. We walked around the corner, and I opened the stairway door.

Ethel was right. Not even eleven o'clock and it felt like the inside of a pizza oven.

With cement slab stairs, concrete walls, and no air vents, it was as if the architect had designed it to trap and hold the heat.

"OK, baby, we're going to trot right down and get through this as quick as we can. Then we're going to find something good to eat."

Like ice.

At the word "eat," Lucy's tail picked up steam. So we had a plan.

Five floors later, I was rethinking the whole trip. My canine companion was skipping down the steps like a prizefighter in training. I was a sweaty wreck.

The only thing that kept me going: By that point, it was only four flights down to the ground. But it was five flights up to the penthouse.

Lucy, gamboling beside me, was none the worse for wear.

When we made it to the bottom, I threw the door open and staggered out like I'd survived a trek across the Mojave. I craved water. And oxygen.

At this rate, who needs an early morning exercise class?

*   *   *

A little while later, after a successful beach outing that included scooping up shells and walking in the surf (for me), and chasing seagulls and barking at waves (for Lucy), along with running in the wet sand (for both of us), we returned to the air-conditioned comfort of the condo.

The pup made a beeline for her new water bowl—now in my sister's space-aged kitchen—then raced for the sofa, hopped up, turned around a few times, and settled in for a nap.

Mission accomplished.

I slipped out and made my way back down nine flights of stairs to the pool. That's when I spotted Ethel Plunkett on one of the landings, standing next to a fluffy, snow-white dog who couldn't have weighed twenty pounds. Mrs. Pickles.

"Beautiful morning, isn't it?" Ethel said cheerily.

As I hit the landing, the little dog ran over, sniffed my ankles, and stared up at me with twinkling black button eyes. With pristine fur and a cute clip, she looked like a little teddy bear. A smiling teddy bear.

"It is that," I said, as I bent down and scratched behind one furry ear.

"You were right, by the way," Ethel said, buoyantly. "I called the county this morning. No rules about pets in elevators at all. They never even heard of such a thing. The poor man in the zoning department probably thought I was crackers. I kept asking 'Are you sure?' So as soon as those elevators are up and running, Mrs. Pickles and I are riding in style. No more stairs for us!"

"That's fantastic," I said. And it would take some of the wind out of Leslie's sails. I wondered how many other rules and regs she'd been inventing over the past few months. I'm guessing as word spread, the residents of Oceanside might take it on themselves to find out. If that was the case, a few government offices would be fielding a lot of phone calls.

"Sure will make my life a lot easier," Ethel said happily, as she stepped lightly up the stairs, with Mrs. Pickles hopping up the steps beside her.

As she exited the stairwell, I swore I heard her singing.

From my poolside office in the shade, I searched a couple of different databases and hit a certain well-known, name-brand search engine for good measure. I found plenty of people with names matching the candidates—including sixteen guys named Manuel Garcia—in the greater Miami area. But none of the names traced back to an address at Oceanside.

But if Ethel was right and they had all moved in fairly recently, that would track. And people of means often supplied their office addresses or even postal boxes on forms, rather than their actual homes—anything to give them an extra measure of privacy.

So I went at it from a different angle. I pulled up the property tax rolls, typed in Oceanside's street address, and looked for matches to the four candidates' names. Nada.

But a number of the units were owned by corporations. Including Annie's penthouse. Someone had been taking advice from our lawyer brother.

It was a common enough practice. And, for recognizable names like my sister's, it offered an additional layer of protection in case an overly enthusiastic fan wanted to show up for tea.

I decided I'd have to get more creative.

In Florida, voter registration records are public. And some websites post them online, too. It's a bonanza for telemarketers and reporters. Not so great for privacy advocates and people hiding from telemarketers and reporters.

But I reasoned that if someone was civic-minded enough to serve as condo president, they'd probably registered to vote. And this was one place you couldn't list a corporate address or box number.

Twenty minutes later, I discovered that there were quite a few guys with those four names voting in the Miami area. But none of them lived at Oceanside.

If Leslie's opponents were transplants, it's possible they were still voting at their old polling places. It's also possible that they'd never registered to vote in the first place. But it was kind of odd that out of four candidates, all four were absent from the local voter rolls.

Something definitely smelled. And it wasn't fresh doughnuts.

CHAPTER 17

"No doubt about it, Red. That does sound fishy," Trip drawled after I'd relayed the story of the enigmatic board candidates.

I was also relieved to hear he'd gotten some sleep. In fact, he sounded more rested than I did.

"Most politicians will show up at a ribbon cutting just to soak up the love and listen to the sound of their own voices," he continued.

"Well, to be fair, these guys aren't politicians. They're just four schlubs who put their names forward for a thankless job that actually pays less than mine."

"How much less?" he asked.

"Zilch."

"OK, so just a little less."

"I'm sorry, we all don't live in historically significant neighborhoods with private chefs and in-house bakers at our beck and call. Seriously, how's Nick doing?"

I'd seen my brother drag himself home from Ian's kitchen looking like a zombie after baking half the night. And that's when his commute was just shuffling across the street. I was seriously worried about him driving from Fordham to Georgetown in the wee hours.

"Comes home all hours, stinking of cheap perfume and covered in even cheaper lipstick."

"Good, because I was afraid he was working too hard," I said.

"That boy does put in some serious hours. Between him and Tom, I feel like a lazy layabout."

"This from a guy who only gets three hours' sleep."

"They put me to shame, the both of them," Trip said. "But they also feed me well, so I'm not complaining."

"Well, if you ever light out for pancakes in the middle of the night, just be sure to let someone know where you're going."

"I heard about that. Sounds like Lucy is officially a teenager now. Pretty soon she'll be blasting her stereo, skipping school, and dating boys."

"There's only one boy in her life. And don't tell Nick, but I think she misses him like crazy. We were exploring the neighborhood yesterday morning and way off in the distance there was a tall blond guy in shorts, a T-shirt, and flip-flops. All of a sudden, her head comes way up, her tail starts to beat double time, and she's dragging me down the sidewalk toward him. When we got close enough and she realized it wasn't Nick, it was like she melted. Head, ears, tail—all drooped. I just felt so bad."

"She's a one-man dog," my best friend said.

"That she is. So, have they at least started in on the kitchen?"

"Wow, look at the time! Got to make that staff meeting."

"Chase Wentworth Cabot the Third—spill," I said through clenched teeth.

"The contractor says your wiring isn't grounded. It's a fire hazard, and they're going to have to redo the whole place."

"Noooooooo!"

"And she wonders why I don't tell her anything."

"That house has been standing for a hundred years," I said. "If it hadn't been grounded, it would have burned down by now."

"Especially with you in the kitchen," he quipped.

"Exactly!"

We fell silent as I digested the new information. It was like a Rubik's Cube—whichever way I looked at it, nothing made sense.

"Look, it goes without saying, but I'll say it anyway," Trip said. "You guys are welcome to stay at the townhouse or the farm for as long as you like."

Trip hailed from money. His family home was a five-hundred-acre spread in the heart of Virginia horse country. Anyone else would have labeled it an estate. His family called it simply "the farm."

"Rewiring the whole house? Trip, that's going to take forever."

As houseguests, we Vlodnacheks have a short expiration date. Like yogurt.

"The contractor told Nick it would take a couple of weeks," Trip said. "Unless there's black mold."

"Because the black mold cancels out the bad wiring? Like two negatives make a positive?"

"Because then they have to schedule specialists to come in and remove that first," he explained. "Then the contractor can start."

"Two teams of experts, months of construction, boatloads of money, and that doesn't even include the changes Nick needs to bring the kitchen up to code," I said, sighing. "And I haven't got the money for any of this."

"Look at the bright side," Trip said. "If the place is as much of a fire trap as they claim, maybe it'll burn down."

"Don't tempt me."

CHAPTER 18

I had no idea what to do about my house. So I decided to kick the can down the road a bit and just enjoy the Miami sunshine. Even if that came with a side of sizzling heat.

Annie had gone to a business meeting at one of the fashion houses. So I figured Lucy and I could explore the glories of South Beach in the summer. And if we happened to bump into some food, so much the better.

I looked through my purse. Cash—check. Small note pad and pen—check. Extra bags for Lucy—check. Treats for Lucy—check. Water for Lucy—check. Pooper-scooper—check.

The pup was even wearing all four of her booties.

"OK," I said as we ducked into the stairwell, "it's gonna be like an oven in here, but we can do this."

Her tail wagged enthusiastically. I noticed that for Lucy, any trip out was cause for celebration.

My new vacation motto.

Which lasted all of thirty seconds. Idiotically, I'd hoped that, after what felt like a dozen trips up and down the stairs, the trek might actually get easier. But I hadn't counted on the afternoon heat.

Encased in cement, the stairwell was sweltering. Forget

frying eggs on the sidewalk. Nick could have used this place to bake scones.

Lucy, good sport that she was, trotted down the steps like a champ. I just tried to keep up.

When we exited I felt a welcoming rush of cool air. Lucy, pulling me toward the front door, didn't even break stride.

But when we cut through the lobby, I could see a crowd gathered in front of the elevators. From a distance, I couldn't hear what anyone was saying. But the body language told me they weren't happy.

"Hey, with all the money we shell out, these should work one hundred percent of the time. And if they don't, there should be a guy here in overalls with a wrench in his hand fixing the danged things."

"Women can fix elevators, too, Charlie."

"I don't care who's wearing the overalls, as long as they're fixing the danged elevators."

"Has anyone called the management company?" another woman asked. I recognized her from the party as Mrs. Ernie.

"An hour ago," a glamorous brunette in a lavender sheath dress replied. "They said we need to speak with Leslie."

"Good luck with that," said a forty-something bald man in a blue blazer. "I called her three times. It just keeps going to voice mail."

"She's probably out giving away T-shirts and kissing babies," Ernie grumbled. "Gonna have to take the service elevator."

"There's a service elevator?" I asked, stunned.

"You can't," the brunette said. "I already tried that. Someone's moving out. And they've got it locked up for the next couple of hours."

"Well, it's only one flight up to the restaurant," Ernie said, turning to his wife and offering her an arm. "How about an early dinner and a nice bottle of wine?"

CHAPTER 19

The next morning, I was up at dawn to walk Lucy. And this time, we were taking the freight elevator.

Because the two main elevators still weren't working. Big surprise.

Annie had tried Leslie a few times herself last night. But, just like the guy in the lobby, her calls went straight to voice mail.

She even phoned an after-hours number for the management company. But when she finally reached an actual human, they weren't any help, either. Basically, unless her name was Leslie McQueen, they didn't have the authority to share any information about what was (or wasn't), going on at Oceanside.

So this morning, I came prepared. Annie had given me directions to the service elevator. And if someone was moving today, I was just going to hitch a ride with their bookcases.

Anything was better than nine flights in the hot box.

From the tenth floor, finding the freight elevator was relatively easy. It was hidden behind a locked door marked

"Authorized personnel only." One swipe of the fob, and we were inside.

I was carrying the leash and our directions from the elevator to the lobby in one hand, and the scooper in the other. I also had an overstuffed beach bag—with water and extra poop bags—slung over my shoulder, and another of Annie's wide-brimmed sun hats on my head. So it took a bit of maneuvering to navigate the heavy steel door.

Once we exited the elevator on the ground floor, finding our way through the building's storage area and out to the lobby was a little more complicated.

According to Annie's directions, you had to wind through a maze of storage lockers and—if you took the correct combination of right and left turns—you were rewarded with the door that accessed the hall that dumped you in the lobby.

I think Indiana Jones had less trouble finding the Ark. And he wasn't traveling with a pup who needed to get outside in a hurry.

"I just use the stairs," my sister had confided. "It's easier. Plus, it's good exercise."

I was honestly beginning to miss my black-mold-tainted, all-on-one-floor bungalow. Dodgy wiring or not.

Turns out the storage area, like the stairs, was definitely lacking in the cosmetics department. I'm guessing it would never be on the home tour for potential buyers. This was the part of the place you'd see only after you signed that mortgage on the dotted line.

Over our heads, square insulated ducts crisscrossed the ceiling, along with a variety of plastic and metal pipes. Lighting, provided by overhead fluorescent tubes, was sparse. And I noticed about a third of the bulbs were dead—giving the place a dark and shadowy vibe.

But hey, at least it was air-conditioned.

Large chain-link cages on each side of the concrete pathway were sectioned off, numbered, and locked. Each resident owned at least one, and they could rent more if they wanted, Annie had explained. It was where they stashed items like holiday decorations, sports equipment, or old files. Things they needed but didn't use everyday. Or didn't have space for in their homes.

The storage area also looked like it hadn't seen a cleaning service in a long time. Dust bunnies skittered across our path and more dangled from the overhead lights. In the corners, a couple of giant spiderwebs decorated the walls.

"C'mon, Lucy," I said, picking up the pace.

Given the size of the webs, I definitely didn't want to meet those spiders.

I rounded a corner and heard footsteps. The whole place was like an echo chamber, with sounds bouncing off the concrete. I couldn't tell where the steps originated. Was someone in front of us? Or behind us? And who was it?

I stopped to listen. And I wasn't the only one. Lucy rotated both of her large satellite-dish ears. In different directions.

We stood stock-still in the silence.

Would it kill them to add a few more lights in this place?

"Anyone there?" I asked.

"Wuff!" Lucy added for good measure. "Woof wuff!"

"Good girl!" I whispered.

Suddenly, a clattering sound. Like something had fallen. Or someone had dropped something.

I swear I heard a muffled scraping sound. Then, nothing.

"C'mon," I whispered to Lucy. "Let's get the heck out of here."

We hustled through Annie's series of left and right turns, until finally a big steel door labeled "Ground Floor Hall" appeared in front of us.

I don't think Indy was half as happy to see that Ark.

CHAPTER 20

Later, after the thrills and chills of the storage area, the pool was kind of anticlimactic.

It was still the cool of the morning. Or at least as cool as Miami gets in July.

A few of the tables were occupied. Mostly by what appeared to be retirees. A couple of younger residents had brought coffee, tablets, phones, or laptops. The office to-go.

After a few days here, I recognized some of the faces. Including Ethel and Mrs. Pickles. If Leslie was going to chew me out for bringing Lucy to the pool deck, at least I was in good company.

I grabbed a small table next to Stan, Ethel, Ernie, and Mrs. Ernie, as Lucy and Mrs. Pickles circled each other excitedly.

First Lucy sniffed Mrs. Pickles. Then they switched. After that, they started chasing each other in ever-widening circles.

"Is that your dog?" Ethel asked. "She's a cutie."

"That's Lucy," I said, as I raised the sun-colored umbrella over my table and locked it into place. "She actually belongs to my brother. But I'm keeping her for the week."

"What kind of dog is she?" Ernie asked. "Never seen one like that."

"She's a Lucy," I said cheerily. "Mixed breed. The exact formula is a closely guarded secret. Kinda like KFC."

That's when I looked over and noticed that the pool had an odd greenish tinge.

"Any idea what's going on with the water?" I asked.

"We think it's the filter," Stan said, sipping from a cardboard coffee cup. "Or it could be algae, if it's low on chlorine. Wouldn't swim in it, though."

"And they're not coming to fix it anytime soon," Ernie added.

"Let me guess," I said. "The pool company needs to speak with Leslie."

Ernie nodded grimly.

"Don't they have some kind of agreement for regular maintenance?" I asked.

Either Leslie McQueen was a total control freak, or this management company was totally lazy.

"My Marilyn here even called the pool company directly," Ernie said proudly, pointing to his wife.

"They claim we're already three months behind with the bills," Marilyn added. "They're not lifting a finger until Leslie cuts them a check."

Wow.

"She's still not answering her phone, either," Ernie said. "Everybody and their monkey's been calling her. Nothing but voice mail. I even went up and knocked on her door this morning."

Marilyn smiled. "Knowing you, it was a little louder than a polite knock."

"Hey, she could be hard of hearing, for all I know," he said.

"My sister tried calling the management company itself

last night," I admitted. "But they refused to tell her any-thing. They said the only one they can talk to is Leslie."

"They told me the same thing this morning," Ethel said. "Except they said 'Ms. McQueen or the board's attorney.'"

That got my attention. Usually when people started referencing lawyers, it meant a lawsuit was in the offing.

"That's odd," Marilyn said.

Ethel nodded. "I thought so, too."

Finished with their game of chase and tag around the green pool, Lucy and Mrs. Pickles trotted over and settled themselves on the blue-and-yellow beach towel I'd spread out in the shade.

I reached into my bag and placed a treat carefully in front of each of them.

Two tails wagged in unison.

I grabbed the phone out of my tote and snapped a photo. I'd send it to Nick later with the caption "Lucy makes a friend."

That way, my brother would have at least one less worry on his mind.

"So who is the board's attorney?" I asked.

"No idea," Ernie said.

"I don't think we have one," Ethel said. "We have a president, and a secretary, and a treasurer," she added, ticking them off on her fingers.

"Yeah, I think that was one of the things the management company was supposed to provide for us," Stan said. "You know, to save us money and keep everything on the up-and-up."

"That swamp sure ain't on the up-and-up," Ernie said, waving a paw at the pool. "I don't care how many champagne parties McQueen throws. She's crazy if she thinks folks are gonna forget this, come election day."

"So it's a board of three," I summarized. "Who are the other two board members?"

I figured if Leslie McQueen was temporarily indisposed, maybe the other two could fill in. Or at least fill in some of the blanks.

"Secretary's that guy on six," Stan said, looking at Ernie. "You know. The one with the green Jag."

"Chu," Ernie said, snapping his fingers. "Dennis Chu."

"That's the one," Stan said, happily. "British racing green, tan leather interior, all the toys. Must have cost him a mint."

I remembered seeing Chu on the tax rolls. Lucy and I might pay him a little visit after five.

"And who's the treasurer?" I asked.

With missing payments and a missing Leslie, I had a sneaking suspicion that money might be the key to unraveling this whole mess.

"Geoffrey Gallagher," Ethel said. "He lives in the unit right above me. Nice, quiet boy. Keeps to himself."

"I heard he's an accountant for some big corporation," Marilyn said, as Ethel nodded.

Make that two visits this evening. And if I was going to get two corporate types to open their doors to a stranger after a long day at the office, it might pay to invite Annie along for the ride.

CHAPTER 21

Late that afternoon, Annie and I held a strategy meeting over tall tumblers of ice cream. Chocolate mint chip for me. Peanut butter fudge for her. Lucy was totally absorbed with a canine version Annie had picked up at the local grocery store. Also peanut butter flavored.

"Oh, I know Gracie and Dennis," Annie said between bites. "But I don't remember Geoffrey Gallagher at all. I wonder if he's new?"

"Stan didn't even mention that Dennis had a wife," I said. "But I think he's in love with the guy's car."

"Oh yeah, the Jag," my sister agreed. "It is nice."

"Gallagher lives just upstairs from Ethel, so his apartment should be easy to find. Even if we have to take the stairs."

Air-conditioned or not, I wasn't too anxious to revisit the creepy storage area. I'm guessing that pool maintenance wasn't the only area where Leslie had been cutting corners.

Lucy and I had been climbing stairs all day. By the time this vacation was over, we were both going to have legs like mountain goats.

"So what are we going to ask these people tonight?" Annie inquired.

"In reporting, this is what we call 'string gathering,'" I said. "No set list of questions. No pressure. We just want to chat and see what we can learn."

"Low-key," Annie said.

"Exactly. Instead of squeezing them for Leslie's whereabouts, we ask if there are any provisions for arranging for repairs and services when the president is indisposed."

"Oh, I like that," she said.

"As a conversation starter, it beats 'Where did she go with the dough?'"

"Do you really think she took off?" Annie asked. "I mean, she was just so . . . enthusiastic."

"More like relentless," I said. "And there's no telling at this point. We need a lot more information. Hopefully, if we do it right, we can get some answers this evening. It would also be nice to find out what the relationship is between Leslie and the management company."

"What do you mean?" my sister asked.

"Well, from what Ethel said, it sounds like they lawyered up. Or they think Leslie did. Which means they might just be the *former* management company."

"Oh geez, that would explain a lot," Annie said. "Including why they won't come and fix anything."

"But it still doesn't account for why Leslie's not answering her phone," I said.

That's when something clicked. I jumped up from my empty glass, loped to the sideboard, and fired up my laptop.

"What?" Annie asked.

"I'm an idiot. Everyone around here keeps calling the phone number that Leslie shared with them. And she never answers it. But I forgot—Leslie is a real estate agent. And every real estate agent I know is crazy-glued to their work cell. It's economic survival. Because if you don't answer your phone, your clients will call someone else. What's the name of Leslie's company?"

"SouthShell Realty."

I found the site, hit "About us," and scrolled through "Our staff." Almost instantly I was confronted with a grinning mugshot of Leslie McQueen. With the same carnivorous expression that had welcomed us to her party. But the smile never quite reached her eyes.

I clicked on the photo, and that brought up all of her contact details. Including three different phone numbers—office, mobile, and home.

"Three phone numbers," I said, holding up as many fingers. "Which one have you been dialing?"

"At this point, I know it by heart—(305) 555-0125," Annie said.

"That's the one she lists as 'home,'" I said. "I'm guessing it's a landline or maybe the cell she keeps at her place."

Annie grabbed her phone and joined me in front of the laptop.

She dialed the number Leslie listed as her "mobile," got voice mail, and left a short message. Then she tried the office line.

"Hi, this is Anastasia Vlodnachek. I'm calling for Leslie McQueen."

My sister paused. "Well, it's rather urgent. Do you know how I might be able to reach her? No, I really need to speak with her personally."

She paused again. "Oh my, that is worrisome. Yes, me too. No, no, that's all right. If you hear from her, just tell her I called. I will. OK, thank you."

Annie had an odd expression on her face as she put down the phone.

"No one at the realty company has heard from Leslie since the night of the party. She had a closing the next afternoon, and she never showed. She's missed a bunch of appointments. Clients are calling left and right. And no one seems to know where the heck she is."

CHAPTER 22

I didn't want a repeat of the other night. So this time we arranged a dog sitter. Or, more accurately, a doggie play-date.

After a nice long walk, we'd dropped off the pup at Ethel's place for a few hours with Mrs. Pickles. I figured if Lucy was happily occupied, she'd have less time to plot her next escape.

"By the way, I should have warned you—the sun is pretty intense here," Annie said, as we headed back to the stairs. "Especially in the summer."

"So I've noticed," I said ruefully.

"What helps is reapplying the sunblock every hour or right after you come out of the water."

"OK, that explains a lot."

She smiled. "Hey, what's a big sister for?"

I had a sudden flash of inspiration. "Do you know what Leslie drives?" I asked.

"A cute little sky-blue Mercedes convertible," Annie replied.

"Do you know where she parks it?"

"That's brilliant!" my sister said, catching my drift.

"Well, we know from Ernie she's not answering her door. And her office hasn't heard from her. I just thought it might be interesting to see if her car's still in the lot."

"If it's there, that doesn't mean she's still here, though," Annie said. "A lot of us use ride shares and cabs. Heck, even when I'm back in Manhattan, my electric Mini's still in the garage under the building most of the time. And the way this neighborhood's laid out, you can get pretty far on foot, too."

"Nothing's conclusive. It's just one more piece of the puzzle."

And one more detail for the cops. Because at this point, I was pretty sure we'd be calling them soon. Either to report a missing Leslie or the missing money.

A few minutes later, we exited the stairs into the garage. I have to say, the lighting was a lot better than the storage area. And it was clean. At least, for a garage.

I said as much to Annie.

"Well, this is one of the first things prospective residents see," she said, as we made our way through the parking lot that housed a virtual fleet of luxury Beemers, Benzes, and Lexuses—peppered with the occasional new economy car here and there. "And most of the homeowners are using it two and three times a day. So if the board made cutbacks here, people would notice. And complain."

"I can't believe the board didn't pay the pool cleaners," I countered. "I mean, that's major."

"Maybe they didn't plan to let it go this long."

"That makes more sense," I reasoned. "You let a couple of payments slide because you can. I mean, this is a big place. They're probably a major client for the pool service. So the pool company lets it go a few times. But then something happened. I'd love to know what."

"We all pay our association dues religiously," Annie said. "The new board instituted a pretty steep fine schedule for late payments. And a lot of us have it on auto-pay, anyway. We thought the management company was using that money to pay utilities, maintenance, and upkeep on this place. But if that's not happening, who's got the money and where is it?"

"That's what we're going to find out," I said. "And I have a feeling we'll locate Leslie in the process."

"You really do think she ran off with it," she said, concerned. A statement, not a question.

"Not necessarily. I just have a strong hunch the two issues are connected. There are a lot of possible explanations at this point."

None of them good.

"Over there," Annie said, pointing. "Right in front of the elevators."

I looked up and saw a shiny, light-blue two-door Benz. The white cloth top was up. As we approached, I reached into my purse, retrieved a Kleenex, and tried the driver's door. Locked.

I rested the back of my hand on the hood. It was cool.

"What?" Annie asked.

"It hasn't been driven in the past few hours, that's all."

At this point, I was reasonably certain the police would be dusting this car for prints in the not-so-distant future. And I didn't want them finding mine. I had enough problems.

"Good lord, she's even got the spot marked," I said, walking around to the back of the car. " 'Reserved for the President?' All she needs is some velvet rope and a security detail."

"It is ludicrous," Annie agreed. "We all have reserved spots anyway. But the board gave her this a couple of months after she was appointed. The story was that she needed to be able to zoom in and out quickly during the day to meet vendors and contractors for condo business.

Honestly, I thought it was just a little perk in lieu of a salary."

"Whose spot was it before?" I asked.

"No idea," my sister admitted, shrugging.

As she walked around to study the front of the car, I gave the trunk and back bumper area a discreet sniff. Lucy would have been proud.

Luckily, nothing but gasoline and rubber.

A real detective would have been popping that trunk about now. For me, there wasn't enough money in the world.

CHAPTER 23

Since Geoffrey lived on three, that seemed like the logical place to start. Plus, as the treasurer, he was the money guy. I hoped having my sister in his home would dazzle him enough to spill a few pertinent details.

It was a cheap ploy. But it was pretty much all we had.

As Annie stood in front of his door, I took a giant step to the side—out of range of the peephole.

"What?" my sister asked.

"One woman looks like a meet-cute. Two looks like we're collecting for the PTA. Or recruiting for one of those storefront churches."

She grinned, smoothed her shiny hair, and rapped lightly on the door.

I could have sworn I heard a TV. But a lot of people leave the television on while they're at work. It's supposed to discourage criminals. I think it just advertises that you have a nice TV.

After half a minute, Annie rapped again—louder this time.

"Geez, Geoffrey, there's a supermodel on your doorstep," I hissed. "Talk about opportunity knocking."

"Shhhh!" she warned.

A half minute more and nothing.

"Let's go," my sister said, suddenly bolting.

"Give it one more try," I said, as I trailed her back down the hall and into the stairwell. "He might have been in the bathroom. Or changing his clothes."

"There was someone in there," she whispered, once the stairwell door closed. "I could see shadows moving behind the peephole. And I swear I saw an eyeball."

As we hit the second landing, we passed Marilyn Doyle.

"Well, hello, girls," she said brightly. "Boy, these stairs are really something," she added, putting one hand to her abundant chest. "Just going down to visit Ethel. I hear she has an adorable houseguest."

"I just hope Lucy's behaving herself," Annie said. "She can be a handful."

"Ethel says the same thing about Mrs. Pickles. I swear that little snowball has the biggest personality. And she always looks like she's smiling. Well, see you later." And with a friendly wave, she was off.

When we ended up in the sixth floor hallway, I pulled my sister aside. "You didn't say anything to Ethel about what we were doing tonight, did you?"

"What do you take me for?" she asked incredulously. "If I did that, it would have been halfway around the building before we even knocked on Geoffrey's door. We haven't got much going for us at this point, but at least we have the element of surprise."

Did I say she was smart, or what?

"Hey, I'm just trying to figure out why he didn't open the door to a supermodel," I said.

"Maybe he prefers brunettes. Or maybe he's shy. Or maybe he's gay."

"Or maybe he has Leslie trussed up in his bathroom," I said.

"In that case, he also has my sympathies," she said. "Come on, Dennis and Grace's place is this way."

Annie knocked, and the door opened almost immediately. A tall Asian man with a phone to his ear looked first at Annie, then at me. He was wearing jeans, a navy golf shirt, and had bare feet.

"Hi, Dennis," Annie said in her most engaging tone. "This is my sister, Alex. Do you mind if we come in for just a minute?"

"Aw, not you too," he said softly.

"No, Bob, not you," he shouted into the cell. "Look, I'm telling you, for the last time, I have no idea what's going on. And if I knew it was going to be like this, I never would have volunteered for the damned board!"

He clicked off from his phone call.

"I wish I could turn this damned thing off," he said, staring at the phone. "It's been ringing nonstop all afternoon. Like I'd know where the hell Leslie McQueen is holed up."

I stood there with my hands behind my back, trying my best to look friendly and nonthreatening. But the smile was frozen on my face. And one of the muscles in my cheek started to twitch.

"We won't be a minute," Annie continued. "But I honestly think we might be able to help."

"Suit yourself," Dennis said. With that he turned and stalked into the living room.

Annie followed him, and I closed the door behind us. So far, so good.

"So how's Grace?" Annie asked.

"Pregnant and irritable," he said, tossing the phone into a soft green basket atop an old wooden steamer trunk that served as a side table. "She'll be home in half an hour, and if I don't have this place straightened up by then, I'm going to be in the doghouse."

I looked around the room. Other than a newspaper spread

over the dining room table next to a laptop, a soda can, and some manila files, the place looked neat as a pin to me.

But maybe living in a mold-infested firetrap had lowered my standards.

Dennis sank into a large chocolate-brown easy chair and motioned us to a tan velveteen sofa.

"Look, before you start," he said, putting both hands out in front of him like he was stopping an invisible train, "I don't know where the heck Leslie is. I don't know when she's coming back. And I didn't even know she was gone, until my phone started blowing up."

"Well, of course not," Annie said, flashing the million-dollar smile that had sold everything from toothpaste to designer labels. "No one knows where she is. Or why she took off—especially in the middle of the election. But Alex and I were chatting, and we thought of something that might calm things down a bit. We figured you might be having a bit of a hard time, so we dropped by to share."

I nodded, smiling. But by this time, the twitch was turning into a spasm. He was going to think I had Tourette's.

"Leslie, for whatever reason, is temporarily indisposed," my sister continued breezily. "We were just wondering if there was something in the board's bylaws that would allow for services and maintenance to continue while she's absent?"

"No idea," Dennis said dismissively. "Look, what nobody seems to understand about the board? It *is* Leslie. She runs this place. Hell, I don't even know where any of the paperwork is. Leslie negotiates contracts, pays the vendors, hires and fires, handles fines—she does it all. Geoff and I pretty much just rubber-stamp everything. And up until now, she was doing a pretty damned good job."

"What about the management company?" I asked softly.

He looked confused. "Management company? Oh, we fired them almost four months ago."

As a reporter, I interviewed people for a living, but right now I was having trouble maintaining a poker face. My big sis? No such problem.

"Any idea why?" she asked, smiling, as though this situation were the most natural thing in the world.

"Leslie believed they were misappropriating money. Definitely overspending, possibly skimming. Couldn't prove it. But it gave her an idea. She called it 'a grand experiment.' She wanted to try handling their job ourselves for a few months. Just to see what it involved. And if we could save money. She convinced Geoff and me that, at worst, we'd know exactly what we needed when we hired the next management company. Her proposal was that we'd do it for a couple of months on the q.t. As a test. We'd document the results, then we'd reveal everything to the homeowners and show them how much money we'd saved. We'd be heroes."

Annie and I nodded encouragingly.

"Of course, what that really meant was that Leslie was doing all the work."

Annie shook her head sympathetically. "That must have been quite a load for her."

My sister had missed her calling. She should have been an actress. She was a natural.

"You'd think so," Dennis said, sagging. "But she had it all perfectly organized. And when we looked at the books every month, we were saving tons. I mean, basically, she was managing this place for free."

He shook his head. "And when it comes to pricing labor, you can't beat free."

"All she asked for in return was a special parking spot," I commented. "That's a bargain."

"The parking spot was just the beginning," Dennis said, grimacing. "Then it was a break from her association dues. Then it was picking up her resident services tab."

"I was seriously beginning to wonder if it might be time to turn things over to a professional again," he said, putting one hand to his forehead, shielding his face. "But Geoff was against it. Basically, if Leslie was against it, Geoff was against it. Two against one. Always two against one. Now I'm hearing rumors that bills haven't been paid. My phone won't stop ringing. The elevators are out. The pool's green. And Grace's in the middle of a tricky pregnancy and can't handle any extra stress. Or stairs. I don't want her finding out about this. And I don't know how much more of it I can take. At this point, if I could just move us out of here and rent this place, I would."

I almost felt sorry for him. Not only was Leslie's "grand experiment" unlikely to make them heroes, I was pretty sure it was five kinds of illegal. But telling him he might be looking at prison time wasn't likely to keep him talking.

"Maybe call the old management company and see if they'll step into the breach?" I suggested.

Dennis shook his head. "Trust me, Leslie burned that bridge. She may not have been able to prove any wrong-doing, but she threatened to sue them and explore criminal charges if they didn't let us out of our contract."

"And they agreed?" I asked.

"Squeaky wheel," Dennis said, leaning forward on his elbows and staring down at the spotless hardwood floors. "It's easier just to give Leslie what she wants. Otherwise, she will make your life a living hell."

"Who called for the special election?" I asked gently.

"Leslie raised the issue," he said, looking from Annie to me. "A couple of residents had approached her and wanted to run for board president—thought they could do a better job. And they didn't want to wait until December. Leslie didn't seem to care. Her attitude was, 'Let 'em try.' So she collected the entry forms, and suddenly it looked like we had a five-way race. Hell, I was hoping one of them would win. Then we could hire another professional management company and get off this roller-coaster. The special election was one request I was happy to rubber-stamp."

Suddenly, he looked at his watch and jumped to his feet. "I gotta get moving. Grace is going to be here any minute."

"Of course, we understand," my sister said, waving her hand. She pulled a card out of her purse, scribbled something on the back with a gold pen, and handed it to Dennis.

"This is my personal cell number," she said. "Grace already has it, but keep this where you both can grab it. When you need anything—help with the stairs, a quick casserole, a ride to the doctor—you just call. Anytime, day or night."

She patted him on the shoulder. "We're all going to get through this. Don't you worry."

Dennis's face relaxed into a grateful smile. He looked like a totally different person.

"Thanks," he said. "You two really are good neighbors. I actually feel better for the first time all day."

CHAPTER 24

Once we'd collected Lucy, I'd reasoned that—since we were only one flight off the ground—we might as well take the pup down for her evening constitutional. Forty minutes after that, we were sitting on the patio of a local restaurant with margaritas in our hands.

Paco's looked like a rambling, wood-sided house that had probably been built right after World War II. Now painted bright turquoise with pink and orange trim, it served—according to my sister—the best Tex-Mex in Miami.

Along with some first-rate margaritas.

We sat on the big patio, illuminated by lanterns and string lights, with half a basket of fresh tortilla chips between us, alongside bowls of red and green salsa.

I put another chip on the ground in front of Lucy. She stepped on it with a delicate paw and wolfed down all the pieces.

"I hate to tell you this, but I think your friend Dennis could be looking at prison time," I said.

"Not if he has a good lawyer," my sister countered.

"Know someone who could recommend one?" I teased.

Our older brother, Peter, specialized in tax law, so he didn't do criminal cases. But he knew plenty of attorneys who did.

"I knew Grace was pregnant," Annie said. "And it was a long time in coming—they really had some trouble. I was so happy to hear she was expecting, it never dawned on me that it was a high-risk pregnancy."

"That doesn't excuse what Dennis did," I said. "Those three didn't just cross a line, they pole-vaulted over it, swam the moat, and kept on running."

"I know," Annie said. "It's pretty bad. And when Dennis said he didn't even know where the board paperwork was? That means he probably doesn't know where the money is either. Some of the residents have put their life savings into those condos."

I'm guessing Stan, Ethel, Ernie, and Marilyn were among them.

"Maybe if we find Leslie, we can find the money," I said. "And I'd still like to talk to your friend Geoffrey the Eyeball."

"One thing doesn't make sense," Annie said.

"Just one? Seriously, I feel like every time we get even close to an answer, someone just raises another question."

"The Dennis I know through Gracie? Always a straight shooter. He's one of those people who sees things in black and white. Right and wrong. To the point where it drove her a little crazy sometimes."

I nodded and snagged two chips. I put one in front of Lucy.

"The idea of his becoming a rubber stamp for Leslie?" my sister continued. "That just doesn't seem like him."

"Yeah, I had a thought about that," I said.

Surprised, Annie looked up at me. "What?"

"The whole time we were talking to Dennis, his words were angry. Angry at Leslie. Angry at Geoffrey. Even angry at the other residents. But his body language was conveying something else—shame."

"Well, yeah, he pretty much sold out everyone who lives at Oceanside," Annie said.

"Yes, but why?" I asked. "When he was telling us what the board did, he never made eye contact. He was looking at the floor. Or hiding his face with his hand. Trust me, I've interviewed enough guilty people to know that reaction was pure shame."

"You're right," Annie said, cocking her head to one side.

I placed another chip in front of Lucy, who made it disappear in record time. Another magic trick she'd mastered.

"You think he knew what they were doing was wrong and did it anyway?" Annie asked. "Honestly, that's not the Dennis I know."

"I believe you. I mean, the guy was very upfront about what he did. It practically came pouring out of him. As if he couldn't wait to tell someone—to unburden himself. He's an honest man. He doesn't like keeping secrets. And you were great, by the way."

My sister smiled.

"But the reason behind it?" I continued. "The reason he caved to Leslie in the first place? I don't think that was strictly voluntary. I think Leslie knew something about him. Something that made him ashamed. And I think she used it as a bargaining chip to get his cooperation."

"You think Leslie was blackmailing Dennis?" Annie asked doubtfully.

"Can I prove it? No. Do I believe it, based on what I saw tonight? Yes. Annie, that man was literally sagging under the weight of guilt and shame. So much so that he wanted to take his pregnant wife and flee their home."

"Yes, but as you pointed out, he could be facing charges," my sister countered.

"You said he was conscientious. And what I witnessed

tonight confirms that. But if what he's saying is true, he and Geoff gave Leslie complete control of Oceanside and its money. And they fired the only people who were policing her. Without asking questions. Without taking it to the residents for a vote. Without making a peep. That's a pretty big ask. Especially of a straight shooter like Dennis. I think he did it because he felt he didn't have any other choice."

"I don't know," Annie said. "I think that's a stretch. Body language or no. But you know what I find weird?"

"Cronuts?"

"Bite your tongue," she said, dipping a chip into the fiery green salsa. "Cronuts are delicious. What's weird is, other than the three people on the board, no one knew about Leslie's little experiment for four months. Four whole months! Oceanside is a tight community. And you know how gossip spreads around that place."

"From what Dennis said tonight, I don't think he told Grace, either."

"He can't have," Annie agreed. "She wouldn't have stood for it. I think he's terrified she'll find out now. Could that be the shame you noticed? Having to admit to Gracie that he made a whopper of a mistake?"

"That still doesn't explain why he did it in the first place. Why does a smart, honest man go along with something so obviously sketchy? Dennis doesn't seem like the type to play with other people's money."

"Leslie does, though," my sister concluded.

"Yup, Leslie definitely does," I agreed, grabbing another chip for myself and coating it thoroughly with red salsa.

"Something else doesn't make sense," Annie started.

"So far, nothing about this whole situation makes sense to me," I admitted, popping the chip in my mouth.

"Leslie wanted to be board president. That was clear from her attitude. And her campaign."

"No argument there."

"So why even hold a special election?" Annie asked, as I put a large crispy chip in front of a very eager Lucy. "I mean, without it, the post was hers until next January. At least. And she could have run again then. Could she have been pressured into it?"

"You mean, did someone find out about her little 'experiment' and threaten to go public?" I theorized. "Possible. But if that was the case, you'd think the whole scheme would be common knowledge by now. I mean, if I were a candidate and I knew—I'd make sure everyone in the whole building knew. Instead, nothing."

"I just realized something," Annie said, leaning forward in her wicker chair. "We have an election in two days. And all five candidates seem to be in the wind."

CHAPTER 25

On the way to the stairwell with Lucy the next morning, I stopped in front of the elevators and reflexively poked the button.

Despite everything I knew, I still hoped.

Nada.

A few minutes later, as Lucy frolicked on the lawn in front of Oceanside, my purse rang.

I dug through it, rescued the phone from the bottom of my bag, and checked the number. Nick.

"OK, so what's wrong with my house now?"

"Good morning to you, too," my brother said.

"Sorry, it's been a really weird couple of days. The elevators are kaput, so every trip out takes a little more planning."

"What floor are you guys on, anyway?"

"Tenth."

"Yowch! How's Lucy taking it?" Nick asked.

"Like a champ. I don't think she really liked the elevators anyway."

"Well, I'm pretty sure she didn't sabotage them, but I'm still willing to provide her with an alibi."

"Good to know. So how are you holding up? And how's the commute?"

"The townhouse is great. The commute's no walk across the street, but it's OK. Kind of like you and the elevators—a little more advance planning. The good thing is, I'm driving into Fordham in the morning when everyone else is trying to get out. And by the time I'm ready to head back, there's virtually nobody on the road."

"The beauty of the reverse commute," I said.

"Exactly! Thanks for the pictures of Lucy, by the way."

"Did I mention that she's going be featured in the *Tribune*? They want a piece on dog-friendly travel to South Beach. With lots of photos."

"I told you my baby's a star," Nick said. "So, how much of that moola do I see? You know, as her agent and all."

"At this point, I haven't seen any of it myself. And I'm kind of glad you called. We need to talk about the kitchen."

"I know. You can't afford it."

I felt like a slug. Or maybe one of those little tiny mites that lived on a slug. I'd promised my brother a clean, safe, dry place to rest and rebuild his life after he moved back to town. And it turns out my house wasn't any of those things.

"Look, I'm taking this payment from the sale of the emu farm and using it on the wiring and the other stuff here," Nick said. "I'll get the last installment in from the university in three months. And we can use that for the new appliances and the upgrades. Ian doesn't mind if I bogart his kitchen a little longer. Heck, I think he'd keep me permanently, if he could."

Nick's first business venture was half an emu farm in the Arizona desert. When he discovered his slacker partner had used their tax payments for pot (and had actually started growing the stuff when that stash ran out), Nick destroyed the illegal crop, put in a few vegetables, and demonstrated the benefits of emu dung as a soil additive to prospective buyers. One of the universities bought the place as a green research station. They'd arranged to pay for it in three installments—and promised that the emus would have a good home for life.

"Nick, I can't ask you to do that," I said softly. "And I'm sure at some point, Ian is going to want his kitchen back."

My issues with Ian Sterling aside, the guy had been very generous to Nick.

"Not according to Harkins. And I'm on Ian's tour, too—the one he gives prospective clients and groups who are thinking of booking the inn. We have this routine where we time it so he brings them through the kitchen just as I'm putting something really good on the cooling racks. Then I let him talk me into giving everyone a big taste. And let me tell you, we are reeling them in."

My brother, the shill.

"I never told you, but I had a part in the last murder mystery weekend, too," he said proudly.

"Was it Baker Nick in the kitchen with a rolling pin?"

"Hey, you laugh, but those folks ate it up. Literally. We moved a ton of baked goods that weekend. And those people *tipped*."

"Look, I can't let you pay to fix my house," I said. "I've been thinking about it, and I'm going to try for a second mortgage. I've only been in the place for a little over two years. But I made a healthy down payment and the house has probably increased in value, so I should have a little equity."

What I didn't tell him: I'd been considering the move already to buy a new car. But my ancient Chevy wagon could grow a little more ancient. And maybe I'd actually let Nick attack the sides with a can of Krylon. Like he'd been threatening to do for the past four months.

"It's totally your call," Nick said. "By the way, who's your home inspector?"

"Why? Are you going to report him for malpractice or pay a late-night visit to his house with a few rolls of toilet paper?"

"I just want to see if there's anything else he might have noticed that could make a difference," my brother explained.

OK, something was up. But from a thousand miles away, I wasn't going to quibble. Especially when he'd just offered to use his last bucks to fix my wonky house.

"His name's Dan Jankowitz, and he's in my address book. You know, that little blue book in the top drawer of the roll-top desk."

"Right, Grandma, because it's not online."

"Hey, you'd better be nice to me if you want to see the latest batch of Lucy pics. Annie and I took her to a local Tex-Mex joint last night. And the owner let her wear his cowboy hat."

"That's my girl," Nick said. "Charming in every culture."

CHAPTER 26

An hour later, just as it was starting to get hot, I steered Lucy back toward Oceanside. I figured if Annie was still home, I'd fix all three of us a nice breakfast. Then I could grab the laptop and work poolside.

Green or not, it still beat the pool I had at home. Which is to say no pool at all. And at least at Oceanside, all the mold was outside.

Besides, on the eve of the election, the pool and restaurant deck were guaranteed to be Gossip Central. And I wanted to see if there had been any Leslie sightings.

But when we hit the lobby, there were a bunch of people clustered around the elevators. As I got closer, I could see a guy in a gray work shirt, blue pants, and heavy tan boots. He was leaning on the wall and speaking rapid-fire into a walkie-talkie. And the entire area around the two elevators had been cordoned off with Day-Glo orange cones and yellow emergency tape.

I recognized one friendly face.

"They're fixing the elevators," Ethel said excitedly.

"Did Leslie finally show up and call them?" I asked.

"No, Stan did," she said, clearly tickled. "He remembered

the name of the company that comes to service them. So he gave them a ring. Turns out, we have a maintenance plan. And here they are."

Since elevators are inspected and pretty well-regulated, I'm guessing this was one corner even Leslie McQueen couldn't cut.

Lucy sniffed around Ethel's feet and looked up, puzzled.

"Well, hello, sweetie," she said, reaching down to give the pup an encouraging scratch under the chin. "You just missed Mrs. Pickles. I dropped her off at the groomers. At this rate, she might get to ride home in a nice, shiny elevator."

She looked over at me. "Won't that be a lovely change?"

"Definitely," I said. "So has anybody heard from Leslie? Or any of the other candidates?"

The election was tomorrow. If one of them didn't pop up soon, this was going to be the first election ever that was cancelled due to lack of interest. From the candidates.

If that happened, I'm guessing Oceanside was going to be stuck with Leslie McQueen for either the next five and a half months, or until the story broke about her little financial "experiment." Whichever came first.

"Not a peep," Ethel said. "And the election is tomorrow. I mean, we all have our ballots and everything. But this is really very strange."

I heard a burst of static and what sounded like mumbling from the walkie-talkie. Suddenly the repair tech stood up straight and adjusted the device. "Say that again, Phil," he called into the squawk box. "I didn't get that."

Without any interference to mask it, Phil's voice boomed across the lobby, echoing off the marble walls. "I said, I found out what shut off the cars. You need to call the cops, pronto. We got a body down here."

CHAPTER 27

I don't know who beat it to the scene quicker: the cops or the residents.

I ran upstairs to drop off Lucy and give Annie the news.

When we hustled back a few minutes later, the stairwells between the second floor and the garage were jammed with people. As the overflow spilled out into the elegant lobby, curious retirees mingled with harried business types and the more casually dressed work-from-home crowd, trading observations, speculation, and gossip. With coffee cups and excited chatter, it felt more like a cocktail party than a crime scene.

There was even a rumor that someone up on the pool deck was taking bets on the identity of the body. And with an entire slate of board candidates missing, it's not like we had a shortage of possibilities.

But since Annie and I had already scoped out Leslie's car—and knew she hadn't been to work in days—I was pretty sure it was her.

"The real action's down in the parking garage," said a guy in a pink linen shirt and khakis with a stainless steel travel mug in his hand. "The cops have the whole place sealed off. No cars in or out."

"How am I supposed to get to work?" asked a tall man in a blue suit with a leather briefcase.

"Cab," said the man with the mug. "Everybody's calling cabs, drivers, and ride shares. At this rate, they're gonna be stacked up out front like pancakes."

"Dammit, I've got a meeting in twenty minutes," briefcase snarled. "If I'm late, there goes my whole third quarter."

Ethel was in the lobby near the door, chatting with Marilyn.

"Do they know who it is?" I asked.

Both shook their heads.

"They won't even say if it's a man or a woman," Marilyn said.

"I'm going to head downstairs and see what I can find out," I said.

"Want me to come with?" Annie asked.

"No, I'll be right back. And you might pick up something interesting here," I said meaningfully.

"Gotcha," my sister said.

The sheer mass of people in the stairwell made the normally hot cement space feel stifling. I was glad I'd left Lucy in the cool apartment. I was also glad I'd had a shower this morning. I was going to need another one before the day was out.

Something caught my attention on the stairs above me. A flash of blond hair and a leopard-print miniskirt. Here, then gone. And, for some reason, familiar.

"Excuse me, excuse me, coming through, excuse me," I repeated like a yoga mantra, as I inched my way through the throng down the last flight of stairs toward the garage.

When I got to the bottom I had to weave my way through the crowd.

The police had roped off everything beyond the landing in front of the stairs, which had now become a makeshift observation deck for the residents—and me.

Beyond the tape, the garage was a hive of well-organized activity. Police cars with flashing lights blocked every exit, throwing a bluish strobe onto the scene. One elevator door was open, but its car was gone. Crime techs swarmed the area with cameras and equipment.

"What happened?" I asked no one in particular.

"Somebody fell down the shaft," a thirty-something brunette in a powder-blue business suit replied.

"Mother of all lawsuits," said a blond guy in a T-shirt and swim trunks. Wearing flip-flops, he had a towel slung over his shoulder, and his hair was still damp. Since no one was using the green pool, I'm guessing he'd just come from the beach. "Man, if this building gets sued, that'll mean a special assessment for sure."

"Not if the elevator manufacturer is at fault," said an older African-American man with a resonant voice, a well-tailored gray suit, and a smart black attaché case. I pegged him for a lawyer.

"Do they know who it is?" I asked, hoping to prime the pump.

"If they do, they haven't said," replied a twenty-something guy in jeans and a white T-shirt with a good view from the curb. "But I thought I heard one of the elevator repair guys refer to the victim as 'she,' so it's probably a woman."

Leslie McQueen.

Well, this was going to put a crimp in the election.

CHAPTER 28

Like a lot of residents of Oceanside—the ones who weren't going to an office today—Annie and I migrated up to the main restaurant.

"Does anyone in this place have a job? Or are you all independently wealthy?" I asked as we crammed ourselves into a table for two in one corner.

"This is the modern workforce," my sister said, smiling. "During the summer, a lot of people either take Friday off or work from home."

When the waiter approached, we each ordered a large glass of orange juice.

"You want anything in that?" he asked.

"What do you mean?" I asked.

He shrugged. "After what happened downstairs, most of these folks are taking their morning sunshine with a little rum or vodka. Tequila's also pretty popular."

"Just juice on the rocks for me," I said.

Annie nodded. "Same here."

"OK, ladies. But just say the word if you change your minds."

As he disappeared into the kitchen, I leaned closer so

that Annie could hear me over the general thrum of background conversation.

"It has to be Leslie."

"I don't know of any other women missing from the building," she said.

"Do you think there will still be an election tomorrow?"

"Well, I guess we could go ahead with it. There are four other candidates. But it all seems a little macabre now. The board could cancel it. Or postpone it."

"Say they don't cancel," I said. "And one of the four new guys wins. What happens to your friend Dennis then?"

"You have an idea," Annie stated.

"Well, you want to keep Dennis out of prison. And Dennis probably wants to keep Dennis out of prison. If he and Geoffrey the Eyeball cancel the election—or even just postpone it for a while—we could take a stab at finding the missing money. If we succeed, those two could pay the bills due on this place and then hire a new management company. No harm, no foul."

"That's a great idea, if it works," my sister said. "The best part is that the people who invested their life savings in homes here won't see the values plummet because of some scandal over condo mismanagement."

We both looked over toward the bar, where Stan and Ernie were holding court at a table with Marilyn, Ethel, and several other neighbors.

The waiter returned, slid our juice glasses onto the table, shrugged, and vanished.

"Do you think we can really do that?" Annie asked. "Find the money, I mean?"

"No idea. But Dennis is motivated. And your friend Geoffrey's supposed to be some kind of corporate accountant. So he should be able to help us. And both of them ought to be willing. I mean, if this mess comes out, they're both in pretty hot water. I say it's worth a shot."

"We'd be bending the law a bit ourselves, though," Annie said.

"Leslie broke the law. We're just trying to glue it back together. And limit the collateral damage. We'd be finding stolen money and returning it to the rightful owners. Technically, that's legal."

"Why do I think Peter might have a slightly different read on that one?" she asked.

"You want to call him for a second opinion?"

"Too afraid of what he'd say," Annie said, shaking her head. "If I don't ask, I can at least claim ignorance as a defense."

"And you know what they say: Ignorance is bliss."

We clinked glasses.

CHAPTER 29

"So what does Dennis do for a living?" I asked as we strolled down the sixth floor hallway. "Do you really think he might be home today?"

"He's a corporate exec for a food company. And I hope he's home, because if we're going to make this work, we've got an election to cancel."

"What do we say if Grace is home, too?"

"I have no idea," Annie said. "I hope we don't have to say anything. She's my friend, and I don't want to lie to her."

"You also don't want to stress her. And you don't want her husband going to jail. We don't have a lot of good options here."

"One step at a time," my sister said, knocking on the door.

Dennis opened it in the same clothes he'd been wearing last night. Except they were a little more wrinkled. And his eyes were bloodshot. He didn't look happy to see us.

"What's up?" he asked.

"Is Grace home?" Annie inquired brightly.

"The elevator thing was getting to be too rough on her. She's staying with her parents across town for a few days."

He didn't invite us in.

"Good news on that front," I said. "They're fixing the elevators now."

"Fantastic. Is that what you came here to tell me?"

"Dennis, we need to come in for just a minute," Annie said. "I wouldn't ask, but it's important."

He stepped back, opened the door wider and ushered us inside. The once neat condo looked more like a dorm room during finals week. The dining room table was covered with files, paperwork, his laptop, a deflated bag of Cheetos, and an empty ice cream carton on its side with the spoon still in it.

He'd decorated the sofa with a blue blanket and two bed pillows. The TV was blaring. Dennis grabbed the remote from the couch and turned the sound off.

"Leslie's dead," I said.

"What?" Dennis looked at me as if he hadn't heard me. Or the words hadn't registered.

"Apparently she fell down the elevator shaft," Annie said, as Dennis sank slowly onto the sofa. My sister sat down next to him, and I took the overstuffed chair.

"They found her this morning when they came to fix the elevator," my sister continued.

"Gracie left me," he said simply, cradling his head in his hands.

For half a minute, none of us said anything. Although the bed pillows pretty much told the story. That and the comfort food.

When Gabby dumped Nick and went back to her old boyfriend, we went through a lot of Cheetos. And ice cream.

"Look, I know you're going through hell right now," I said. "But you have a chance to set things right. Leslie is gone. You and Geoffrey, the . . . uh, treasurer, can cancel the election. Or even just postpone it for a month or two.

Then, the four of us try to find the paperwork and the money Leslie collected on behalf of the board. You and Geoffrey can pay off the bills that are due and hire a new management company. That way, when the new president is elected, everything is back where it should be. And no one is the wiser."

"Gracie is," he said, looking me straight in the eye. "I told her what we did. That's why she walked out. She was furious. I know some of it's the hormones. But she's really angry."

"So you make it right," Annie said. "And we'll help you. But it has to be your decision. We're not here to talk you into anything."

I didn't know about my sister, but that was exactly what I was here to do.

"Did you tell her why you helped Leslie?" I asked.

"No! I mean, what do you mean?" Dennis said indignantly.

"Look, I don't know you from Adam, but my sister does. She says you're a decent, moral guy. And she knows about things like that."

He looked at Annie, who smiled encouragingly.

"So it's pretty much a given that you didn't just jump on board with Leslie's little 'let's rip off the residents of Oceanside' plan," I continued. "She obviously had something on you. What was it?"

He put his hand behind his head and rubbed his neck as he stared at the floor.

"Pictures," he said quietly. "She had pictures."

"Does Grace know?" I asked.

He shook his head.

"She's mad enough as it is. If she saw those photos, it would be over. Our marriage would be over. One stupid mistake. I didn't even go through with it. But if she saw the pictures . . ."

"How did Leslie get them?"

"Damned if I know. But I think she had them before she even asked me to step up as secretary for the board."

"Leslie plans ahead," I concluded. "What about Geoffrey? Do you think she has something on him?"

Dennis looked up. "I never thought of that. He was always so positive about everything we were doing. Enthusiastic. And since he was an accountant, I figured maybe it wasn't such a bad idea after all. Geoffrey kept saying we were being innovative."

"Decide what you want to do," I said quietly. "But if we're going to take a stab at fixing this mess, we don't have a lot of time. We need to cancel that election."

He got up from the sofa and walked over to one of the bookcases. He removed a book and carefully extracted something from inside. I thought it was a photograph until he handed it to Annie. It was from an ultrasound.

"We're having twins," he said.

Annie beamed. "That's wonderful! Congratulations!"

"I want to fix this," Dennis said, nodding. "For Gracie and our family, I need to fix this. Let's go talk to Geoff."

CHAPTER 30

This time, Annie and I both stepped back and let Dennis knock on Geoffrey's door. Eyeball or no, we figured he might be more welcoming of a friendly face. Especially if he'd heard the news about Leslie.

He opened the door a crack. I could see one blue eye and a sliver of a pale face.

"What do you want?" Geoffrey asked.

"We've got some news. Good and bad. We need to come in for a minute."

Geoffrey appeared to think it over for a split second before he stepped back and opened the door all the way.

Dennis marched right in, and we followed like a trail of baby ducks.

"I'm Annie. I live upstairs. This is my sister, Alex."

Tall and gangly, Geoffrey bore more than a passing resemblance to a praying mantis. His silver-blond hair was swept straight back from his forehead, revealing a prominent widow's peak.

After a few seconds, he gestured at the jaunty red Scandinavian-style sofa and loveseat in his living room, as if hospitality were an afterthought.

Annie and I settled on the loveseat, while Dennis and Geoffrey occupied opposite ends of the long sofa. I just hoped they weren't at opposite ends of this issue.

"The bad news," Dennis said evenly. "There was an accident downstairs with the elevator. And Leslie is gone."

"Gone?" Geoffrey asked.

"She's dead," Dennis said.

The blue eyes blinked as he brushed a hand over his silvery hair. "What? That can't be!"

"It probably happened a few days ago," Annie said softly. "That's why the elevator hasn't been working."

"Are you sure?" Geoffrey asked, looking stricken.

I was afraid he might actually cry.

"Are they sure it's her?" he asked, almost pleading.

Dennis nodded grimly.

"That's why we're here," Dennis continued. "We need to cancel the election."

The accountant side of Geoffrey's brain seemed to kick in as he considered the idea. I could see the wheels turning behind his almost translucent skin.

How does he stay that pale living in Miami? What kind of sunblock is he using? And where can I get a gallon of it?

"Yes, that's probably a good idea," Geoffrey said finally.

"Good," Dennis said. "I can put a notice on the community's electronic bulletin board."

"I don't know how tech savvy some of the residents are," Annie said. "It might be a good idea to put up paper notices in the lobby and at some of the gathering spots—like the pool and the gym. And maybe the hallways, too."

Right next to the elevators?

Dennis nodded. "Can you two handle that?"

"Sure," I said. "We should probably let the other candidates know, too. Any idea how to get in touch with them?"

Dennis shook his head. "Leslie handled all the election

stuff. From collecting the candidate applications to distributing the voting ballots. And I don't remember meeting any of those guys. You?"

Geoffrey shook his head. "Leslie kept all of the resident information. Names, addresses, contact numbers. She was so organized. She handled all the board paperwork."

"Do you have any of the bills or the bank statements?" I asked.

"She kept all that," he said softly. "We just signed off on things when it was necessary. Huh, I guess I'm the president now."

"What do you mean?" I asked.

"That's how it works. First, the president. Second, the treasurer. And third, the board secretary. And if one is missing, we all go up a step. So I'm the president now."

Annie, Dennis, and I looked at each other.

"Uh, Geoffrey, what you don't know is that the board finances are in a bit of a mess at the moment," I said. "Leslie's been collecting association dues and fees. But she's let the bills slide. We have to find that money and get those bills paid."

"Do you know where the money is?" Dennis asked.

"Sure, it's in the board account. At Primary Federal Bank—down the street. Leslie and I went there together and opened it. As treasurer, I had to sign off on the paperwork."

I had a bad feeling about this.

"As an accountant, I'm sure you know all about fiduciary duties," I said, hoping to appeal to his professional side. "Leslie's not paying those bills could cause problems for the board, the residents—even the association's credit rating. I'm sure she didn't do it on purpose. She had a lot on her plate. But some of those bills are three months behind. So that's got to be the first order of business."

Geoffrey seemed to snap back to reality.

"I can get copies of our bank statements," he said. "I don't need the account numbers if I show my ID. And that should also give us the names of a lot of the vendors."

"Then we can call and have them email us the invoices," Dennis said.

I didn't quite trust Geoffrey, accountant or not. He seemed a little too fond of Leslie. And a little too eager to assume her old post. I remembered what Dennis had said about Geoffrey always backing Leslie "two against one." Could they have been in on it together?

Annie must have read my mind.

"OK, gentlemen, it sounds like we have a plan," my sister said. "How about I call for a car, and we can visit the bank?"

CHAPTER 31

Sun-washed South Beach or not, Primary Federal looked like every other suburban branch of every other bank I'd ever visited.

Situated at the very edge of the neighborhood, it was a squat, white stucco building with blue trim and a stable of drive-through lines on one side.

Inside, there was a coffee service with stale cookies in the lobby. And a bowl of brightly colored lollypops on the teller counter.

I'm not exaggerating. The cookies may have looked like chocolate chip. But they tasted like cardboard. I don't normally eat bank cookies. But since all I had in me this morning was coffee and a glass of orange juice—after walking miles with Lucy and climbing umpteen flights of stairs—I was getting a little desperate.

"You've got crumbs on your chest," my sister said, as we waited in matching blue cloth chairs in the lobby.

"That's because they're so dry," I said, coughing.

"It's going to take them a minute to get the bank manager," Annie said. "Try the coffee."

"No thanks. If they can do this to chocolate, there's no

telling what they've done to a poor, unsuspecting pot of coffee."

Sitting across from us, Dennis looked grim. But Geoffrey was calm and unflustered. Like visiting the bank with his three new buds was the most normal thing in the world.

I was afraid he might be in for another shock. But I hoped I was wrong.

"Ah, Mr. Gallagher," a small, round man in a gray suit said as he approached, extending his hand. "I'm Gerald Booker. I'm the branch manager."

We'd all agreed in the car that no one would mention Leslie's demise. As it stood, Geoffrey was entitled to see the account statements. No need to complicate things unnecessarily.

Geoffrey offered his hand and displayed something that could have passed for a brief smile.

"I'm Dennis Chu. Geoff and I work together on the board. And this is Annie and Alex, also from Oceanside."

"So nice to meet you," Annie said, flashing her million-watt smile.

"Lovely to meet you all," Booker said. "Why don't we all step into my office?"

As Geoff presented his ID, Dennis and I dragged a couple of extra chairs into Booker's tiny workspace. Describing it as an office would be like calling my bungalow Buckingham Palace.

Branch manager or no, it was a cubicle with walls and a minuscule window set near the ceiling. A half-dead plant withered on one corner of his Formica desk.

"So, what can I do for you good people today?" Booker asked genially, surveying our little group.

"I just wanted to get hard copies of the last four account statements," Geoffrey replied.

"Of course," Booker said. "Let me see if I can pull that up."

He put on reading glasses and turned to his computer. "Ah, here we are. And . . . let me see. Oh yes, print."

My palms started to sweat. What we were doing was pretty much legal. But it felt like I was here to rob the place.

Booker poked a button, and a small printer in the corner rattled to life.

After a few minutes, he gathered a stack of papers from the tray, placed them in a manila file folder and handed it across the desk to Geoffrey.

"Naturally, there's a small charge for hard copies. Five dollars per statement. We'll just deduct that from the account."

"Of course," Dennis said smoothly. "We appreciate your time. Thank you."

Another round of handshakes and we were out the door. I eyed the cookie plate again as we exited.

"Don't even think about it," my sister warned. "We'll grab lunch after we swing by the apartment."

In the back seat of the SUV, Geoffrey opened the file, scanning the pages. His face crumpled.

"This can't be right," he said, so softly I almost didn't hear him.

"What?" Dennis asked.

"This is the most recent account statement," Geoffrey said, as two pink splotches bloomed on his pasty face. "The current one. According to this, the association has thirty-four dollars and twelve cents."

CHAPTER 32

Two hours later, Annie and I had papered Oceanside with hot-pink fliers.

We kept the message simple. In light of recent tragic events, the board election had been postponed. And we included Dennis's cell number, in case anyone had any questions.

I was half hoping some of the other candidates would call. No such luck.

But just about everyone else did.

"My phone hasn't stopped ringing," Dennis complained when we met up at his condo that afternoon. "Mrs. Sakowitz's garbage disposal is on the fritz. Mr. Jenkins on four wants me to let in the furniture delivery guys. And Quinn Whitmore thinks we should organize a memorial service for Leslie."

"What did you say?" I asked.

"Not my problem, I don't have a key, and that's up to her family."

"Does Leslie have family?" Annie asked.

"No idea," Dennis said. "I didn't know her that well."

I looked at Geoffrey, who was perched on the edge of the sofa as if he might actually take flight.

He shrugged. "She never said. I think she was kind of alone."

"Too bad, so sad," Dennis said. "Dude, we have to track that money. It's the only way we're gonna stay out of jail."

"What do you mean?" Geoffrey asked.

"The board is responsible for that money," he said. "And it's gone. We signed off on everything. *Everything!* Leslie may be dead. But we're still here. And we're going to jail."

Geoffrey leaned forward and started making a strange whooping sound.

"He's hyperventilating," Annie said. "Do you have a bag?"

I reached into my purse, pulled out an empty foil potato chip bag—barbecue, of course—and handed it over.

My sister put it over his nose and mouth. "Just breath slowly. In, two-three-four. And out, two-three-four."

He seemed to be getting better. Then he started coughing.

"Barbecue dust," he rasped, between coughing fits.

Annie went to Dennis's kitchen and came back with a glass of water.

"Drink this slowly," she instructed. "Little sips. You'll be fine."

"Thank you," Geoffrey said gratefully.

If my sister wasn't careful, she was going to acquire a new pet. And Lucy was a lot less work. Pooper-scooper or not.

"My life is over," Dennis said flatly. "I'm going to jail."

"Prison," I said. "Jail is just a holding cell when you're first arrested."

I'd seen lots of jails. Compared to where he was going, jail was nothing.

Dennis and Annie both glared at me. Geoffrey busily sipped his water like a baby bird.

"Look, the situation hasn't really changed," I said. "We knew the money wasn't going to be in the account when we went over there."

"I didn't know that," Dennis said.

"Me either," Geoffrey squeaked.

"OK, let me spell it out for you," I said, wondering, not for the first time, how these guys were pulling down enough to live at Oceanside while I couldn't even get a car loan. "Leslie took over the running of the board. Then she convinced you two that the management company was overspending. Or possibly taking more than their share. Right?"

"Right," they said in unison.

"So she persuaded you to fire the management company. Now there's no one looking over her shoulder. She's super-efficient, and you guys are just signing whatever she puts in front of you. For whatever reason," I said, looking at Dennis.

He glanced at the floor.

"So money's going in and out of the account, just like you'd expect. Only she's not using it to pay bills. That means she's probably stashing it somewhere. Our job, before the bill collectors show up, is to find that money and pay off the debts. It's the same thing we all agreed to do this morning. It's just going to take a little more work."

"But how did she take the money out of the account?" Geoffrey asked.

"That's the key," I said. "And you're an accountant. You're going to help us figure that out."

"Because if you don't, you're going to be keeping me company in jail. Oh, excuse me," Dennis said pointedly to me. "Prison."

"Why?" Geoffrey whined. "I didn't take any money."

"You said it yourself," I reminded him. "You and Leslie signed up for that account. Your name is on all the documents. You and Dennis signed off on everything she put in front of you. And, presumably, you looked at the books every month for four months."

"But Leslie moved the money," Geoffrey protested.

"If we find it, we might be able to prove that," I said. "Or you two can just pay off the bills, hire a new management company, and go on with your lives. But as it stands now, if someone new comes into office and all you have in that account is thirty-four bucks—minus twenty in bank fees—there's going to be an investigation. And since Leslie's gone, who do you think they're going to charge?"

"I think I'm gonna be sick," Geoffrey said, as Annie folded him forward with his head between his knees.

"Not on the area rug!" Dennis shouted. "I'll never get the smell out. And Gracie bought it on our honeymoon. She'll kill me!"

It only took us fifteen minutes to come up with a plan. Minus the time it took to soothe a freaked-out Geoffrey.

Dennis would answer resident calls, help anyone he could, mollify anyone he couldn't, and basically reassure everyone that even though Leslie was gone, everything at Oceanside was fine.

In other words, lie.

Geoffrey would use his skills to scour the last four months of bank statements, gathering clues on where the money should have gone and where it did go. And Annie and I would run down any leads.

In the meantime, we would also follow up with any residents who had a connection to Leslie. I figured if we could fill in more of the blanks on who she was and where she was from, that might help us find out what she did with the money.

There was no telling how long we could keep Leslie McQueen's house of cards going. I think all four of us realized we had a few days, at best. After that, we were going to have to give up, call in the cops, and let Dennis and Geoffrey—as well as the home values at Oceanside—take their lumps.

CHAPTER 33

As mourners go, we looked great. Annie was kitted out in a navy sheath dress with a matching bolero jacket. And she'd loaned me a fitted gray coat dress that accented my red hair.

Still, I was dubious.

We'd decided to visit Kelsey first. Technically, we were "paying condolences." In reality, we were digging for dirt. Or, more specifically, dough.

One of Leslie's tennis friends opened the door. Fiftyish, tan, and gristly, she'd opted for the classic "little black dress." But to me, she'd always be Tennis Thing One.

"We just stopped by to see how Kelsey is holding up," my sister said sympathetically, holding out a casserole we'd picked up at a local market.

For a condolence call, it was the price of admission.

"Oh, as well as can be expected," Tennis Thing One said. "Kelsey, Anastasia from upstairs is here. She brought a casserole. Are you up for a visitor?"

Kelsey must have said yes, because her friend opened the door, collected the casserole from Annie, and whisked it into the kitchen.

Tennis Thing Two, also in black, was draped across the sofa holding a Kleenex box in front of Kelsey.

"Oh, that's so sweet," Kelsey said cheerfully. She was decked out in a short-sleeved black crêpe de chine number with a ruffle at the knee, and four-inch black pumps. Her dark hair, parted in the middle, was gathered in a low chignon.

Her eyes were red-rimmed from crying. Or maybe just soap.

Call me jaded, but if any of these people had known what Leslie was truly like—and what she'd been doing with their money—I suspected there'd be a few less tears.

Annie, who seemed to know the script, alighted in an adjacent chair. I sat on the only other space that wasn't someone's lap. An ottoman.

"We were so sorry to hear about Leslie," Annie said. "We just wanted to stop by and see how you were."

"Oh, I'm holding up," Kelsey said, brandishing a wad of tissues in one hand, and a lowball glass in the other. An identical glass rested on the coffee table. With a coaster, of course.

"It seems to come in waves," Kelsey continued. "One minute I'm fine. Then I think of something I want to tell her and reach for the phone and . . ." She paused to blot her face. "It hits me all over again."

"You poor dear," Annie said. "Naturally, we wanted to send flowers to the family, too. But I didn't have an address."

I sat forward and watched, fascinated. For all anyone in this room knew, I could have been mute.

Kelsey looked startled. "Oh. Well, of course. I guess everyone will be wanting to do that. But I don't know if they're up to it quite yet. The family, I mean. But when they are, I don't mind sharing their contact details."

"Of course," my sister agreed. "This was all very sudden."

"So where was Leslie from originally?" I asked. What the heck—if polite wasn't getting us anywhere, I might as well throw a grenade in the punchbowl.

"Charleston," Kelsey said, taking a slug from her glass. "But Leslie's been in Miami for ages." She looked over at Tennis Thing Two.

"Simply ages," her friend echoed, nodding.

The other one reappeared with a full tumbler of amber liquid and claimed the far end of the sofa.

No one had offered us so much as a stick of gum.

"She was a Miami girl at heart," Kelsey said, and all three of them nodded. "She always said, 'Life begins in South Beach.'"

For Leslie, a life of crime, maybe. Or did she end up here when things got too hot back home?

"At moments like this, it pays to remember the happier times," Annie said, smiling. "How did you and Leslie meet?"

"Oh, that *is* a funny story," Kelsey said, taking another long draw from her glass.

Nine times out of ten, when someone has to tell you a story is funny, it's not.

"Almost two years ago, I was renting not too far from here. And I wanted to buy. Well, I *am* in finance, but of course, this was several promotions ago. You know how it is. Not long out of college. Tons of student loans. Of course I'd been salivating watching them build this place. But I knew I couldn't afford it. Then I met Leslie at an open house, and that was it. When she learned Oceanside was my dream, she wouldn't let me give up. We found a smaller unit coming onto the market. The list price was still waaay above my budget. But Leslie's a champ. A total champ. She got the price knocked down and even helped me secure a deal on the financing. And we've been best friends ever since. I wouldn't be here if it weren't for her," she finished, mopping her dry eyes with the tissues.

I noticed the Tennis Twins exchange a glance—and a little smirk—when Kelsey claimed "best" friend status. Trouble in paradise?

"She was such a people person, and so attractive," Annie said, settling into her chair. "It's a wonder she never married."

"Oh, she did," Kelsey said. "Fred McQueen."

Tennis Thing One and Tennis Thing Two shook their heads in unison. I'm guessing they weren't big fans of Fred.

"It just didn't work out," Kelsey continued, downing what was left in her glass. "From what Leslie said, I think he was a bit of a player, if you know what I mean. Or maybe they were just too young. That was sooo long ago."

Was it my imagination or did the Tennis Twins blanch slightly? They were about Leslie's vintage. And I'm guessing Kelsey's not-so-veiled comments about Leslie's age—including the marriage that was "sooo long ago"—may have hit a little too close to home.

"Finance is such a fascinating field, especially now," I said, taking a page from my sister's pay-a-compliment-ask-a-question playbook. "What do you do?"

"I'm a manager in investment products at Promethean National Bank," Kelsey said proudly. "I've been there for almost a year."

CHAPTER 34

Next stop, Quinn Whitmore's apartment.

Annie and I figured that anyone interested in staging a memorial must have more than a passing acquaintance with the deceased. So I was curious what Quinn might have to say.

And whether he'd be slipcovered in black, like the last bunch.

"So what's your take on the Leslie-Kelsey friendship?" I asked, as we exited the stairwell on the ninth floor.

"Not as close as she wants everyone to believe," Annie said. "You caught the look between her two friends? Plus, she obviously has no idea where Leslie's family lives. I asked for their address, and she was stalling."

"Or just trying to control the flow of information," I said. "Absent family, she gets to be the chief mourner and center of attention."

Annie shook her head, smiling. "So young and yet so cynical."

"You, by the way, are scary-good at information gathering," I said.

My sister grinned. "So I could have been a reporter, huh?"

"You could have been a spy," I said, then instantly regretted it.

"Did you know about Dad?" I finally asked.

"Did I know what about Dad?"

"That he was a spy."

"For real?" she asked. "How did you discover that? And what did Mom say?"

"I haven't had the nerve to mention it. You know how she gets about Dad."

To put it simply, he was the love of her life. And I know the feeling was mutual. While almost no topic was off-limits in our family—especially if Mom was the one raising it—we tiptoed around the subject of Dad. Especially with her. It was just too painful.

"How did you hear about this?" Annie asked. "Spill."

"You know my neighbor, Ian Sterling?"

"The hunky Brit who has a crush on you? Sure."

"He doesn't have a crush on me," I insisted, as my face went hot. "We're just . . . neighbors."

That much was true. Now.

"Well, I kind of accidentally learned that he's in the business," I said. "Or was. Frankly, I think the place he's running is some kind of covert meeting place or safe house, in addition to being a B&B."

"He's certainly in the right location—Northern Virginia, just outside D.C.," my sister concluded. "Is that why you're giving him the cold shoulder?"

I shook my head. "Not exactly. Anyway, one of his guests? Let's just say she was in a related occupation. And she said I reminded her of Dad."

The woman was a spy married to a spy. She was also an assassin. But no need to get into that.

"Damn," Annie said. "Do you think she was telling the truth?"

"Only one person would know," I said. "And I haven't had the guts to ask her yet. I'm thinking full-on, intervention-style family gathering . . ."

"Definitely with Peter and Zara," my sister added. "Maybe a catering tray and some light refreshments?"

"If we give her some of what was in Kelsey's glass tonight, she might actually tell us."

"Don't kid yourself," Annie said. "I crossed Europe with that woman. She can hold her Scotch. More important, she never has more than one. When we left the MacLeish distillery, she was the only one on the tour who could walk a straight line. Including the tour operator."

"Sounds about right. But am I one hundred percent sure of my source? No. At the same time, the woman had no reason to lie. Not that I'm aware of. So who knows?"

"It would explain all those lengthy business trips," Annie concluded.

"Yeah, but it makes me wonder what really happened on the last one. The heart attack? And if Mom's been keeping secrets all these years, how do we even bring it up?"

"With love," Annie said simply. "She loved him. We all loved him. And we're all adults now. There's no reason not to tell us the truth anymore."

See what I mean about graceful? I'm convinced my sister could do anything.

"So what's the deal with you and Ian?" Annie asked.

"He bugged my house."

"No!"

"My bedroom, actually. But only because that's where I keep the plug-in phone. Not because he wanted anything skeevy."

"So what *was* he after?" my sister asked, folding her arms across her chest.

"His father was missing. I knew where the guy was, but had promised not to tell. And it looked like his father was going to have to go into hiding. Probably permanently."

"So what happened?" she asked.

"Ian found out what was going on. Through the bug. And offered his dad a bit of assistance. I knew the dad's situation, but I didn't know about Ian's . . . industry contacts. Now Harkins and his family are safe. Living out in the open. And Ian has a new baby brother. Alistair."

"So Ian broke the rules to save the people he loved?"

"Yeah, basically."

"Sounds like something you'd do," my sister noted.

I hate it when she's right.

CHAPTER 35

As we sat on the sofa in Quinn Whitmore's apartment, I was struck by how much the place resembled Annie's. Surrounded by walls of floor-to-ceiling windows, it gave me that same sense of floating above the Earth in the deep blue Miami sky.

Quinn could have been fifty or seventy. He greeted us wearing a snow-white guayabera and pressed khakis. His feet were bare. With a square bronzed face, high cheekbones, and graying light brown hair just long enough to be stylish, he gave the impression of family money. Lots of it.

His home was a minimalist's dream. Mostly modern furniture with a few well-chosen antiques; there were just enough places to sit—or set a drink—without blocking the views or feeling the least bit cramped.

If *Architectural Digest* had needed another condo to sub in the month they featured my sister's penthouse, this one would have filled the bill.

"To what do I owe the honor?" he said, carrying a tea tray in from the kitchen. "It's not every day I get two lovely ladies knocking at my door."

"Dennis wanted us to find out a little more about what

you had in mind for a memorial service for Leslie," Annie said.

Since we didn't know just what his relationship was to Leslie McQueen—or whether we needed another condolence casserole—we had decided to mask our fact-finding mission as a fact-finding mission.

"I had the definite impression that Dennis Chu was less than interested in the ideas of this old duffer," he said, pouring three cups from a white bone-china pot.

Annie smiled. "He was a little overwhelmed. That's why we volunteered to help out. I guess you've heard— Grace is having twins."

"I hadn't heard it was twins," Quinn said amiably. "Double trouble—good for them!"

I spied a plate of sliced pound cake on the tray and tried not to drool. That promised lunch had never materialized, thanks to the election-cancellation fliers and our "condolence visits." I was ravenous.

"I'm afraid I'm at a bit of a loss," Annie confessed. "I didn't know Leslie all that well."

Quinn chuckled. It seemed an odd reaction.

"She certainly knew you," he said finally, shaking his head. "Vacuumed up every story in every gossip column. Constantly pumping the neighbors for tidbits. A bit obsessed, I'm afraid.

"Oh, not in a bad way," he added when he saw what must have been the shocked look on my face. "No, she was just curious. And I think she rather saw you as something of a rival."

Annie's expression was hard to read. And I knew her. But she was used to drama. I'd noticed she just tended to float above it.

"I wish I'd known," she said. "I'd have made more of an effort to be friends."

"My dear," Quinn said, "I don't think it would have

made a damned bit of difference. Leslie was what she was. And she was a firecracker, that's for sure. She certainly livened up this place."

"How did you meet?" I asked, finally snagging a piece of cake.

"Here at the pool," he said. "She wanted to host a poker evening and was looking for a couple of extra players. I said it sounded like just the thing. We all had such a good time, she ended up hosting the game a couple of times a month. And I was a regular. You'd be amazed what you learn about someone across a card table."

Especially if they've had a few cocktails.

"So where was she from originally?" I asked. "We'd like to send flowers to the family."

"No real family anymore," Quinn said. "She has an ex-husband. But from the sound of it, they didn't get on too well. From what she said, he's some kind of bank executive. And they lived in Charlotte. But that was a long time ago."

Not all that long, if he was helping her hide money. Could Leslie McQueen have a partner in crime?

"I guess you've heard they postponed the election," Annie said. "Just for the time being."

"Ah yes," he said, smiling broadly. "The election. No doubt how that would have turned out."

"It did look like Leslie had a lock on the competition," I said, trying to sound neutral.

"Of course she did," Quinn said, laughing. "Her competition didn't exist."

"I'm sorry?" my sister asked.

Quinn leaned forward and dropped his voice. "Those other four fellows? Totally fabricated. They were straw men."

The pound cake halted halfway to my mouth.

Quinn sat back, a broad smile on his tanned face.

"No one knew them, so no one would vote for them," I summarized.

He nodded. "It's all about name recognition. Brand recognition. Who's the best-known candidate on the ballot? The most popular brand? Leslie McQueen."

I dropped the cake onto my saucer. "And to be on the safe side, she spreads a few stories to her friends about rotten things the other four have been caught doing recently, then lets the gossip mill take over."

"Just so," Quinn said, folding his hands in his lap.

"That's why she called a special election," I said, snapping my fingers. "So many of the snowbirds and building regulars are away from here in July. So they wouldn't be around to ask questions or maybe throw their hats in the ring. They'd just send in their ballots. And for the price of a cocktail-party-slash-campaign-rally, Leslie would get an extra year as president of the homeowners' association."

Quinn nodded, grinning from ear to ear.

"You knew about this?" my sister asked him, astonished.

"My dear, it was my idea."

CHAPTER 36

Annie had been stony since we'd exited Quinn Whitmore's place.

"That's vile," she whispered finally, as we approached the door to the stairs. "Absolutely vile."

"That's politics," I said, wishing I'd been quicker on the draw with that cake.

"Why would he help her? She was stealing from the building."

"Well, first of all, I'm guessing he's a sociopath. And second, it's possible he didn't know about the money stuff. Or maybe he sensed a kindred spirit."

"I wonder what he does for a living?" my sister pondered.

"Advertising or marketing would be my guess, based on the terms he used. Possibly campaign management. These days it's all the same thing."

We headed through the door and, as we started to turn to go up, I glanced down. Several floors beneath us, I spotted a woman jogging jauntily up the stairs. Huge, wide-brimmed hat. Big dark sunglasses. A white pool cover-up with a rich tan and sky-high espadrilles.

It hit me like a thunderbolt.

"Gabby!" I screamed.

She stuck her head over the railing, looked up and grinned. "Sister girl? Oh my gosh, it is you!"

Gabby DuBois, Nick's ex-fiancée, came running up the stairs and threw her arms around me. "I can't believe you're here! What are the odds?"

Annie had heard about Gabby, but she'd never actually met her. I figured I'd better make the introductions. "Gabby, this is my sister Annie. Annie, this is my friend Gabby."

My brother's most recent ex- gave us each the once-over. "Wow, Nicky was right. You two really do look alike."

"Thank you!" we both said in unison.

"What are you doing here?" I asked. "What happened with Rick?"

After a whirlwind Vegas courtship, Gabby had left my brother to go back to the love of her life, a pro wrestler named Rick, who promptly proposed. It was the right move for everyone. But Nick had taken it hard for a while.

"Oh, sugar, he's joining me here next weekend," she said, flashing a big smile. "He and the boys are doing a big tour down the East Coast. All the guys on one of those super-cool buses, a different city every night. But he loves it! So I popped over here for a little vacay, and we're going to meet up when he gets to town."

With Gabby, things were never exactly what they seemed.

The first time we'd met—when she was engaged to my brother—she was picking pockets and operating an online boutique funded with stolen credit cards. Like Robin Hood, she only stole from the rich. Gabby was also the one who'd discovered Lucy eating out of a garbage can, coaxed her into her arms and carried her home.

The second time we met, Gabby was involved in a conspiracy to steal, forge, and switch art treasures. But since the art had been looted by the Nazis—and Gabby and her merry band were returning the pieces to their rightful own-ers—I actually wanted to help.

My almost-sister-in-law may have skirted the law, but she had a moral code. Of some kind.

The question was, surrounded by sun, fun, and the super rich, what was she really doing in South Beach? And, more specifically, at Oceanside?

"I've heard of that junket," Annie said, snapping her well-manicured fingers. "A couple of the guys were talking about it at one of the fashion houses the other day. The Total Testosterone Tour!"

Gabby nodded, grinning. "A bunch of big, smelly men packed into a tricked-out tour bus. Honestly, it's a man cave on wheels."

"So how is Rodeo Rick?" I asked, remembering the photos she'd shared of the hunk in a cowboy hat, tiny trunks, and a pair of six-guns.

His wrestling alter-ego was a cowboy hero dubbed "Rodeo Rick Steed." His real name was Richard Stumpel-fig. But with a granite jaw and muscles to match, he looked more like a Rodeo Rick.

Gabby shook her head. "He's one of the bad guys now. Evil Edvard, the Mad Duke of Destruction. This one has a crown and a scepter and a little red velvet cape. I know it sounds silly, but he's their most popular villain, and I'm so proud of him. And he's having the time of his life."

She paused. "So how's Nicky?"

"Nick's good," I said. "Really good. His bakery's taking off. He's still running it from the inn, but we're trying to retrofit my place. And he's dating again. He's happy."

Her face relaxed. "I'm glad. High time he got back in the saddle. So how are things between you and the English stud muffin?"

"Complicated."

"Honey, I know complicated. But if there's something there, give it a chance. I did. And it's been worth it."

Was there something there? Ian and I had shared precisely one kiss. OK, a great kiss. But then life intervened.

And there was the business of that pesky little microphone. Plus whatever he was really running out of that inn.

"Listen to the lady," Annie said, poking me in the ribs with an elbow.

"Oh, and Harkins and Daisy got married," I said, hoping to change the subject. "And you should see Alistair—he's growing like a little weed."

To Annie, I explained, "Gabby was helping Harkins and his family when they thought they were going to have to make a run for it."

"Gabby, we're going upstairs for a very late lunch," my sister said. "Why don't you join us? You two can catch up, and we can fill you in on what's been going on in the building for the past couple of months."

"Yeah, I heard that real estate lady fell down the elevator shaft," Gabby said, shaking her head. "You wouldn't think that could happen in a classy place like this."

"You have no idea," I said.

Something finally clicked.

"You're the duchess!" I exclaimed.

"What?" Gabby asked.

"Annie and I went to a cocktail party. And a couple of the neighbors were gossiping about a duchess who was staying in the building—an American woman who'd married a European duke. I'd bet money they were talking about you."

"Well," Gabby drawled, looking very pleased with herself, "who'd have thunk it?"

CHAPTER 37

Lucy spent the first few minutes of our return trying to jump into Gabby's arms. Or lap.

"My little girl's all grown up now," Gabby said. And I swear she was tearing up.

"That's what Nick calls her, 'the little dog,'" I said. "But the vet says she'll probably top out at forty-five or fifty pounds."

"She looks good," Gabby said, giving Lucy a double-handed, double-ear scratch.

"She plays in the yard, gets lots of walks around the neighborhood, and has a regular circle of doggie friends she visits," I said. "They even put in an agility course at our dog park."

Lucy being Lucy, she'd adopted an à la carte approach to that one. Some of the agility stations she'd hit twice, some she skipped entirely. But she loved the place.

Even after half an hour of dedicated Lucy time, including a quick "break" on the front lawn of Oceanside, the pup remained steadfastly glued to Gabby's side.

As my sister buzzed around the kitchen throwing pasta

into a pot and chopping vegetables, Gabby and I sat at the white marble breakfast bar watching the show.

"Your kitchen is like something out of one of those fancy TV home makeover thingies," Gabby said, looking around in wonder.

Annie smiled. "Thank you! Whoever designed these places did an amazing job—everything you need and all in just the right spot."

"So how come you're here in Miami?" Gabby asked me, reaching down to stroke Lucy. "Are you on vacation too?"

"Kind of," I said. "That was part of it. Also, there was something weird going on with the condo board election here at Oceanside. And Annie wanted a second opinion."

"So what's weird about it?"

While Annie minced garlic, I filled in Gabby about why I'd first come to town—and what we'd discovered this morning.

"You mean she staged the whole thing?" Gabby asked, eyes wide.

I hoped we weren't giving her any ideas.

"Lock, stock, and fake competition," I said.

"That's awful."

"Exactly what I said," my sister added. "But the worst part is that she hung poor Dennis and Geoffrey out to dry."

"Yeah, and neither of them would do too well in prison," I said.

"Why would they go to jail?" Gabby asked. "Your friend Leslie is the one who faked an election. And they can't exactly arrest her."

"It's not the fake election," I explained. "It's why she faked it. Apparently, Leslie had taken over managing the association's money. The other two just signed off on whatever she gave them. But she wasn't paying the bills, and now the association account has about fourteen bucks in it."

"Shoot, sugar, are you sure no one pushed her down that elevator shaft?"

She had a point. But the police were treating Leslie's death as an accident, and who was I to quibble?

"The problem is, we have to find the money," Annie said. "If Leslie hasn't already spent it."

Gabby's face took on a crafty expression I knew all too well.

"What?" I asked.

"Well, I'm no expert, but it sounds like what you all need is a little reconnaissance mission."

CHAPTER 38

Annie's spaghetti was great. Gabby's idea gave me heartburn.

In a nutshell, we would go into Leslie McQueen's apartment and nose around a little.

Or, "have a little look-see," as my never-quite-sister-in-law phrased it.

The only thing I could see happening was the three of us joining Dennis and Geoffrey in a holding cell. But at least Gabby and Annie would look great in their mug shots.

The phone rang. When Nick's number popped up, the heartburn went into overdrive.

"I have to . . . uh . . . take this in my room," I said, scurrying down the hall. "It's my editor."

"What's wrong now?" I hissed into the phone, firmly closing the bedroom door behind me. "Termites? Rats? A family of mimes living in my crawl space?"

"The place is totally solid," my brother said. "Not a thing wrong with it."

"No black mold?"

"Nope."

"What about the wiring?"

"You could host one of those electric-light events next Christmas. Your original home inspector knew what he was doing. And we know this because a second inspector—one who doesn't even know the first guy—confirmed it this morning."

"But what about what the contractor said? The extra tests? And the specialists? And the second mortgage?"

"BS, no, no, and we don't need it," Nick said. "Look, this one was my fault—totally. I made a bad hire. The contractor may have had skills and great reviews, but he was not a good guy. When I first spoke with him, I explained that I was doing the necessary stuff now with the money I had in hand. But I wanted to leave the door open to taking a little from the next payment to do a couple of really cool upgrades in a few months. Unfortunately, he heard 'second payment' and decided to double his money while halving his workload. Hence the ever-expanding budget."

"Oh geez," I said.

"Yup."

"So what happens now?" I asked, feeling like I'd just woken up from a nightmare.

"Now we start over with a new contractor. But, honestly? I'm taking a breather for a while. I've kinda had it."

"No lie," I agreed. "So how much do we owe him?"

"Zip."

"He came out and did tests," I said. "Even if we didn't really need them, he's still going to charge us."

The last thing I wanted was some angry contractor filing a lien on my home. My snug, wonderful little home.

"Yeah, I don't think so. Instead we played *Let's Make a Deal*. The deal is I don't report him to the police and the local building association, and he calls it even. I'm looking at a receipt with his signature that says, "Paid in full.""

My brother would have made a great lawyer. Or possibly a crime boss.

"You're kidding."

"Guess who paid for the second home inspection? Hint—it wasn't yours truly."

"Nicholas Edward Vlodnachek, you are the man," I said.

"Don't I know it."

CHAPTER 39

That night was the first time I'd ever taken an elevator to a break-in.

Apparently, with no Leslie McQueen to get in the way, the elevators were now working perfectly. I wish I could say the same about the condo board.

Dennis was doing a pretty decent job of glad-handing the residents and the bill collectors. Despite that, he remained stubbornly convinced that he was going to prison.

Geoffrey was a wreck. But he'd managed to track down a lot of the services and vendors Leslie had stiffed during her grand experiment—even with time out for panic attacks. Unfortunately, he'd had zero luck in following the money. And spending hours with Dennis Chu wasn't exactly decreasing his anxiety levels.

At this rate, I didn't think either of them would make it through the weekend without running screaming to the cops.

So we decided to spare them the knowledge of tonight's little excursion. Besides, if we did it right, no one would be any the wiser.

Gabby was magic. She twirled some little silver gadget

in the lock, depressed the handle, and opened the door. In less time than it had taken Annie to open her own door with her own key.

"Girl, you've got skills," my sister said.

Gabby beamed.

To be on the safe side, we'd each chosen a pair of gloves from my sister's collection. So as not to look too suspicious, Annie and I donned ours only after we were inside Leslie's apartment.

Gabby had picked a practical pair of black leather driving gloves. Annie had selected some little blue flannel ones—for gardening, I think. And for some reason, I'd gone with elbow-length white silk opera gloves.

What can I say? It seemed like a good idea at the time.

We'd even brought a couple of large shoulder satchels, in case there was anything we needed to pack out with us. At this point, all we needed were black eye-masks and empty sacks with big dollar signs on the side.

Leslie hadn't been seen since the night of the party. Now I noticed that her blinds were closed, and the lights in her place were all on. So it looked like she'd probably died sometime that night.

Plus, the elevators weren't working the next morning.

Oddly, champagne campaign rally or not, everything was perfectly neat and tidy. Not a balloon, not an election T-shirt, not an inch of red-white-and-blue bunting. Not even the little step-stool where she'd made her stump speech.

"It's a little like your home only smaller, and the stuff isn't as nice," Gabby noted. "But the layout is like the place where I'm staying."

"Airbnb?" my sister asked.

"Pretty much," Gabby said breezily.

Ahead of time, we'd decided to give the whole place the once-over together; then we'd divide and conquer.

I'd seen the kitchen and the living room the night of the

party. And I was pretty sure that Leslie wasn't keeping bank books on the balcony.

"Let's hit the bedrooms first," I said.

Leslie's room was like the rest of the house—expensive but cold. All color-coordinated, in varying shades of gray and lavender.

"This looks like a mid-level room at one of the big-bucks Vegas hotels," Gabby said.

"I was thinking model home, but yeah," I agreed.

There wasn't a book or piece of paper in sight. At my house, you couldn't go three feet without stumbling over a stack of paperbacks. And notebooks, pens, and magazines pretty much were my décor.

I opened a shallow white cabinet mounted on the far wall, revealing a huge TV screen. Five feet, at least. The matching deep cabinet beneath it housed a DVR and a DVD player, along with a couple of gizmos I didn't recognize.

"Wow," Annie said. "She didn't skimp on the electronics."

It reminded me of something. But I couldn't quite place it.

"Damn, girls, you should see this closet," Gabby called from across the room. "It looks like a boutique."

She wasn't wrong. In shades of pink and chocolate brown, it did look like one of those chichi little clothing shops in the mall. The floors were dark brown marble, the wooden shelves a rich espresso, and the walls and ceiling were covered in pink satin. Except for the one wall that was completely mirrored. In the middle of the ceiling hung a large crystal chandelier.

"Is that a chaise?" I asked, pointing to a pink velveteen thing jutting out from one corner.

"Fainting couch," Annie said. "All the rage in the eighteenth century."

Surrounding us on shelves and racks, Leslie's wardrobe and shoes were organized by color.

"I could live in here," Gabby whispered reverentially.

"I want to go home," I muttered.

"OK, probably nothing here," my sister concluded. "So we keep this in mind, and we can always double back later."

Leslie's office turned out to be much more utilitarian. The desk was a modernist contraption of glass floating on metal. Like her bedroom, not a stray sheet of paper or a random ballpoint pen. But there was a computer monitor.

"I'll take this," Annie said, settling into the chair. "Hmm? Password protected? Who on earth puts a password on their home computer? Especially when they live alone?"

"Maybe she's got a nosy cleaning lady," I said. "Or maybe she doesn't always live alone."

If someone else had keys to this place, I prayed they wouldn't be home anytime soon.

I opened the closet door. No bordello chic this time. A printer, a shredder, and two polished oak file cabinets. The cabinets got my attention. Especially the brass locks.

I'd worked in offices. So I was used to secured cabinets. The ones I'd seen had dinky locks you could open with a paper clip.

Not that I'd know.

But these were different. Thick amber wood with heavy-duty brass fittings and substantial locks. Custom-made, I'd guess.

So what was worth that kind of protection?

"Gabby, I think we might need your expertise over here."

"Gotcha, sugar," she said, ambling over and sizing up my find. "Your real estate lady really loves her locks, doesn't she?"

"Can you get into it?"

"Sure thing," she said, digging through her bag. "I just need the right tool."

Pulling out something that looked like a dental pick, she went to work on one brass lock. After two seconds, I swear I hear a soft *ping*.

"Is that it?" I asked.

"For the first one. Sugar, this thing is double locked. One lock on the entire cabinet, then separate locks on each of the drawers. Whatever's in here, your lady didn't want anybody getting their hands on it."

Please let it be bank books.

I heard a second ping, and Gabby grinned. "First drawer is open. Just a shake, and I'll get the other one."

After another soft click, she stepped to the second filing cabinet and started all over again.

While she worked, I yanked open the top drawer of the first cabinet. Only one item: a large, worn, leather-bound organizer. I carefully lifted it out and opened it.

It appeared to be set up numerically. I flipped to a random page.

#2516: No dog. Sec sys: 2516#. Loves jazz & tequila. Family summers in the Hamptons—conservative! 2nd mort. Secretly gay (photos). Occasional pot—gym bag MB clst. Regular 9 to 5. Gym M, W & F: 6:15 to 7:30 am. Out late TH nites. MB ovhd lt.

#2517: Stupid dog—Pickles. No sec sys. $$$ in savings. Painkillers—MBth med cab. Petty cash—LR flower vase. Walks dog @ 7, 12 & 5. Other outings irregular. Sometimes dogwalker. LR elec out nr balcony.

Number 2517 was Ethel's place! Painkillers and petty cash—that's what the burglar stole from her unit.

The notes went on and on—page after page. Thumbnails

of schedules, likes and dislikes, and gory personal details—usually followed by "photos." Whatever that meant.

And what was her obsession with dogs?

The book was heavy. But it was also a blueprint of Leslie's mind. And, with any luck, her movements. I hoisted it carefully into my satchel.

"Ooooh, girls, check this out," Gabby said. She turned and unlatched the second file cabinet's doors. But though this looked identical to the first cabinet, it was very different. The entire front face swung open in one piece, revealing a pegboard decorated with keys. Each key and peg was carefully labeled and numbered.

Annie lifted one out and read the tag. "Six seven one two—this is Dennis and Gracie's place! That witch!"

"You said she was pushing you for keys to your unit. It looks like you're not the only one. And some of the residents complied."

"Of course they did," my sister said indignantly. "She claimed she was collecting them for the management company."

"Yeah, and she claimed the money was for the homeowners' association," I said.

I tapped the satchel. "She's also got a slam book that details everyone's personal profiles, schedules—and some other weird stuff I can't quite decipher."

"She was going into people's homes," my sister seethed.

"Looks like," I said. "At least, the ones who gave her keys. That's probably how she got whatever she got on your friend Dennis."

Gabby's eyes widened. "She was blackmailing him?"

"That stays between us girls," Annie said quickly. "That's how she got him to sign off on everything. He made a stupid mistake. But he swears he didn't go through with it, and I believe him. And now he and Gracie are starting a family."

"Gotcha," Gabby said blithely. "So what do we do with these?" she asked, gesturing at the key cabinet as if it was a game-show prize.

"Leave them," Annie and I said at the same time.

I moved on to the bottom drawer in my file cabinet. Nada.

But the space was only a few inches deep. And the drawer went at least a foot. I knocked on the bottom. Hollow.

It took me a minute, but I finally figured out that the "bottom" of the drawer folded back like a partition, revealing two items: a gold key and a small rubber mallet.

Most door keys I'd seen were cut with a series of divots. That's how they turned the locks. But this one was completely smooth.

Gabby glanced over my shoulder. "That's a bump key, sugar."

I'd heard of bump keys, but I'd never actually held one in my hand. Theoretically, you stuck it in a lock, hit it with something heavy—like a mallet—and boom, you were in the door.

"It's not as nice as the thingies I use, but it'll get the job done," Gabby said with professional detachment.

"Will this open any door?" I asked.

"Any door that uses that kind of lock," she said, studying it. "It looks like the model they used for this whole place."

"So with this . . ." I started.

"Your real estate lady wouldn't need a key," Gabby said. "She could open any door in the building."

CHAPTER 40

The three of us spent the rest of the night in Annie's apartment poring over Leslie's leather binder.

Leslie had just four phone numbers listed in the back. Each with a different first name. No last names. And nothing that pointed to where the money might have gone.

We did puzzle out some of her shorthand, though. "Sec sys," obviously, was "security system." And the poor guy in number 2516 apparently used his apartment number as his system password.

"Rookie mistake," Gabby declared, yawning.

Annie worked out that LR was "living room," and MB was "master bedroom." That meant Ethel kept petty cash in a flower vase in her living room. And her pills were, obviously, in the "MBth med cab"—master bathroom medicine cabinet.

"No wonder Leslie went ballistic when Ethel hired her own locksmith to change the locks on her door," I said. "If he used a different brand, even Leslie's bump key wouldn't have worked."

"Then Leslie socked that poor woman with a five hundred dollar fee—and pocketed it."

I finally worked out that "ovhd lt" was "overhead light" and "elec out" was "electric outlet."

What did it mean that Leslie's shorthand was a lot like my own? And why was she so obsessed with lights and outlets?

But the book—and Leslie's office setup—did explain her weird antipathy for dogs. It was a lot harder to go strolling into an apartment if there was someone on the other side of the door with sharp teeth and a nice, loud bark.

I flipped through the book looking for Annie's place. It was near the back:

#10001: No dog. Sec sys? Irregular visits, irregular hours. Always guests. Airbnb?
Need more info!

I showed it to Annie.

"Airbnb? I asked.

"No, but I lend it out to anybody I know who's coming to Miami," she said. "And the models are always camping out here."

Unfortunately, the more we learned about Annie's neighbors, the less we wanted to know.

Larry on two really did have a drinking problem. He also had three DUIs, a suspended license, and a case of cut-rate bourbon under his bathroom sink.

One couple on five was headed for the rocks. The stay-at-home mom lost most of their kid's school tuition playing online poker. The dad had two secret credit cards and a sports car hidden in a garage across town.

A single woman on four had a crush on Dennis Chu—and invited him to her apartment when Grace was out of town. Apparently a glass of wine had turned into an extended snogging session. Like a lot of the juicier bits, that one also had the mysterious notation "photos."

Including the notes on Dennis and Grace:

#6712: No dog. Sec sys: #0214. Both 9 to 5. DC
home F's. Multiple rounds IVF. $ trouble. 2nd mort-
gage. DC drunken make-out with #4315 (photos).

"That's awful," Annie said. "I mean, I know all of that
already. Well, except for the bit about the girl on four. But I
know it because Grace chose to confide in me. This is just
wrong. Leslie was stealing people's lives. She had no right
to any of this."

"From what Dennis said, she wasn't just stealing secrets, she was monetizing them," I said.

Gabby had gone silent, which wasn't like her at all.
That's when I noticed she'd fallen asleep sitting on the
floor with her back against the sofa. Lucy's head was in her
lap.

"She can have my room," I said, nodding toward our
new guest. "I can take the sofa."

"Nonsense," Annie said. "The sofa in my office pulls
out to a queen. And it's comfy. I slept there before the beds
were delivered."

We returned to the book. I kept hoping something in it
might somehow show us where Leslie had squirreled away
the missing money. But what if she'd just spent it on mortgage payments, home electronics, and that awful pink
fainting couch?

In the back of the book, Leslie's mysterious phone numbers all belonged to men. First names only. Andy, Jake,
Eddy, and Thom. With their extension numbers following
their phone numbers. I'd be calling them later. Could be
family, friends, or coconspirators, take your pick.

She also had several pages of strange notations. Groups
of numbers—which looked like condo numbers. But, at the
very top of each column, some weird combination of let-

ters that didn't look familiar. And some of the condo numbers were listed under more than one cluster.

I'd looked at them when we first got our hands on the book. And I'd been puzzling over them in my head off and on for the past forty minutes, but none of it made any sense. Not to me, anyway.

"Here, look at this," Annie said, pointing a perfect blush nail at Leslie's synopsis of #3612. "We've deciphered it, but it doesn't make any sense. Leslie has a note here at the end that translates to 'master bedroom phone.'"

"Oh geez," I said.

"What?"

"I know why Leslie McQueen was obsessed with electric outlets and lights. And phones. She was planting bugs. And, as I learned the hard way, a listening device needs juice. You have to put them somewhere people won't find them. But you also need a power source."

"So she was breaking into people's homes and bugging them? That snake!"

"An overhead light would have a good line of sight on the bedroom," I said. "We might be looking at cameras, too."

"Her notes mention photos."

"She'd need pictures to get any leverage in a case like Dennis's," I said. "Otherwise, it's just he said/she said. But we were all over that office of hers. We didn't find any photos."

"They're probably on the computer—and it's password protected," Annie said, her face a thundercloud. "I swear if that woman wasn't already dead, I'd strangle her myself!"

CHAPTER 41

"We need a technology expert to crack that computer," Annie said as she spooned coffee into her coffeemaker the next morning.

Gabby was sleeping in after our late night.

I'd already taken Lucy for her morning constitutional. And we'd come back with doughnuts.

"I've been thinking about that," I admitted. "For someone who uses electronics and bugs, Leslie seems to have preferred old-school storage methods. How old do you think she was?"

"Leslie? I'm guessing midfifties. Why?"

"Young enough to make the most of technology. Old enough not to trust it completely. I mean, the woman kept her blackmail profiles in a leather-bound organizer."

"Easy to pick up and carry," my sister said. "You think there's another one of those things with photos?"

"I think she was going to a lot of trouble to gather information on people. And some of the folks in this building have some serious money and technical know-how. If one of her pigeons realized that she was storing her blackmail goodies on a computer, they could have possibly hacked in and wiped her files."

"But keeping hard copies?" my sister asked. "That would take an awful lot of space. And we've already searched her apartment."

We had, too. After we locked up Leslie's key cabinet, Gabby, Annie, and I had spent the next hour going through every inch of Leslie McQueen's impersonal, yet expensively furnished digs, looking for anything resembling a bank book.

Nada.

I'd found a stack of mail—or, more correctly, junk mail—in one of her kitchen drawers. I put it in my satchel, just in case. It wasn't as if Leslie was going to need it anymore.

With Gabby's help, I even trolled through the electronics store in Leslie's bedroom. The DVD player was empty. And the DVR player must have been new because she hadn't even had a chance to record anything on it yet.

"What about her storage locker?" I asked.

"That would be perfect," my sister agreed. "But how do we find out which one is hers?"

"Are they coded? You know, by apartment number?"

Annie shook her head. "Totally random. First come, first served. At least, that's what we were told. And now we all know what that's worth."

We fell silent.

My sister eyed me with concern. "What strength of sunblock are you using?"

"The sunblock's fine—it's SPF 45. But apparently I wasn't as regular with it as I should have been when we first arrived. So the sun kinda got a head start. I'm being really careful now though."

I was, too. Not that it seemed to make any difference.

"Look," I said, finally, "if what we deciphered is right,

Ethel has a bug or a camera planted in her living room wall outlet."

"I know," my sister said. "I'd love to rip it out. But I don't know how to do that without letting her know it's there. And if we tell her . . ."

"Then we have to explain everything else—including what Dennis and Geoffrey did," I finished. "But I think I might have an idea. And it'll let us test our theory about Leslie's surveillance equipment at the same time."

Annie smiled. "So what kind of gloves will I need this time?"

"You? None at all," I said. "All you have to do is invite a nice neighbor and her pup for tea."

CHAPTER 42

While Annie entertained Ethel Plunkett, Gabby and I broke into her condo.

Annie and I had worked out a code ahead of time. I'd text her "❤" when we were clear of the place. And she'd text me "911" if Ethel and Mrs. Pickles cut out early.

I just prayed Ethel's earlier brush with burglary hadn't prompted her to install some kind of silent alarm. Or a camera of her own.

Red hair looks lousy with an orange jumpsuit.

"Oh, sugar, this place is cute," Gabby said, glancing around. "Neat as a pin and homey, too. I could move right in."

I was hoping that was a figure of speech. But, given what we were doing already, I wasn't about to ask.

I headed straight into the living room. Next to the balcony door there was an electrical outlet. Bingo.

"This has to be the one," I said.

"Where's the fuse box?" she asked.

"Why do you need the fuse box?"

Gabby grinned and shook her head. "If I don't cut the power first, your nice neighbor lady is gonna come home and find a couple of crispy critters."

"Hallway?" I guessed.

"Got it!" she called from the other room a minute later. "They hid it in a closet. And we have to reset the clocks before we leave. Otherwise, that's a dead giveaway."

Clearly, this was not her first rodeo.

"OK, sugar, we're good to go," Gabby said, reappearing in the living room.

I fished a screwdriver out of my satchel and unscrewed the plate on the outlet. I had no idea what to expect. The extent of my knowledge on the subject—aside from the bug I'd pulled off the base of my own phone—was searching "hidden listening devices" on Annie's computer this morning. Too bad I couldn't call Ian for a quick lesson.

Unfortunately, when the plate came off, it brought powdered wallboard with it, forming a tell-tale pile on the floor.

"Don't worry, I've got a little hand vac for that," Gabby said, patting her oversized purse.

I didn't know whether to be concerned or grateful. Instead, I peered into the outlet.

"Yowza!" Gabby exclaimed, looking over my shoulder. "Is that . . . ?"

"Yup—a big ol' nasty bug," she said happily.

"Can you tell if it's a microphone or a camera?"

"Looks like just a microphone," Gabby said. "But I'm no expert."

Could've fooled me.

"Do I just yank it out?" I asked.

Hand it to Ian, the one he used in my house was a lot easier to remove. Although, I'd been pretty steamed at the time.

"Honey, let me," Gabby said, stepping in smoothly.

It took her less than a minute to produce wire cutters, clip what looked like stray threads, and lift the bug out of the wall.

"All set."

As I replaced the plate, she turned the device in her hands, studying it.

"Why on earth would a real estate big-shot want to bug a sweet little old lady?" Gabby asked.

"No idea," I admitted. "But I think Leslie was popping into people's apartments and swiping stuff. She discovered Ethel kept prescription meds in her bathroom and some spare cash in the living room. I'm guessing the mikes helped her keep track of when people were away from home. And if she picked up a little information she could use, that was icing on the cake."

It also explained how Leslie McQueen had known the minute Ethel Plunkett changed the locks.

Now if we could just find the money Leslie had looted from the association. And her stash of photos.

CHAPTER 43

Gabby placed the tiny microphone in the middle of Annie's living room table.

Luckily, Lucy had zero interest in it. Wedged between Gabby and me, she was fighting sleep. And losing. Apparently, two long morning walks followed by a playdate with Mrs. Pickles had left the pup pooped.

The rest of us were relying on sugar and caffeine. Three coffee mugs littered Annie's table. Along with an empty bag of orange Milanos.

"So that's what a bug looks like?" my sister asked.

Gabby and I nodded.

"One of them, anyway," I said. "The model Ian used was different."

I didn't want to say it in front of Gabby, but given Ian's contacts, he probably had access to better stuff.

"I learned something interesting from Ethel," Annie said. "Remember that fine she had to pay for the new locks? Well, it turns out that Leslie had her write out that check a little differently."

"What do you mean?" I asked.

"When Leslie went to Ethel's condo demanding the

fine, she had Ethel make out the check to a different entity."

"The Leslie McQueen Ugly Furniture Fund?"

"Oceanside HOA," Annie said. "We normally just make out our monthly association checks to 'Oceanside.' But according to Ethel, Leslie was very insistent that 'HOA' had to be included. She even ripped up the first check and made Ethel do it again."

"The other account!" I said. "Annie, you're brilliant!"

My sister grinned.

"Any way Ethel could get us a copy of that check? If we could get the number of the account where it was deposited—or even just the bank—we could find out where Leslie's been hiding that money."

"Already on it," Annie said. "I told Ethel it was possible we might be able to get her a refund—in light of the fact that Leslie was playing a little fast and loose with the rule book. I promised her I'd look into it, but told her I'd need a copy of the check. She's calling her bank this afternoon."

"But, sugar, what are you going to do when that nice lady wants to know what's up with getting her money back?" Gabby asked.

Annie smiled guiltily. "I already called my local bank. They'll be mailing her an anonymous cashier's check for five hundred dollars."

CHAPTER 44

Life at Oceanside was changing fast. For one thing, there seemed to be a lot more dogs. It was as if someone had waved a magic wand and they'd all come out of hiding.

The elevators had become mini doggie meet and greets. Especially at prime pup-walking times. Even Lucy didn't seem to mind riding in the things anymore. She was too busy getting to know her canine neighbors.

But not all the changes were good.

I'd bundled Annie's garbage and hauled it to the trash chute, which was inside a little room at the end of the hall. Apparently all the floors had one. But when I opened the door to the chute room, it smelled like a dump. And when I opened the chute door, I discovered why: Garbage had backed up all the way to the top.

Add trash collection to the long list of services Leslie McQueen had neglected to pay.

At this rate, they'd have to start throwing the stuff in the pool. Which was now a disturbing shade of dark green.

And from what I was hearing, the parking garage was turning into the Wild West. Reserved spots were a thing of the past. The lot was a free-for-all. Released from Leslie's iron grip and armed with the knowledge that she'd been reading from a rule book of her own invention, residents were getting even for past slights—perceived or otherwise. And it was amazing how many of those grudges involved parking.

The new rule: There were no rules.

On the bright side, no one seemed to care when—or if—there would be another election. Having escaped one overreaching board president, homeowners seemed none-too-anxious to appoint another one. Green swimming pool or not.

And they didn't know the half of it.

Geoffrey had gone through the last four months of bills. Right after they'd first fired the management company, Leslie was paying everyone. But, slowly, over the next few months, she let more and more bills slip. So now the building owed pretty much everyone in town—from the water company to the carpet cleaners. And the amounts were staggering.

Geoffrey being Geoffrey, he'd turned it into a color-coded wall chart to demonstrate the building's current level of indebtedness.

"That's actually kinda pretty," Gabby said, studying his pastel poster after one of our emergency confab sessions.

"Thank you," he said proudly.

Candied hues or not, Oceanside was in the red.

Dennis had had a little luck staving off the bill collectors and keeping some of the more necessary services—like water—flowing. But that was only because he kept promising them money that we didn't have.

Heck, if I wanted to do that, I could've just stayed home.

Then Ethel Plunkett showed up at Annie's with a copy of that check. Two bad photocopies of a fax and it had cost the poor woman fifteen bucks. I could read it, but just barely.

Still, it gave us a bank name: Warranty National. And that gave me an idea.

I'd dialed all the contact numbers in the back of Leslie's organizer. Some of the numbers weren't in service. Others were places that seemed unlikely contacts for a Miami real estate agent. A nail salon in Portland. A coffee bar in Denver.

Not a Caymans moneyman or Swiss banker in the bunch.

And none of them had ever heard of Leslie McQueen. Or the men whose names Leslie had written by each number.

"Do you have the copy of that account printout Geoffrey gave us?" I asked Annie, as she studied Ethel's check.

"In here," she said, handing me a file folder. "But, much as I hate to admit it, Geoffrey's chart *is* easier to understand."

"The mark of a skilled professional—simplifying the complex," I said, as I pulled the paper out of her folder. "I still don't understand how she pulled the wool over his eyes. I mean, Dennis, OK, she had something on him. But Geoffrey almost seems above it all. Like a space alien."

"More like a young space alien," Annie added. "He needs someone to look out for him. I get the feeling he's kind of naïve."

"This is it!" I shouted, pushing the photocopy and the book toward her. "Check this out."

"What am I looking at?" Annie asked.

"The first contact number in the back of Leslie's book. Next to the name 'Andy.' The phone number is the same as the number for the HOA's account at Primary Federal. The one Leslie opened with Geoffrey. That's why these phone numbers don't make any sense. They're not phone numbers. They're bank account numbers."

"Alex," she said, squeezing my shoulder, "you found the money!"

"Not yet," I said. "We know the one for the account at Primary Federal. And we know one of these other three is probably code for the account number at Warranty National. But where are the other two? And what's with the men's names?"

"You said it—codes!" Annie exclaimed triumphantly, bouncing on the sofa.

"PIN codes!" I shouted. "She disguised the bank account numbers as phone numbers and listed the PIN codes in letters instead of numbers."

We decided to test our theory with low-hanging fruit. I dialed the customer service number for Primary Federal and punched in the association's account number.

"For your security, please enter your four-digit PIN and press pound," the electronic voice commanded.

I held my breath and spelled out 'Andy' on the keypad, carefully pressing 2-6-3-9.

"Your account has a balance of fourteen dollars and twelve cents."

I grinned at Annie. "Now all we have to do is figure out where these other two are—and Oceanside will be back in business."

CHAPTER 45

Lucy, Annie, and I decamped to a juice bar down the street that specialized in fresh tropical juices, hot sandwiches, and organic coffee. With a view of the water, the place was a picture postcard of Miami.

But all I cared about was the Wi-Fi.

Because, at this point, that put the place one step ahead of Oceanside.

Chalk it up to one more bill Leslie hadn't paid. So while residents had Wi-Fi in their homes (if they'd subscribed), the public coverage that blanketed the pool, lobby, restaurants, bars, cafés, spas, and workout room, was a thing of the past.

Dennis had been fielding phone calls all morning—telling angry residents that it was a technical glitch that would be fixed "as soon as the company could get a guy out to the building."

What he didn't tell them: The company wasn't sending anyone until Oceanside cut them a check.

Annie, naturally, had Internet in the penthouse. But she was afraid that I was missing the best part of my Miami vacation. So she convinced me we could work just as easily at the juice bar.

"They have these great grilled cheese and shredded chicken sandwiches," she promised. "With roasted peppers and caramelized onions."

We'd gotten a table in the shade, under a big blue umbrella. Lucy, resplendent in her booties—all four of them—was delicately lapping water from her collapsible bowl under the table.

As offices go, it was pretty cool.

While we waited for our order, I was pondering our match-the-account-numbers-with-the-banks puzzle.

This morning, I'd tried a couple of Leslie's phone numbers with Warranty National. And though I struck out with the first one, I hit pay dirt with the second. (PIN code: Eddy.)

It had a sizable balance. Or, at least, more money than I'd make in a few years. So with any luck, we could send it back to Primary Federal and get the Wi-Fi switched on, call the garbage collectors, and have the pool decontaminated.

But by my calculations, this was nowhere near all of the association's missing money.

Times like this made me realize how much I really missed investigative reporting. As a freelancer, I'd been writing a slew of feature stories. And I'd enjoyed a six-week stint as a newspaper agony aunt. It was fun, and it paid the bills. But I felt like my news skills were getting rusty.

Suddenly, I was rooting through documents, searching for the truth. And people were depending on me to find it—and get it right. It was scary. And kind of exhilarating.

What no one understands about reporters: Everyone thinks if they tell us a juicy story, we'll just print it verbatim.

That's hearsay, not news. And I'm nobody's stenographer.

For us, your intriguing tidbit is just the beginning. A tip, a lead, a piece of string to follow.

After you share it, that's when we start digging. Tracking clues, looking for needles in haystacks, and fact-checking stuff your mamma told you was gospel.

Most of the time, those tips come to nothing. But when they pan out, even the tipster might not recognize the end result.

One of my favorites was a municipal secretary who indignantly excoriated my former paper—and me—for printing only bad things about her city. Instead, we needed to write about how her director-boss was putting in all his spare time off the clock. No matter the hour, she loyally informed me, the guy was always on the job.

Turned out he worked the same nine-to-five everyone else did. But he was driving his city car after hours and on weekends. Ditto his city-issued credit card.

So the fact that I had a few slim leads—like numbers for accounts when we didn't know the banks—didn't bother me all that much.

Time to pull a little string.

CHAPTER 46

That evening, Gabby "borrowed" Lucy.

She'd planned a jaunt to a dog-friendly beach followed by a "little shopping spree" at a South Beach pet boutique and a trip to a dog spa.

I just hoped the pup wouldn't come home with pink nails or a rhinestone collar. I didn't know how I'd explain either one to Nick.

After they'd left, I was sitting on the floor of Annie's living room, with a notepad and pen on one side and a stack of mail on the other.

"What on earth are you doing?" my sister asked.

"Welcome to the glamorous world of reporting," I said, glancing up. "I'm going through Leslie McQueen's junk mail."

"Why?"

"Promise not to laugh?"

Annie nodded.

"I'm looking for clues."

Of course, she laughed.

"Where did you get all that?" Annie asked, eyeing the pile. "We never found her mailbox key. I wouldn't even know which box is hers. Besides, isn't stealing mail a fed-eral crime?"

She actually sounded worried.

"If I take it from her box before she collects it, that's a federal crime. I stole this from her kitchen. After she col-lected it. So that's just a regular crime."

"Much better," Annie said, shaking her head.

"Look, if this were for a story, I wouldn't have done that. Couldn't have. But if you want to get back the money Leslie stole and keep Dennis and Geoffrey out of jail, I'm running out of options."

"Sorry, Cissy," she said contritely, as she sat on the floor beside me, neatly crossing her legs. "How can I help?"

I handed her half the stack. "We already know that Leslie was doing business with Primary Federal, which is here in town. And Warranty National, which is based in Richmond. What we're looking for are any clues to the identities of her other two banks. Trust me, when you open a bank account anywhere, you go on a ton of mailing lists. Which means lots of junk mail. And if there's a healthy bal-ance, the bank is also going to try to sell you on its other services. So I'm hoping some of this might give us a few hints."

We sorted in silence.

"Gutter cleaning, nail salon, dentist," I muttered, reject-ing three in a row.

"'We'll remortgage your home at three percent,'" Annie read from a letter on creamy paper.

"OK, that sounds promising," I admitted. "Who's it from?"

"Transcontinental Bank and Trust in Boston. But it's just a form letter. Oooh, and here's another one from the same bank—promoting their luxury auto loan program."

"Oh yeah, sounds like someone knows Leslie has a little money to burn. So 'Jake' or 'Thom' could be Transcontinental," I said, scribbling notes on the pad. "Where did Quinn Whitmore say Fred McQueen worked?"

"He didn't. The closest he got was the city—Charlotte. But Kelsey works at Promethean National."

"Might be helpful to have a friend at the bank," I said, making notes. "Especially one who feels like she owes you a favor."

"Do you think Kelsey was involved?" my sister asked.

"No idea. Off the top of my head, I don't think so. I don't think she's got the nerve for the kind of games Leslie was playing. But I've been wrong before."

Boy, had I.

"Wait a minute," my sister said, snapping her fingers. "Kelsey said she's a manager in investments."

I nodded, tossing aside a flyer for a meal delivery service and another for a discount pharmacy. I looked up and noticed the color had drained from my sister's flawless face.

"If Leslie has already invested that money," she breathed, "it's going to be impossible for us to get it back."

I'd pictured the possibility of Leslie McQueen moving her ill-gotten gains overseas. Switzerland. The Caribbean. Macao. But for some reason I'd never seriously considered a scenario in which she'd park that money close to home and just transfer it into something a little less liquid, like stocks, bonds, or—heaven help us—real estate.

While the cops could follow the trail and—eventually— return everything to Oceanside, that would be long after the scandal decimated the value of this place. And possibly Dennis and Geoffrey right along with it.

"Look, we don't know anything yet," I reasoned. "Let's try the account numbers and see what Leslie still has in cold, hard cash. Then we can panic."

"Deal," my sister said resolutely.

After we looked up the customer service numbers, I dialed Promethean National first. For some reason, I punched in the fourth account number. The one for 'Thom.'

I took a deep breath and poked 8-4-6-6.

It had a balance. Not as much as the account at Warranty National. But Dennis and Geoffrey could definitely use that money to pay some of the building's bills.

I dutifully jotted down the amount, hit 3 so the automated system repeated the balance (just to be sure), and quickly hung up the phone.

I showed Annie the pad, pointing to the dollar amount.

"Cissy, this is great!"

"I'm feeling lucky. What say we check Transcontinental, too?"

I called the bank's customer service number, entered the account number, and carefully spelled out J-A-K-E on the keypad.

The balance was staggering. I wrote it down, made the system repeat the information—and quickly hung up the phone. Then, just to be safe, I shut it off.

I handed Annie the pad.

"Oh my gosh, Cissy," she said, leaning forward and throwing her arms around me. "You did it!"

Chapter 47

We banged on Dennis Chu's door. For a long time, nothing happened. Then I saw a shadow in front of the peephole. The door opened, and he stuck his head out furtively.

"Hurry up, if you want to come in," he said, stepping back inside. "There's gonna be another gang of them any minute."

"Gang of what?" I said, as he closed the door behind us and turned both bolts.

"Angry residents. You name it, if it's in this building, it's broken, missing, disconnected, or malfunctioning. I've been yelled at—actually screamed at—three times tonight. Once by a buddy of mine. I don't know how much more of this I can take. My nerves are shot. I can't eat. I can't sleep. I'm thinking it might be time to turn myself in."

"Alex found the money," Annie said.

"Really?" he said, looking hopeful. "You're not playing, right? Because, I mean, I've been promising people money all day. But that's total BS."

"Really, truly," I said, nodding. "Leslie had three secret bank accounts. And the balances roughly add up to what

Geoffrey figures you should have in the association account."

"Hot damn, let's pay some bills!" he said, grinning.

"First we have to move the money back into the board's account," I said. "And I think we're gonna need Geoffrey's help with that. We've got the account numbers and the security codes. But I think there are some rules about moving money. You know, so that we don't inadvertently call attention to ourselves while we're trying to return what Leslie stole."

"Good thinking," Dennis said. "Oh man, the first thing I'm gonna do when this is over is resign from the board and sleep for a week. And beg Gracie to forgive me. And I mean grovel."

He looked happier than I'd ever seen him.

Fifteen minutes later, Geoffrey had joined us. With his candy-colored chart.

"Yes, this is everything," he said, studying the account totals. "I mean, to be absolutely sure, we could call for an audit, but . . ."

"Look, is it fairly close to what we're missing or not?" Dennis asked, exasperated.

"Well, I'd say so. I mean, it's definitely within five hundred dollars."

"I'd pay five hundred dollars for all of this to be over," Dennis said. "I can't believe I'm finally gonna get my life back."

"We need to move the money back into the board account," I said. "That way, Geoffrey, you'll have the authority to use it to pay the bills. And then you two can turn over what's left to the new management company."

Geoffrey stopped, a startled expression on his face. "Hmm, oh yes. But we need to transfer the funds in amounts of less than ten thousand dollars. Otherwise, well, that would be bad."

"Define 'bad,'" Dennis said, looking a lot less happy.

"Mandatory government reporting and investigation," Geoffrey said. "Bad. Very bad."

"Oh geez," Dennis said, slapping his forehead.

"But if we keep it under ten thousand, we should be fine," Geoffrey concluded happily.

"This is a lot of money to move," I said. "So I'm guessing we'll make multiple transfers?"

"Exactly," Geoffrey said, smiling.

"I've been thinking about that, too," Annie said. "And I was wondering if we should also take a few precautions to cover our tracks electronically. So to speak."

Geoffrey actually beamed. And Annie was right. He looked exactly like a young space alien. All he needed was a silver suit and some antennae.

"Excellent idea," he said. "What did you have in mind?"

CHAPTER 48

Let's just say that Annie's idea involved a brand-new electronic tablet, some special software and public Wi-Fi.

Even though Geoffrey had the expertise to make the transfers himself, Dennis insisted on keeping him company. Or keeping an eye on him.

After what Leslie had done, trust was in short supply on Oceanside's HOA board.

Annie went along to help them with logistics. And make sure they didn't kill each other.

Left to my own devices, my mind kept returning to those blackmail photos. I hated loose ends. And it bothered me that they might still be discovered and made public. It was as if Leslie was still spreading poison from the grave.

So where would she put them?

It was clear from Leslie's condo that she liked keeping the evidence of her little enterprise close at hand. And, if her slam book and those oak filing cabinets were any indication, she preferred old-school storage methods.

So a storage unit in the building would be the perfect hiding place. But if she had one, where was it? And how would I find it?

I tried working with the facts I had. Leslie wrote down account numbers and passwords. In tiny, neat handwriting. She labeled the keys *and* the pegs on her resident key pegboard. Everyone who knew her said that she was remarkably efficient and organized.

So, chances are, she'd written it down somewhere.

I retrieved Leslie's book from my satchel and flipped through the sections. There were only four listings under "contacts," and we now knew they were the bank accounts. And we'd deciphered all the goodies about various residents in her "profiles." Unfortunately.

But the columns of condo numbers still didn't make sense. At least, not to me.

I turned to that section.

Then it struck me: Leslie knew everything there was to know about these people. But she never listed them by name. Instead, they were all numbers. Unit numbers. Easier to depersonalize them that way? Or just concealing evidence?

So if each of the numbers in the column represented a resident of Oceanside, what were the strange words written across the head of each column?

C BOBO

D BOBO

E BOBO

F BOBO

Numbers! Leslie, ace cryptographer, substituted letters for numbers to hide her bank PIN codes. Why not here too? If that was true, BOBO was probably 2020, and the letters in front stood for months. So now I had a handle on how she catalogued her blackmail photos—where was the stash?

In Annie's kitchen, I grabbed a flashlight and checked the clock. I had at least an hour before Gabby and Lucy were due. Like it or not, I was going to pay another visit to that scuzzy storage area.

CHAPTER 49

I was hoping that maybe, in my haste to get Lucy out for her walk, I'd exaggerated the creepy quotient of the storage area.

No such luck.

If Leslie's storage locker was anything like Leslie's parking spot, it would be conveniently located fairly close to the elevator. And, reasoning that Leslie McQueen wouldn't be caught dead on the service elevator—ironically—this time I started my search just inside the hallway lobby door.

But my sister had warned me that the first-floor storage area wasn't the only one. There were more storage lockers on three, four, and five. Oh goody.

Annie's superstrong flashlight lit up the dim pathway. Well enough that I could see evidence that one of the giant spiders had eaten recently.

Too bad they didn't have a craving for dust bunnies.

Idly, I wondered what was going on at home. Ever since Nick had delivered the good news about my house, I hadn't heard from him. I'm guessing he was making up for lost time with the bakery. Weirdly, I hadn't heard from Trip, either. I hoped everything had gone OK with the hotel bigwigs. First thing tomorrow morning, I was calling both of them to catch up.

As I approached the first storage cage, I swung the light in a wide arc, peering through the chain-link. I felt like an archeologist searching for a lost tomb.

Instead of an ancient sarcophagus, I discovered a collection of hockey sticks and roller skates. Along with a set of crutches and a dusty-looking walking cast.

Probably not Leslie's.

The next one held a lawn mower, an assortment of rakes, and a child's plastic playhouse. White with blue shutters and a pink roof.

Definitely not Leslie's.

Something scuttled across my path, and I aimed the light at my feet. A roach scurried by and suddenly took flight.

I jumped back and shuddered.

I waved the light across the pathway. Just to make sure the cigar-sized arthropod wasn't part of a mass migration. Something shiny shimmered in the edge of the beam. In front of one of the locker doors.

I prayed I hadn't found its nest.

I stepped back, focused the beam, and realized that it was two tiny bits of confetti. A red piece and a blue one.

Just like someone might use in a campaign balloon.

CHAPTER 50

Lucy bounced through the door with an extra spring in her step. Maybe because she wasn't wearing the booties.

"No need, sugar," Gabby drawled. "The ride-share guy let us off right in front of the building. She even took a little comfort break in the grass, if you know what I mean."

As Lucy pranced around the living room, Gabby filled me in on their trip. "First, we went to the beach. And hoo boy, this little girl ran me ragged. Then we stopped at this local hamburger joint. And let's just say that somebody worked up an appetite. Then we hit the doggie spa. Oh, it was the cutest place. And she loved it. She had an oatmeal shampoo, and an egg conditioner and a little clip, and a blow dry. Oh, and a mani-pedi. Or, in her case, I guess it's a pedi-pedi."

I tried to get a look at Lucy's dancing paws. No pink that I could see. Or polish of any kind. Just trimmed and smooth.

"And the collar is Coach," she said proudly.

"Gabby, she looks great!" I said. She did, too.

My ex-almost-sister-in-law beamed.

"Some good news on the condo front," I said. "We finally found that money Leslie McQueen stole from this place. Annie and Dennis and Geoffrey are transferring it back as we speak. But that's strictly on the q.t."

Gabby mimed locking her lips and throwing away the key. "I won't make a peep, sugar. What about the blackmail stuff?"

I told her about the storage locker. And the confetti. I left out the part about the Jurassic cockroach. Then I uttered eight words I'd never thought I'd hear myself say.

"So, are you up for a field trip?"

CHAPTER 51

I'd been worried because Annie only had one flashlight. But that wasn't a problem because apparently Gabby never left home without one.

Which made me wonder, not for the first time, why she was really here. A little vacation and romantic meet-up? Or was something bigger afoot?

We'd left Lucy in the comfort of Annie's penthouse. Bad enough I had to revisit the dusty, insect-infested storage area. No way was I dragging the pup down there.

As we left the lobby and headed down the back hallway, I had a sudden attack of the guilts.

"Gabby, I wasn't exactly honest with you here," I started.

"What is it, sugar?" she asked, looking concerned.

"The rest of this building is really nice. Even the garage. But the storage area? It's kind of a mess. And there are some bugs in there that belong in a museum. Or a sci-fi movie."

Gabby giggled. "Gotcha, sister girl. Big ol' bugs and lots of dust. Kind of like someone's attic."

I noticed she didn't say whose.

"Boy, they sure didn't waste any money on mood lighting," Gabby observed as we pushed open the heavy metal door and made our way into the storage area.

"Annie says most people only come in here a couple of times a year," I said, keeping my voice down so it didn't echo off the cement. "My theory is this is one of the first places Leslie started cutting corners."

"Looks like," Gabby agreed. When her flashlight grazed the occupied spider's web, I swear she shivered. But give her credit, she never stopped moving. Or even slowed.

"It's right up here," I said, gesturing with my beam. "That one on the right."

Gabby handed off her flashlight and reached into her purse.

"OK, sugar, just hold both lights on the padlock, and we'll be in there in two shakes."

She wasn't lying.

The inside of the storage locker was nearly as well organized as Leslie's office. Against the back of the unit, she'd stacked a handful of moving boxes. All neatly labeled. Campaign supplies—T-shirts. Campaign supplies—balloons. Campaign supplies—buttons. Campaign supplies—bunting.

I folded back the corner of one box. Exactly what the label said. "Leslie McQueen for President" T-shirts. Dozens of them.

A small stepladder rested against the chain-link fencing in one corner. In the center, she had one of those industrial folding tables that reminded me of high school art class. With a battery-powered camping lantern and blue cloth-covered rolling chair, I'm guessing this was her de facto desk when she was sorting through her blackmail stash.

All she needed was a dead plant and a barely there window and she could be a branch manager at Primary Federal.

A rolling stainless clothing rack with six black, zippered

hanging bags had been positioned on the opposite side of the unit. I guess the boutique-sized closet wasn't quite big enough.

Unfortunately, nothing was labeled "blackmail photos."

Gabby unzipped one of the dress bags. "Sorry, sugar, but I do love her clothes. I've just got to see what she has in here."

"Knock yourself out," I said, wondering if I'd been totally off the mark in coming here.

"Huh, that's funny," she said.

I turned and saw that, except for a couple of bulky hangers, the bag was empty.

I stepped forward and unzipped the next one. Ditto.

And it was the same story for the next three bags we attacked. Hangers only.

But the sixth bag was different. Inside, it had one of those organizers with multiple clear pockets for shoes.

Only there weren't any shoes. Instead, there were homemade DVDs and dozens of USB sticks.

The first pocket was labeled "D BOBO." I reached in and pulled out a DVD. The label read "D BOBO," followed by several apartment numbers. The next DVD was the same. And so were the memory sticks.

A few pockets down, the labels switched to "E BOBO." Also followed by different unit numbers.

"Gabby, this is it," I whispered, holding up one of the homemade DVDs. "If I'm right about what I saw in Leslie's leather book, these are her blackmail files."

CHAPTER 52

Annie was already home when we arrived. She was stretched out on the sofa, clad in a pink silk T-shirt and black yoga pants, cradling a tall glass of iced tea. Lucy was curled up asleep with her head in my sister's lap.

"All's right with the world," she told us. "We paid the bills straight out of Leslie's many accounts. And Geoffrey came up with a couple of good work-arounds to put the rest of the cash back without stirring up trouble. The guy really wanted to make things right. I honestly don't think this could have gone on one more day. Poor Dennis was ready to crack."

"So how was the odd couple getting along tonight?" I asked, remembering the prickly atmosphere this afternoon.

"Let's just say I don't see a buddy movie in their future," Annie said. "So what have you guys been up to? And by the way, Lucy looks wonderful."

Gabby grinned. "The little girl deserves some pampering. Especially if she's going to be a media star."

"You've got to take me to that doggie spa tomorrow," I said to Gabby. "That place is definitely going in my travel piece."

"You got it, sugar. They'd love the publicity. Now go on and give your big sis the big news."

"Big news?" Annie asked.

"We found Leslie's blackmail stash," I said.

"You're kidding! That's wonderful! Where? And how? Don't tell me you found more clues in her junk mail?"

"Close. I walked the first-floor storage area with a flashlight. And I found a few pieces of that confetti from her campaign balloons. Once I knew which unit was hers, the rest was just down to Gabby and me searching the thing. Good old-fashioned shoe leather and elbow grease."

"So what did you do with the stuff?"

"Leslie kept it on DVDs and USB sticks, so it's going to take a while to destroy," I explained. "Right now, it's parked in your hall closet. In a black suit bag."

"Oh geez," my sister said. "There's no telling what's in there."

"I don't want to watch them. I just want to get rid of them. Any suggestions?"

I'd noticed that, where Leslie McQueen was concerned, every solution seemed to present a brand-new problem.

"My shredder will handle the DVDs," Annie said. "USB sticks? No idea."

"Water, sugar."

"Really?" I asked. If that was true, then for the price of a punchbowl full of Miami tap, we could make our neighbors' lives a lot easier.

"It might not totally get every teensy, little bit," Gabby said. "But it'll make them pretty near worthless. Besides, with these nice people, you're talking about a few little sins and indiscretions, right? Not top secret files."

"Uh, right," I said.

Now I was truly itching to know: What the heck was Gabrielle DuBois really doing in Miami?

CHAPTER 53

That night, Annie, Gabby, Lucy, and I had a shredding party.

It's sort of like a slumber party with doughnuts. And dog treats. And a shredder.

Thanks to Gabby, we even had a bucket of water for the memory sticks. And I dumped in some salt, just to be on the safe side.

One thing I'd learned during my stay in Miami: Salt water corroded everything.

Before I consigned the contents of the leather binder to Annie's shredder, I was curious about one more thing.

I flipped through it, searching for a specific apartment number: 3517.

Because, while Dennis's cooperation with Leslie made sense (given what she had on him), I couldn't fathom how she'd snared Geoffrey.

At first, I thought it might have been one of Leslie's charm offensives or her alpha-female, authority-figure behavior. Or maybe, like a lot of people around here, Geoffrey just found the prospect of defying her too scary.

But before this blasted book was gone forever, I wanted to know.

#3517: No dog, no sec sys. @ office 9-6 M-F. Home nights, weekends. Stolen software. HO ovrhd lit. Comp—keylggr.

Leslie had actually put a keylogger on Geoffrey's home computer! And she'd found something. Or thought she had. Because, try as I might, I couldn't picture Geoffrey Gallagher stealing anything.

The question was, had she been using it against him? Or just keeping it in reserve for a rainy day?

A few hours later, thanks to Annie's superpowered shredder, we'd traded the lone suit bag for a neat row of small black trash bags. Which we would dump as soon as the garbage collectors came to call.

"So are you going to tell Dennis that this stuff's history?" I asked Annie, when Gabby ducked into the kitchen to top up her coffee.

"I'm thinking yes," she said. "I mean, some of these people may not know Leslie even had anything on them. And others will realize that with her gone, the blackmail stops. So that's good. But with Dennis, we know he's still worried, and now we can set his mind at ease."

"I wish we could put up another flyer," I said. "Attention, everyone Leslie McQueen was blackmailing: The stuff's been destroyed. Have a nice day!"

"With a smiley face," my sister added.

"Definitely a smiley face."

CHAPTER 54

I agreed with Dennis. Now that Leslie McQueen's reign of terror was over—and Oceanside was back up and running—I wanted to sleep for a week.

But the little dog had other ideas.

When I woke up the next morning, the sun was shining, the birds were singing. And Lucy was looking up at me with an urgent expression I recognized all too well.

"You've been very patient through this whole rotten mess," I told her, as I tugged on my jeans and grabbed one of the white T-shirts from my duffel.

"Let's get you out for walkies, and I'll grab my coffee at the pool deck this morning."

Thanks to a sizable check from Oceanside's association, the pool would soon be a sparkling blue. Which meant life was returning to normal. And the sooner we could get rid of that collection of bags in Annie's hall closet, the better.

I was beginning to understand why Leslie had kept the stuff in her storage unit. Housing even the shredded remnants of blackmail material in Annie's condo was making me nervous. But they'd be gone soon enough.

When I pressed the elevator button, nothing happened.

The expression on Lucy's face told me we didn't have time to waste.

"Freight elevator," I said decisively. More like the fright elevator, thanks to the well-fed arachnids in the storage area. But beggars can't be choosers.

Even without Annie's directions, I managed to navigate my way to the lobby. As we trotted through, I noticed the elevator doors were roped off, and there were "Out of Service" signs on each door.

Odd.

Turns out, I got Lucy to that patch of grass out front just in time.

"Come on, little one," I said, after she'd had a lengthy romp through the grass. "We're going to have some fun today. We'll go grab a coffee. Then we can meet up with your Gabby for a nice long walk through South Beach. And get some bacon and eggs. Won't that be fun?"

From the thoughtful expression on her face, I have to say Lucy—still sassy from her spa visit—did appear fond of the idea.

Last night, fresh off our high from destroying Leslie's illicit enterprise, Gabby and I had arranged to meet up and take Lucy for a long walk—and bring back breakfast. Later, we were going to the doggie salon to snap some pics and gather a little information for my travel piece.

Finally, I felt like I could relax and let the vacation begin. Even if it was pretty soon time to head home.

On our return trip through the lobby, I had to wonder: Had Dennis and Geoffrey inadvertently missed one of the bills?

This time, I steered Lucy toward the stairs. We were only going up one flight to the restaurant. And at this point, I could use the exercise.

I thought we were up and out early. But the pool cleaner was already on deck when Lucy and I arrived.

Stan and Ernie were watching the show from the bar

while having their morning orange juice. And providing a running commentary.

"I hope he brought the super chlorine," Stan said. "'Cause the regular stuff's not gonna cut it. Course, chlorine's only going to do so much. He's gonna have to use the net first to strain out all the debris. When you have a pool, that's the real enemy. Debris."

"Doesn't matter," Ernie growled. "No matter how he tackles it, no way he's gonna have it cleaned up all in one trip."

I had to agree with him. The water was now a brackish, piney green more reminiscent of a sludge pit than a swimming pool.

"Morning, guys," I said happily. "Beautiful day, isn't it?"

"You're pretty chipper this morning," Stan said. "Got a new boyfriend?"

"No, I'm finally looking forward to starting my vacation. You know, spending some quality time by the pool. And at the beach."

"What have you been doing this whole time?" Ernie asked.

"Well, I was kind of tied up," I said. "With a work project. But now it's pretty much finished."

And thank goodness for that.

They both nodded.

"Guess you heard the news?" Stan asked. "It's all over the building this morning."

"News?" I'd been blissfully ignorant of Oceanside gossip lately. And after what I read in Leslie's book, I kind of wanted to keep it that way.

"It's about Leslie McQueen," Ernie said. "The police are here nosing around this morning. They're taking another look at that elevator. They're thinking maybe she didn't fall down that shaft by accident."

"Nope," Stan added. "They think the dame was murdered."

CHAPTER 55

"Annie, we've got a problem," I said, as I came flying through the front door of the penthouse.

I unclipped Lucy's leash and gave her a pat on the rump. "Go play for a couple of minutes. Then Gabby and I will take you for a nice trot."

She scampered off toward the living room.

"What's up?" my sister said, appearing in the hallway.

"The police are here. Downstairs. Looking at the elevator. Stan and Ernie said the cops think Leslie was murdered."

I watched her face as she absorbed the news.

"I'm thinking it's pretty normal for them to investigate a fatal elevator accident," she said finally. "The equipment might be faulty. And you've seen how gossip works around this place. Just because Stan and Ernie hear something or say something doesn't mean it's true."

"I know, I know. But what if it is? I mean, Gabby said it when we told her what was going on with Leslie. She actually said, 'Are you sure nobody pushed her down that elevator shaft?' Annie, you and I both know that a lot of people in this building had a reason to kill her. We had an entire book full of suspects. Along with pictures, audio and video tape. And we destroyed it. All of it."

"Look, remember what you said before? First, we find out what's what. Then we panic. We don't know anything right now."

"I know I want to get those garbage bags out of this house," I said, pointing to the closet that concealed the tell-tale evidence of yesterday's shredding party. "And I don't want to carry them out in front of the cops."

"Look, we didn't do anything wrong. All we were trying to do was return the money to Oceanside. We didn't know she'd been murdered. And we still don't. You can't put any stock in the rumors around here. Otherwise, I'd be featured in *Penthouse* this month, and your friend would be a duchess."

"Not just in *Penthouse*," I corrected, smiling. "Breaking the Internet."

"Well, that's better," she said lightly.

"All I know is the minute I start to relax, something horrible happens. I mean, I broke into her home. And her storage locker. And I spent most of yesterday eating doughnuts and obliterating evidence. Now the one thing we do know is that the police are back. And they think maybe that innocent little accident wasn't an accident. And you and I both know they have good reason to think that. And the list of suspects is going to be the resident roster for this building. How could this day possibly get any worse?"

There was a heavy knock, and we both stopped, startled, and stared at the door.

"Gabby," I said, exhaling. "She's meeting me to walk Lucy and pick up breakfast. You wanna come? Walking is good for burning off stress."

"I'd love to, but I have to finish some paperwork pronto. It's for a charity fashion show I'm staging, so I have to take care of it."

Knowing who it was, I didn't even check the peephole. "You're just in time, and I've got a little bad news," I said, as I threw open the door.

Nick, Trip, and Baba stood in the hallway, smiling back at me.

CHAPTER 56

For a split second, it didn't even register. Kinda like when you run into your grade school teacher at the mall over summer vacation.

In my dim, sleep-deprived brain, the three of them weren't supposed to be here. They were supposed to be in Fordham. Or Baltimore. Or Georgetown. Or pretty much anyplace but a building where there was possibly a murderer running amok, Annie and I had just destroyed evidence, and the police were sniffing around.

Suddenly a doe-colored flash streaked past my legs and jumped on Nick.

Lucy.

He hefted her into his arms, as she wiggled and wriggled and licked his face and neck.

"Hey, hey, c'mon, you crazy little dog," Nick said, strolling into the living room with his arms full of an ecstatic, squirming puppy. "Yes, I missed you, too. So, are you having a good time with your aunties?"

"We would have called, but they wanted to surprise you," Trip said, a gift box under one arm and a bundle of pink roses in his other hand.

"*Da!*" Baba said happily, wrapping me in a bear hug. I noticed the familiar violet smell that was Baba. Ancient and tiny, coming not quite to my shoulders, she looked up at me, patted my back, and toddled over to Annie—wrapping her in the same full-body hug.

"I'm surprised," I admitted. "Totally blown away."

"Hostess gift for Annie," my best friend said, handing me the flowers, while he deposited the box, wrapped in shiny red paper, on a side table. "So what's the bad news?"

"Huh?"

"When you opened the door, you said you had a little bad news."

"Oh, the elevator's out," I said smoothly, carrying the flowers into the kitchen. "We're gonna have to use the freight elevator for a few hours."

"See!" Nick said, turning from the center of the living room, Lucy still in his arms. "I told you there was a freight elevator. Nine flights of stairs. Nine!"

"Good for legs," Baba said, pointing at Annie's photogenic calves. "See?"

I grabbed my phone off the counter and punched in Gabby's number.

"Honey, I'm almost there," she chirped into my ear through the cheap handset. "But the elevator's out again, so I'm coming up the stairs."

"Actually, I'm going to have to reschedule my appointment," I said neutrally. "My family just arrived for a spur-of-the-moment visit."

"Nicky?" she whispered.

"Yes, I knew you'd understand."

"Gotcha," Gabby said. "Call me when you get the all clear."

"Man, the little dog looks good!" Nick called from the living room. He deposited Lucy gently onto the floor. She stayed put, looking up at him adoringly.

"She had a little spa visit," Annie said, walking to the sofa with her arm around Baba. "Shampoo, conditioner, clip, nails—the works. A friend of ours recommended the place, booked her a spot, and chauffeured her home."

"The celebrity treatment—that's my girl," Nick said, fingering the leather band around Lucy's neck. "Hey, you've got a new collar. Nice!"

Trip, casually attired in a pressed madras shirt and whiter-than-white jeans with loafers, eyed me suspiciously. "OK, what's going on?" he murmured. "And why are there cops in the lobby?"

"You wouldn't believe it if I told you," I whispered. "I'll fill you in on everything later. And trust me, there's a lot."

My best friend grinned and shook his blond head. "Can't let you out of my sight for a minute."

"For the record, I wanted to give you guys a heads-up," he added softly. "But I was outvoted. I should have at least sent a text. So is any of the news juicy? Did we interrupt a hot double date?"

"No such luck. The black cloud haunting my love life followed me all the way from Fordham. But Annie's getting attention from some wunderkind with his own plane and an accountant who lives here in the building."

"Bite your tongue—Esteban's just a friend," my sister retorted. "And Geoffrey is, well, Geoffrey. I'm sure you'll meet him later."

"How's Tom?" I asked. "And where's Tom? He's not parking the car, is he?"

At this rate, if people kept coming through the door, I didn't know where Annie was going to put them all. Heck, I didn't know where she was going to put the people who were here now.

"Tom's fine. The California hotel people were completely gobsmacked. So now he's back to working his regular six-to-midnight grind while they hammer out an agreement. And I am blessed with an abundance of over-time. Which I was reliably informed by my boss I must use or lose. Hence, my sudden appearance in the southern climes."

"I'm really glad you're here," I said, hugging him.

"By the way, I've booked into a nice little boutique hotel down the street. Close enough that I can pop over anytime. But they have room service."

"You're just afraid you-know-who will try to cook," I said sotto voce.

"I am, she will, and I'll show up regardless," he said, barely above a whisper. "But this way I get to sleep in and have a little me time. By the way, the present isn't from me. It's from Lord Sir Bed and Breakfast himself."

"Did you scan it for bugs? 'Cause he really seems to like them. And how come he's got you playing courier?"

"Technically, he's got Nick playing courier. And I think it's his way of trying to apologize. Nick," he called to my brother, "we're double parked."

"You got it, mah man," Nick said, ruffling the fur on Lucy's neck. "OK, now you be a good girl and stay put. Daddy's got to bring up the luggage. Then we'll hit the beach."

"Here, take these," I said, handing Trip my keys. "The fob gets you into the garage and opens the door to the service elevator. It's behind the big blue metal door marked 'official personnel only.' Oh, and there's no assigned parking. It's kind of a free-for-all. So just grab a spot where you can."

Lucy followed Nick to the front door. When it closed behind him, she sat back on her haunches and howled.

"Hey, it's OK," I said softly, patting her head. "He's coming back. He's just getting his stuff from the car. Honest."

Lucy looked up at me with those trusting black eyes. She stopped howling. But she didn't budge from the door.

"Baba, I'm thinking that you can take my room," Annie said. "And Alex and I can double up in the guest room. Then Nick can have the pullout in the office."

"Bah," Baba said, peeling off the black wool cardigan that matched her heavy calf-length skirt. "I take sofa." She pushed on a couch cushion with her palm. "Firm. Nice."

Baba came over from Russia alone when she was just twelve. And while I was convinced she was plugged in in ways I'd never understand, her spoken English was limited.

Not that it mattered. Baba never had any trouble making herself understood.

Annie looked at me with a pleading expression. I rolled my eyes.

"Show her the room," I prompted.

We each grabbed one of Baba's gnarled hands and led her into Annie's immense master suite. We sat down on the bed, and Annie hit the remote to open the blinds. Baba peered out the glass wall at the ocean.

"Nice?" my sister asked.

Baba nodded.

"Show her the TV," I said.

Annie hit another button and a door rolled back, revealing a fifty-inch screen on the wall.

"Watching *Wheel of Fortune* on this would be like having Pat Sajak in the room," I said. "It's practically life-sized."

"And you haven't seen the best part," I added, tugging Baba's hand.

We walked into the massive bathroom. It was, honestly, bigger than my bedroom back home. The long marble counter had two sinks and enough counter space for the cast of *Cats* to prep their makeup. The toilet had its own room.

On one wall, there was a glass steam shower with a full-length bench and more nozzles than a car wash. But the real showstopper was at the end of the room: a huge, jetted soaking tub. Positioned in front of a picture window, it looked out onto the water.

"Come on, admit it, wouldn't you like to have a shot at this baby right before you curl up for a good night's sleep?" I asked. "Those jets will give you a massage while you soak. You don't even have to wash. You put in enough soap, and it'll just bubble you clean."

"Bah," she said. But I noticed she was looking at the tub rather longingly.

"If you're in this room, Alex and I can share the guest room," Annie said. "It'll be just like we're kids again. Come on, what do you say? Please?"

Baba beamed and stole a glance at the soaker tub. "*Da*!" she said, nodding happily. "Okie-dokie."

CHAPTER 57

A little while later, Trip and I made our way out to the pool. Nick had taken Lucy to the beach. And Annie had kidnapped Baba "for a spot of shopping."

We were all meeting up at Diamond Jack's for lunch.

Leary of the midmorning sun, I was wearing one of Annie's wide-brimmed hats, a silk scarf, huge sunglasses, and SPF 45.

It didn't seem to matter what I did; somehow the Miami sun always found me. Every morning my nose and forehead were bright red. And now they were peeling.

"Admit it, you're hiding from the cops," my best friend teased, as we carried our juice to a table with a view of the pool.

The pool guy must have used Stan's super chlorine, because the water was clear and sparkling. But the pool deck smelled like a bleach bottle.

"I'm cultivating an air of mystery," I said.

"Is that what I smell?"

"That's actually the pool. It was a hot mess yesterday. Today, it looks good, but I'd wait a day before I swam in it."

"OK, so stop keeping this idiot in suspense. What's going on around here? And why do you look like an extra from *Sunset Boulevard*?"

I spent the next twenty minutes telling him everything. From the fake election and the champagne campaign rally to Leslie's slam book, surveillance equipment, and secret bank accounts.

His eyes widened when I got to the part about bumping into Gabby, our fact-finding missions-slash-break-ins, the shredding party, and the renewed police interest in the accident that might not be an accident.

"That Leslie McQueen was a one-woman crime spree," he said, after I finally ran out of steam. "Mind you, you're not doing so bad yourself."

"I thought after last night, life was getting back to normal. You know, that I could actually start the vacation part of my vacation. But if Leslie was murdered, that means there's a killer on the loose. And now you guys are here. In the middle of it. Oh yeah, and I talked Annie and Gabby into destroying evidence and obstructing a murder investigation. Which will move us to the top of the suspect list."

"Yes, but from what you said, that list is going to be more like an encyclopedia. And if Leslie's been making blackmail her side gig, there are bound to be suspects with a lot stronger motives than you three."

"Which the police will never know because we destroyed Leslie's blackmail stash."

"That is a puzzler," he said, putting the paper straw to his mouth. "But I wouldn't worry too much about a killer on the loose. From what you discovered, it sounds like Leslie 'the Embezzler' McQueen might just have squeezed the wrong person. Since you and the fam aren't in the blackmail biz, I think we should all be just fine. As long as you don't go near that pool. They could disinfect hospital sheets in that thing."

"I feel like a complete idiot. I wanted to help Annie. And we were trying to keep Dennis and Geoffrey out of jail. And because of that, a killer is going to go free."

"I know, Red. You saw a wrong, and you wanted to make it right. That's not exactly a character flaw."

"It is when I end up putting my sister and Gabby on the suspect list."

The sunglasses were making the bridge of my nose sweat. And the salty sweat was irritating my already inflamed skin. I tried mopping my face with a napkin.

"I'm pretty sure Gabby can fend for herself," Trip said. "Your sister too, for that matter. But we could give them a little help. Just to tip the scales."

"What do you mean?" I said, ripping off the scarf and glasses.

I swear Trip winced.

"How much of that slam book do you remember?" he asked.

"Too much, frankly. Apparently one of the guys on five is into something involving superhero costumes. Every time I bump into him, I can't get the visual out of my head. And I didn't even see the DVD version."

"So, maybe we nose around a little and see what we can find. To be fair, you did stop Leslie's blackmail machine."

"Leslie's death stopped Leslie's blackmail machine. I just tidied up after the party."

"Look, Red, we're already down here with a little time on our hands. And we are ace reporters, after all. Besides, I'll have to come in off the beach sometime. And you appear to be allergic to sunlight."

"At this point, I honestly think it's the stress. Even my own body is turning on me."

"So we'll fish around and pick up a little information of our own. Along with a gallon of aloe vera."

We sipped our juice in silence. Bleach smell or not, the

setting was gorgeous. Whitewashed patio with sunny-yellow umbrellas around a brilliant blue pool.

"I wonder what her endgame was," Trip said, idly stirring his grapefruit juice with the straw.

"I've been thinking about that, too. I think she was going to drain off the monthly fees, beef up the resident fines, and let this place limp along until her bank balance got fat enough. Then take off for parts unknown—leaving Dennis and Geoffrey holding the bag. If she made the most of her next year as board president, she could have potentially gotten away with millions."

"Could those two have killed her? Dennis and Geoffrey? Separately or together?"

"Together they couldn't make a ham sandwich. Separately? I don't know. Dennis made one mistake that was more of a near-miss, and he was nearly consumed with guilt. Plus, giving in to Leslie was really eating him. I honestly can't see him upgrading to murder. Geoffrey? He's a lot harder to read. But I can't picture him actually hurting someone."

"If the elevator was the murder weapon, it's a very hands-off way to do it," he said. "A well-versed killer might not even have to be there at the time."

"And don't forget old Quinn Whitmore, either," I said.

"Yes, but it's harder to blackmail someone who doesn't have a sense of shame in the first place," Trip said.

"True. But we don't know what else that guy's into. And I keep wondering if he and Leslie might have been an item."

"She breaks it off, so he drops an elevator on her?" Trip shook his head.

"Better than a house. Stan Cohen did refer to Leslie as 'the Wicked Witch of the West.'"

"Another suspect. Wonder what Leslie had on him?"

"Don't know. Don't want to know. He claims to have a

girlfriend across town. But I think he really has a crush on Ethel. Oh geez, I almost forgot about Ethel."

"Do tell," he said, leaning forward.

"She said if Leslie had been lying to them about the law banning dogs on elevators, she was going to wring her neck. And Ethel was pretty chipper the next day."

"It's a miracle your friend Leslie lived as long as she did."

"Come to think of it, my sister threatened her, too. But that was only after Leslie was already dead."

"So I think we can rule her out."

"Did I mention that we've got the confettied remains of Leslie McQueen's blackmail tapes in Annie's apartment?"

"You did not. And those I would definitely remove."

"Love to. But garbage collection hasn't restarted yet. The trash chutes are practically backed up to the roof. Plus, I don't know how smart it is to chuck the stuff here. You know, in case the police start going through it all."

"Do you remember what I used to do during the occasional garbage strike?"

"Write a strongly worded letter to your district councilmen?"

"Besides that. I'd throw the bags in my trunk, drive to an apartment complex, and toss them in a dumpster."

"Are you suggesting a road trip?"

"I am," he said, checking his watch. "And if we leave now, we'll still be able to make lunch with your family. Because I, for one, am not going to miss out on those lemon ricotta pancakes."

CHAPTER 58

Lunch was wonderful. The best part: the company. It was great to have two of my three siblings and Baba, Trip, and Lucy all around one big table.

And the pancakes weren't bad, either.

Strangely enough, I missed Gabby. While I was pretty sure Nick was over her, I didn't want to chance raising the issue. It was one thing to move on from a breakup. It was another to see your ex laughing across the table.

But the biggest surprise was Baba. Annie had taken her to the heart of South Beach to get fitted out with the latest in summer fashion, Baba-style.

Tonight, she was decked out in a wide-brimmed straw hat, hot-pink clam-diggers, and a bright multicolored blouse.

"Lee-lee Puh-leet-zer," Baba pronounced carefully, smiling.

"About time somebody in this family brought home a Pulitzer," Nick quipped.

"They're made for vacations, and they'll wash like a dream," Annie said. "You don't even need an iron. Tumble dry and pop them on. That's why I love them."

Baba was still wearing her running shoes. But I noticed she'd traded the calf-high athletic socks for a pair of neat white socklets. And instead of her trademark black leather purse, she was carrying a jaunty straw bag with a red hibiscus decoration on the side.

Summer Baba.

I was also glad to see Annie had made sure our grandmother had a pair of dark sunglasses. They were even bigger than mine—and pretty much covered her face from above her eyebrows to below her cheek bones.

At this rate, someone could replace her with a whole different Baba and we might not notice.

"And the most important part of any summer wardrobe is sunblock," Annie said. "Especially down here."

Trip and I exchanged glances. I was still wearing Annie's sun hat with my sunglasses. I'd left the scarf at home. But it had taken half a pound of concealer just to appear presentable. Or, in my case, human. So instead of peeling red skin, I had peeling pasty skin.

"I discovered this brand that's really top-notch—gentle but supereffective," my sister said, passing baby-blue gift bags around the table. "Anyway, I stocked up and got a bottle for everyone. Call it a 'welcome to Miami' present."

Wouldn't you know it was the same stuff I was using already?

CHAPTER 59

When we arrived back at Oceanside, the elevators were working. But the residents were in an uproar.

Trip dropped us at the curb. That's where we noticed the squad cars.

He looked at me. I could see the question in his eyes.

"We'll be fine," I promised.

"I'll park the car and be right in," he said.

My heart was hammering as we walked through the door. The first thing I noticed in the lobby was the crowd. A clot of people just standing around waiting. Or watching.

Stan, Ernie, and Marilyn were in the thick of it. Facing off with a couple of sets of uniformed police officers. And one guy in a gray suit, who I'm guessing was a detective.

"I'm gonna get Baba and Lucy upstairs," Nick said softly. "You guys want to stick around and see what's going on here?"

"Good plan," I said.

"In the absence of a pool cue, don't be afraid to throw an elbow," he said, grinning.

I knew he was kidding. So why was I so relieved to see the elevator doors close after them?

"Now you just wait a darned tootin' minute!" Stan yelled, waving his wrinkled finger in the face of a young patrol officer. "Ethel wouldn't hurt a fly."

"Sir, please stand back," the man in the suit said evenly. "The officers are just doing their job. And your friend isn't under arrest. She's just helping with our investigation."

"Bull pucky!" Stan spat.

"I'm fine, Stan," Ethel called over her shoulder, blinking back tears as a pair of officers steered her toward the front door.

No cuffs, I noticed.

I'd been through the same thing myself recently. Except no one bothered to tell my neighbors I was "helping" the police. One of them, Mr. Rasmussen, still thought I was Jackie the Ripper.

"I'll get you a lawyer, Ethel!" Stan shouted after her.

"I'll be fine!" she hollered. "Get one for Mrs. Pickles! She's never spent a night away from home! She'll be terrified!"

Ernie patted Stan on the shoulder. Marilyn had clearly been crying. There were streaks of black mascara down her carefully made-up face.

"What the heck's going on?" I asked her. "Why are the police taking Ethel?"

"They want to talk to her about Leslie McQueen," Ernie said quietly. "They think she might have had something to do with her death."

"Why? And what did she mean about Mrs. Pickles?"

"They picked her up a few hours ago," Marilyn said, sniffling as she dabbed her nose with a crumpled tissue. "It was awful. Ethel was so upset. And the worst part is they won't tell her when Mrs. Pickles is coming home. Or if she's coming home. They wouldn't even tell Ethel where they're keeping the poor little thing."

"Why?"

"Because," Ernie said, "when that old witch went toes up, she had some kind a' mark on her arm. The cops think it's a bite. Ethel had had words with McQueen. Ethel was always having words with McQueen. They think maybe it got physical, and Mrs. Pickles bit her. You know, to defend Ethel. And then Ethel was afraid McQueen was going to have Mrs. Pickles put down. So she killed her."

"Ethel would never hurt anyone," Stan said, his voice cracking with emotion. "She's a delicate flower."

With that he made a break for the front door—after the cops and Ethel. Ernie followed him.

"Stan's got a point," I said. "I mean, Leslie was wiry. Toned. I'm guessing she played tennis at least a couple of times a week. And probably worked out in the gym here?"

Marilyn nodded.

"The idea of Ethel shoving her into the shaft—or even being able to get the shaft door open—that just doesn't make any sense."

"Ethel's late husband was an electrician," Marilyn said to me quietly, as we watched her husband catch up with Stan and clap a big paw on his bony shoulder, halting his forward momentum. "Ethel used to go with him on jobs. When they were just starting out. Before he could afford to hire anybody. She's still pretty handy. She installed the dimmer in our dining room. The police think, well, they think she might have rigged the elevator door."

"What do you think?" I asked.

"That's not Ethel. Stan's absolutely right about that. But sometimes when Leslie was in one of her moods? That woman could be truly terrifying. She'd get this gleam in her eyes. And she'd just go off. Like she wasn't even human. More like a volcano or a tornado. Just, total destruction. If that's what Ethel was up against, I could kind of understand it."

I looked and saw my sister out on the lawn, chatting

amiably with a good-looking guy in a navy suit. From the posture and the stance, I marked him as another detective.

Good girl!

Knowing Annie, she was milking him for lots of details.

Across the lobby, Trip was talking with Quinn Whitmore.

As Ethel's patrol detail pulled away from the curb, I half expected Stan to break and run after it. It was turning into that kind of day.

CHAPTER 60

When we got back to the apartment, Baba gave everyone a hug and a kiss on the cheek, and toddled off toward Annie's master suite for an afternoon siesta.

I suspected she was going to fire up that soaking tub.

But after all the carbs, I needed some caffeine. Or I was going to be nodding off myself.

"I'm making coffee," I said. "Anybody else want some?"

"Definitely," Trip said.

"Count me in," Nick said.

"Why not?" Annie said. "Sure."

When she saw me struggling with her megabucks coffeemaker, she grinned. "Want me to show you how?"

"It won't hurt my feelings if you take over," I admitted. "So what did you learn from that cop?"

"I can't believe you noticed that," she said. "Especially with the circus in the lobby. Basically, what the other detective told everyone is true. Ethel's not under arrest. She went in voluntarily. Just to talk."

"But she could be under arrest soon," I said. "Especially if she talks to them without a lawyer."

Unfortunately, this was one area where I did have some expertise.

"She has a lawyer," my sister said. "He should be getting to the station any time now."

"Friend of yours?"

"He handles my contracts down here. The criminal side isn't his specialty, but he'll be there with her this afternoon. And he'll call in someone else from the firm to take over if she needs it."

"What about her dog?" Nick asked, reaching down to pat Lucy, who was glued to his leg. "Can we spring her?"

"From what Detective Alvarez said, Mrs. Pickles isn't in any danger. Even if she did bite Leslie. They just wanted an impression of her teeth. But, if they end up arresting Ethel, they can't bring a dog home to an empty apartment. So they're holding Mrs. Pickles temporarily."

"Could we keep her?" Nick asked. "She's a friend of Lucy's. I mean, I'm going to be here for a couple of days. So I could look after her."

"Yeah, Mom, can we keep her?" I asked.

Annie grinned and nodded. "Of course. But it might not be necessary. If Mike—my attorney, Mike Hathaway—if he can get Ethel released, she and Mrs. Pickles might be able to come home together today. If not, we'll ask to take her in the meantime. I'm sure Ethel would be fine with it."

"Good," my brother said, clearly relieved.

"There's no way that poor woman killed anyone, even Leslie McQueen," Annie said.

"I don't think so either," I agreed. "But apparently she knows her way around an electric outlet. Which is ironic."

"What do you mean?" Nick asked.

I told him about Leslie's bugging spree, and Ethel's knowledge of wiring.

"You don't think Ethel might have found one of the bugs and confronted Leslie, do you?" he asked.

"No," I said quickly.

"I don't know," Nick teased. "I mean, you were pretty furious at Ian. If he'd ended up dead, I'd have wondered."

I glanced at Trip, who shrugged.

I looked at Annie. She nodded.

"Look, this stays right here. Annie distracted Ethel, and I removed the bug, OK? And, according to Leslie's notes, which I also filched, it was the only one in her condo. If Ethel was mad enough to kill Leslie, I don't think she'd have left the thing in place."

"Damn, you've been busy on your vacay," Nick said approvingly. "I thought investigating this whole board election thing was just an excuse to get you down here. And then it was gonna be all margaritas and mojitos in Miami."

"It might have started out that way," I admitted. "Then I met the people in this building. And Leslie. And I just couldn't leave it alone."

"Big surprise," Trip said, grinning.

"OK, so what now?" Nick asked.

"Now we look out for Ethel and Mrs. Pickles, and the police investigate to find out who killed Leslie," Trip said. "Do they even know for certain that it wasn't just a horrible accident?"

Annie nodded. "That's what I was talking about with Logan. I mean, Detective Alvarez. Once they were able to really dig into it with the elevator engineers and take another look at Leslie, they realized that it probably wasn't an accident. But they still don't know for sure. The elevator company could be trying to cover up for faulty wiring. Or some kind of mechanical failure. So they're investigating that, too."

"Uh, is it safe to ride those things?" I asked, suddenly seeing a lot more stairs in my future.

"The police techs have been all over them," my sister

said, waving her hand. "They even brought in their own engineers this morning. As it is now, they're safe."

"As it is now?" I asked. My calves were going to be like granite by the time I left town.

"If no one else monkeys with them," Trip translated. "What about this dog-bite theory?"

"Leslie had a strange mark, an impression, on her right forearm," Annie said. "The police think it could be a bite."

"Could it be human?" I asked. I recalled what Marilyn said about Leslie the tornado. If she'd gotten into a scuffle with someone, they might have bitten her in self-defense.

"The forensic people think it's canine," Annie said. "And they don't think it happened when she died. They believe it happened earlier. Apparently, it had time to heal a bit."

"So sometime before Leslie fell down that elevator shaft, somebody's dog bit her," I summarized. "In a community where gossip runs rampant, I can't believe that story hasn't been making the rounds."

"Well, it gives somebody a motive," Nick said. "They wouldn't want anyone to know about the bite."

"Yes, but this happened *before* Leslie died," I said. "Before she was even missing. So at the time, it wouldn't have been seen as a motive. And a lot of people in this building detested Leslie. Especially the dog owners. Heck, she banned them from the elevators. And according to Stan, she tried to break them with fines. If one of their dogs took a chunk out of Leslie McQueen, that would be bragging rights. I can't believe we haven't heard this story."

Lucy looked up at Nick as he settled in on the sofa. He scratched her affectionately under the chin. "All the puppies aren't as good as you, are they?" he asked.

She laid her head on his knee and sighed.

"The police theory is that Ethel was afraid Leslie would have her dog put down," he continued, stroking the top of

Lucy's velvety head. "That could apply to other dog own-ers, too. Especially if the dog had bitten someone before. They might want to keep it quiet."

"Especially if they were planning to kill Leslie," Trip said.

"So Leslie's blackmailing people left and right but she gets killed because someone's dog bites her?" I floated. "That doesn't feel right, somehow. OK, Nick has a solid explanation for why the dog owner never said anything about the bite. But what about Leslie?"

"What do you mean?" Nick asked.

Lucy had inched her way onto the sofa and was sitting next to him, her head still across his leg. As he stroked her flank, her eyelids fluttered. I could tell that after a morning beach romp and a big lunch, she was struggling to keep her eyes open.

"Leslie hated dogs," I said. "And if one of the ones in Oceanside actually bit her? She'd be screaming about it from the rooftops. She'd have the dog thrown out. Heck, she'd use it as an excuse to ban them all from the building."

"You're right about that," Annie said.

"So how come she never made a peep about it?" I asked.

"What are you thinking?" Trip asked.

"I'm thinking that in the process of planting bugs and running her side business in skullduggery, Leslie was in and out of a lot of places she shouldn't have been. If some-one just got a dog—or maybe didn't tell her about their dog—she might have been surprised. And she couldn't very well say anything. How would she explain what she was doing inside someone's apartment?"

"Gas leak?" Nick said.

"All electric," Annie said. "The whole building."

"That's a good theory," Trip said. "And it totally clears Mrs. Pickles. Because Leslie already knew about her."

"So how'd she get the bug in Ethel's condo in the first place?" Nick asked.

"Leslie kept a schedule of everyone's regular comings and goings in her diary-slash-slam-book," I said. "And Ethel walks that dog three times a day like clockwork, apparently. I'm guessing Leslie went in while they were both out."

"Sheesh," Nick said, shaking his head. "And I thought Lydia Stewart was bad."

"Lydia? What's she up to?"

"Nothing new," he said with a dismissive wave of his hand. "Let's just say she's spending more time at the inn than she is at her own home."

My least favorite neighbor lived in the most historic stately home in our neighborhood. Which made sense because nearly all of the land that was Fordham, Virginia had once belonged to her family. A fact which she never let anyone forget.

A local fixture, Lydia Stewart either led or influenced almost every civic organization, club, and board in Fordham. She also had a serious crush on one Mr. Ian Sterling. And, despite zero encouragement, had been pursuing the guy non-stop since he moved in four months ago.

"None of my business," I said flatly.

"She wants to run Ian's murder mystery weekends. And she's hinting that he needs someone with local contacts to organize his teas. You know, really beef up that part of the business."

"So how did the Lord of the Manor respond to that?" I sort of felt for Ian on that score. Lydia was completely enmeshed in the community, as well as being heavily involved with the local visitors bureau. Her favor could bring a lot of business. And her disapproval could put a real chill on Ian's burgeoning B&B.

And that wasn't counting what her friends could do if she unleashed them online. A few nasty comments could cripple his bookings.

"He just laughed it off," Nick said. "Told her he's not nearly that successful yet. But hopefully one day."

"Hopefully one day she'll be hit by a truck?" I finished.

"You sound awfully invested for someone who hasn't even opened the man's present," my sister said, carrying the coffee service into the living room.

"Hey, harassment is harassment, no matter who's doing it," I said, grabbing a cup and saucer after she set down the tray. "I don't like to see her taking advantage of him."

"So throw the guy a bone and open the gift," Nick said.

Annie nodded.

I looked at Trip.

"I only give advice when asked," my best friend responded. "But I have to say, it's a very nice presentation. And he did have it hand delivered."

"I had it stashed in my sleeper compartment for the whole trip," Nick said. "I was afraid to let it out of my sight. I half expected the conductor to make me buy it a ticket. Now I wanna know what's in it."

"Oh, all right," I said, strolling across the living room.

Trip was right. It was beautifully wrapped. I plucked off the sealed card and opened it.

Alex,
Saw this in a little shop in Georgetown, and it reminded me of you—and that first lovely tea we shared. And the many since.

I hope you can someday forgive my inexcusable breach, knowing that I sought only to protect my family. A reason, but not an excuse, to be sure.

*Regardless, I hope this little sampler will remind
you, as it did me, of happier times. Please enjoy it
with all of my warmest good wishes for you and
your family.*

*My fondest regards,
Ian*

"Out loud, please," my brother heckled.

"Knock it off," Annie said, hitting his arm with a throw pillow.

"Children, behave," Trip said.

As they both tossed pillows at him, I ripped into the glossy red paper, revealing a beautiful inlaid wooden chest. Lucy, now fully awake, jumped up and raced to my side.

"It must be b-a-c-o-n," Nick said.

"Yes, because nothing says love like smoked pork," Annie said. "Men, honestly."

"It's a selection of teas," I called over the din. "A sampler. With little candies and packages of cookies."

"Tea?" Annie rose gracefully from the sofa and joined Lucy and me near the door.

"Ooh, this is the good stuff," she said. "They served it at our London hotel. And it's pricey."

"Hand it to the man—he has good taste," Trip said.

"Definitely," Annie said, looking at me.

"I guess this calls for a thank-you note," I admitted.

So what do you write to the guy you like but don't trust?

"Actually, this is more of a phone call situation," Annie said.

"Seriously?"

She nodded.

"Trip?" I asked.

"Definitely calls for a call," he agreed.

"That's not a present, that's a trap," I protested. "If I'd known that, I wouldn't have accepted it."

"Wanna know what I think?" Nick asked.

"No!"

"Sleep on it," my brother said.

"Actually, that's a good idea," Trip said. "Ian knows he sent it. But he doesn't know that you've opened it."

"Unless there's another bug in it," I said.

"Possible, but unlikely."

I looked at Annie. She nodded.

"I can help, if you want to practice first," she said softly. "And if you want company for the call, I'll sit right next to you."

"Thank you," I whispered, patting her hand.

"OK, so we table this for now," I announced, lugging the wooden box into the kitchen. "Now can we please talk about getting Ethel and Mrs. Pickles out of lockup?"

CHAPTER 61

Later that afternoon, Nick took off for a neighborhood walk with Lucy. I made him promise to take lots of pictures if they stopped anywhere. Annie had locked herself in the guest room to make a couple of business-related phone calls.

We still hadn't heard anything on Ethel. But Annie had left a message for her attorney to see if—failing Ethel's immediate release—we might be able to get temporary custody of Mrs. Pickles.

"So if we're not looking for people with undeclared dogs, what are we looking for?" Trip asked, as we strategized in Annie's expansive living room.

"Well, I for one would like to know who at this place besides Ethel can hot-wire an elevator."

A few hours later, we'd been through dozens of résumés, courtesy of several online databases.

"This reminds me of checking up on old boyfriends online," I told him. "You know, just to see how they're doing."

"That never made any sense to me," Trip said. "If a woman looks up an ex online, what exactly is she hoping to find?"

"Poverty, sterility, and an unfortunate haircut. Or maybe that's just me."

"I've honestly never seen so many people so well-versed in the workings of electric current," Trip said. "Does Ocean-side have some kind of a reciprocal deal with the local brotherhood of power workers?"

"Hey, it's a solid career path. And it pays well. The problem is, résumés won't tell us a thing about the retirees. And that's got to be at least a third of the building."

"I know what you mean. For that we're going to have to rely on good old-fashioned gossip. I'm thinking another trip to the bleach bowl and a few rounds of drinks for your new friends might do the trick."

"Speaking of which, what did you learn from Quinn Whitmore?"

"Nothing helpful. The guy was looking for a few new faces to join him for a poker game. My guess is the old faces are tired of losing all their money. Methinks he's something of a cardshark."

"Shark is right. He's the slime-ball who helped Leslie stage a fake election."

"You think he did her in?" Trip asked.

"He's definitely worth keeping an eye on. And I wouldn't sit across a poker table from him anytime soon. I'm betting he cheats at cards, too."

"I'll take that bet, and raise you yet one more electrical expert," he said, reading from the screen. "Majored in business and communications. Minored in electrical engineering."

He turned the laptop so that I could see the page.

"Oh no," I breathed, as the face smiled innocently from a corporate website.

It was Dennis Chu.

CHAPTER 62

Annie was still locked in the guest room when we left for the pool. I'd have to break the news about Dennis. And soon.

But I didn't have to do it right now.

It was early evening, and the pool deck resembled a cocktail party from a '60s movie. Or an '80s TV show. Residents gathered, wearing everything from swimsuits and flowing cover-ups to cruise wear and casual Friday chic.

Ernie and Stan were camped out by the pool. Marilyn was nowhere to be seen.

"Hi, guys," I said, as we strolled by their table. "Have you met my friend Trip? He's visiting from D.C."

"You can pull up a chair, if you like. The tables are in short supply. I'm Ernie Doyle, by the way. This is Stan Cohen. Didn't we see you earlier in the lobby?"

Trip nodded, pulling out a chair for me and then one for himself. "I was sorry to hear about your friend's troubles. Alex and Annie have been telling me what a kind person she is."

"Ethel is the best," Stan said. "A real lady. They don't make 'em like that anymore."

"Any news on when she's coming home?" I asked.

Ernie shook his head. "Hopefully tonight. We're just waiting for the call; then we're gonna swing by and pick her up. Marilyn's upstairs freshening up."

I nodded.

"There's no way Ethel would do something like that," Stan said, clutching a highball glass that appeared to be filled with orange juice and ice. "No way, no how."

"I agree," I said. "So who around here would know how to rewire an elevator?"

"You trying to figure out who did it?" Ernie asked. "We been chewing on that since the cops showed up this morning."

"Leslie cheesed off a lot of folks," Stan said. "Especially the dog lovers."

"But it looked like she was going to win the election anyway," I said.

I knew Leslie had rigged the whole thing. And how she'd done it. But I was curious what they knew.

"That's politics," Ernie said. "Give the devil her due, she did keep things ticking along like a Swiss watch. 'Course, they say Mussolini made the trains run on time. Wouldn't a' wanted to share an elevator with him, either."

"Ethel can't be the only one around here with electrical skills," Trip prompted.

"Heck no," Stan said. "Frank used to be in construction."

"Frank was a plastic surgeon," Ernie said. "The only thing he constructed were noses, breasts, and bottoms."

"That's Frank on eight. I'm talking about Frank on four."

"Oh, right. And there's that other guy. You know, what's his name."

"Oh him," Stan said. "He left for Vermont last month. They got a house up there. Cute little place. He showed me the pictures."

"Really? I wouldn't mind seeing Vermont this time a'

year. Nothin' to shovel. And it's got a nice roll to the land. Not like this place. Flat. Like living on a sand bar."

Trip and I exchanged glances.

"The Frank on four," I said. "The one in construction. Any idea what his last name is?"

"I think it begins with a P," Stan said helpfully.

"Anybody else you can think of?" I asked. This was beginning to remind me why I didn't like doing two-on-one interviews. It was like herding cats.

"Hey, how about that nice kid who helped you with your whatchamacallit?" Ernie asked, snapping his fingers.

"Oh yeah, I forgot about him," Stan said. "Came in to help me install my new flat-screen and got the remote working. Forty-eight inches. Picture in a picture. A real beauty."

"A name?" I asked. "Do you remember a name?"

"Samsung," Stan said.

"She meant the guy," Trip said patiently. "The expert who helped you."

"Well, he's not really what you'd call an expert," Stan said. "I mean, his father is some kind of electrician. Or maybe it was an electrical engineer. What's the difference between them, anyway?"

Ernie shrugged. "Couldn't tell ya. But the kid picked up a couple of tricks from the old man. Sharp."

"Yup, smart as a whip, that one," Stan said. "Nice kid. But he keeps to himself."

"Do you remember his name?" Trip pressed. "Or maybe what he looked like?"

"Oh, you know him," Stan said. "He's the one who lives upstairs from Ethel. Georgie? Gregory?"

"Geoffrey," Ernie said, snapping his fingers.

"That's it," Stan agreed, smiling. "We called him 'Double Gee.' Geoffrey Gallagher."

Chapter 63

An hour later, Trip and I were sitting poolside. Ernie, Stan, and Marilyn had already left to pick up Ethel and Mrs. Pickles.

"I don't believe it," I said. "I destroyed evidence for a murderer. I helped cover up murder."

"Look at the bright side," Trip said. "It still might be Frank-whose-last-name-probably-begins-with-P."

"I'm going to prison. And I should. When will I learn to mind my own business?"

"From my experience, never," Trip said. "Look, we found umpteen people with the skills and know-how to have fiddled with that elevator. And yes, Dennis and Geoffrey are on that list. But so are a lot of other people. What would you do if this were a story?"

"At this point, nothing. I need more information."

"Exactly. So far, the only thing you've proved is that Ethel's not the only suspect. And the police obviously agree because she's coming home tonight."

"She has a stable address, a regular schedule, a good lawyer, and a small dog with a tiny bladder. Just because she's not a flight risk doesn't mean she's off the suspect list."

"Do you really think Dennis or Geoffrey killed Leslie? Gut instinct?"

"No. But I've been wrong before. Really wrong."

"You've also been right a lot. Keep following your gut."

He stopped and took a sip of his drink—some kind of orange and pineapple juice combo.

"Well, look who the cat dragged in! This is turning into a big-time reunion!"

If I hadn't known the voice, I'd never have recognized her. In a red straw hat with a huge brim, oversized sunglasses, and a white silk scarf around her face, Gabby was unrecognizable. But not exactly invisible. A diaphanous white cover-up barely hid her glamorous red maillot. And sky-high white sandals made the most of her long, tanned legs.

If Nick did run into her, he was toast.

Trip stood and gave her a quick hug.

"Lookin' good!" she teased him. "You enjoying the sights and sounds of Miami?"

"Right now, the sights and sounds of Oceanside are more than enough," he admitted.

"I told him about our little excursions," I said. "Strictly on the q.t."

"Got it, sugar," she said, pulling out a chair. "I've been keeping a low profile myself. But I didn't see Nicky here, so I figured I'd chance it."

"So what ever happened to Leslie's bump key?" Trip asked.

"We left it in her apartment," I said. "I'm guessing the cops have it now."

"Complete with your fingerprints?" he asked.

"Gloves," I said, wiggling my fingers in the air. "We're not a complete bunch of amateurs."

"Besides, I wouldn't give one of those bump keys house-room," Gabby said decisively.

"Why not?" Trip and I asked in unison.

"No finesse," Gabby said. "And if you don't know what you're doing, you can hurt the locks."

"Hurt them how, exactly?" I asked.

"Well, you're not coaxing them to turn. You're using brute force. That can make it hard to open the lock later with a key. Sometimes permanently."

"*Sometimes* permanently?" I asked quickly. "Meaning sometimes the damage isn't permanent?"

"Right, sugar. Sometimes you turn the key a few times, everything falls back into place. Other times, stuff gets bent. And that's when you have to call the locksmith. The thingamabobbies I use are better. But you have to learn how to use them."

My mind was spinning.

The night of the party. Leslie's lengthy absence. Annie struggling with the front door key. And Lucy.

"Oh geez, Leslie was in Annie's condo," I breathed.

"What do you mean?" Trip asked, suddenly sitting forward.

I told them what was buzzing through my head.

"That poor little puppy," Gabby said. "She must have been so scared to see that harpy flying through the door."

"Why would Leslie have risked it? She knew you guys had a dog, right?"

"She was desperate," I said. "She wanted Annie's endorsement. It would have been the icing on her campaign cake. And Annie, being Annie, was politely declining. I watched her do it at the party when Leslie confronted her. So I guess Leslie decided it was time to get a little extra electronic help."

"But Annie's never here," Trip said. "Leslie could have come in anytime."

"That's what I'd have thought, too. But it turns out my sister is always lending her place out to friends and models. There was no telling when someone would show up. At all hours, from all parts of the world. And you talk about not keeping a regular schedule. But suddenly, the only two people staying in that condo were right there at Leslie's own party. It must have seemed like a gift from heaven. Even with the possibility of a dog. So she took a chance. And, give Leslie credit, Lucy loves everyone. At least, she did until that night."

I described the short-sleeved red silk dress Leslie had worn, and how she'd slipped on a navy blazer when she reappeared for her speech.

"I assumed she wanted to look more presidential," I said, feeling like a total dolt.

"She was trying to cover that bite in a hurry," Trip concluded.

"Leslie's right-handed," I mumbled, remembering her handshake with my sister—and our encounter by the elevators earlier that same day.

"Along with ninety percent of the population," Trip said. "What of it?"

"At the end of her campaign speech, she pumped her arm in the air. Her left arm."

"Because if she put the other one up, her sleeve might fall down. And a bite mark invites a lot of questions. It also explains how Lucy got out that night."

I nodded.

"But my baby's not a biter," Gabby protested. "She's never bitten anyone. Even when I first found her. She just tried to run under that smelly old dumpster and hide."

"Leslie was a bully," I explained. "And she had a volcanic temper, according to Marilyn Doyle. I'm guessing she probably screamed at Lucy. Took a swing at her, or maybe grabbed her by the collar. So Lucy bit her and ran out the open door."

"That's self-defense, open-and-shut," Gabby declared.

"Well, yeah," I agreed.

"Do we need to get the little girl out of town?" she asked. "You know, before the cops get wise?"

"Well, I'm not planning on telling them. As far as they know, Lucy's been with us every minute or locked inside the condo."

Trip nodded in agreement. "Which raises another salient question: Did Leslie take the time to plant anything special before she left?"

CHAPTER 64

Annie took the news as well as could be expected.

"That vicious, rotten, conniving little witch!" she spat. "I'm telling you, Alex, if she wasn't al . . ."

" 'Oh, what a beautiful moooo-ooorning,' " I sang loudly off-key.

"If she has a partner, someone might still be monitoring the bug—if there is a bug," Trip explained.

At the word "bug," Baba roused herself from where she'd been napping next to him on the sofa, rolled up the magazine in her lap, and assumed a batter's stance. "Where is bug? Where?"

"Not that kind of bug," Annie explained. "A neighbor of ours might have planted a listening device. Here in the apartment."

"Just like old country," Baba said, shaking her head sadly. Then she stalked off to the kitchen.

"So what do we do now, folks?" Nick asked.

"Well, either we stop talking entirely or we're going to have to have this place swept for bugs," I said. "Or, we could open the outlets and see if we can find them ourselves."

"Like 'you' did at Ethel's?" he asked, using air quotes.

"Uh, why do you say it like that?"

"I'm not a kid. Gabby and I are over. You don't have to hide her. Or edit her out of your stories."

"What gave me away?" I asked sheepishly.

"You can't even work Annie's coffeemaker, and I'm supposed to believe you're suddenly breaking into apartments, cracking open walls, and extracting bugs? Plus, those ads for the Total Testosterone Tour are everywhere."

"I'd have electrocuted myself if she hadn't cut the power first," I admitted. "And actually removed the thing. Basically, I just took off the wall plate and watched."

"See, that's the technophobe I know and love," he said, punching my shoulder.

"I'm not technophobic. I'm just techno-reluctant. Besides, I just didn't want to see you get hurt."

"I got hurt. I got over it. I'm OK. Now, go call her. If anyone can figure out if we've got aftermarket electronics in this place, it's Gabby."

CHAPTER 65

Gabby was happy to help. "But, sugar, I have to pick up a few little goodies first," she explained. "I didn't exactly pack for this."

Nice to know that there was at least one gadget that didn't live permanently in her oversized designer bag.

She promised she'd stop by in a few hours. In the meantime, Annie's house had gotten very quiet.

Baba was busying herself in the kitchen. Nick had taken Lucy for her evening walk. And Annie, determined to keep things as normal as possible, had gone to the gym. She was also going to stop in and see Ethel on the way.

"You don't have to stay for this," I said to Trip, as we sat on the sofa and watched the last of the sunlight fade from the wide blue sky.

"Funny, I said the same thing to Nick. Offered to trade places with him for the duration. Oddly, he declined."

"Geez, you don't think he wants to see her?" I asked, as the fist in my gut tightened like a noose.

"I think he wants to face something, instead of running from it. You know, like an adult."

"Yeah, everybody seems just fine with it. But I had a front row seat to the last crash-and-burn, and I just want to crawl under the sofa."

"You did not cause this," Trip enunciated carefully. "Nick came here of his own free will. He's staying here of his own free will. We'll be polite. We'll get through it."

"If worse comes to worst, when it's over, I'll go downstairs and blackmail Dennis for some Cheetos and ice cream."

"See, that's my girl."

Annie, Nick, and Lucy had just arrived back at the penthouse when there was a telltale knock at the door.

Lucy bolted toward it.

I looked at Nick. He gave a little smile.

"Hey, Gabby, come on in," Annie said, opening the door.

Lucy danced around her legs, overjoyed.

"Sure thing," Gabby said, giving a little wave to the room. "Hey, everybody. And how's the little girl?" she said, bending to give Lucy some love.

Gabby was still Gabby, but she was a little more subdued. In appearance, if not mood. Her hair—or, knowing her, the latest wig—was wavy, long and blond, tied back with a scarf. This afternoon's 1940s bombshell bathing suit had been replaced by a plain pair of jeans and a white T-shirt. But, Gabby being Gabby, they still fit like a second skin.

"She's doing great," Nick replied. "Turns out she needed that spa visit more than any of us knew. I guess you heard what happened?"

"That woman is a stone-cold witch," Gabby said, bending to stroke Lucy while the pup sniffed her shoes.

For a moment, it was as if the three of them were the

only living beings in the room. The rest of us were frozen in space and time.

Then Trip came clattering out of the kitchen with a tray of coffee and Baba toddled after him with a platter of sliced cake, as Annie cleared the living room table.

And just like that, the spell was broken. Normal life returned.

Soon we were all talking, laughing, chattering, and passing the platter, plates, sugar, and creamer around the big table.

Lucy had wedged herself onto the sofa between Gabby and Nick—and was basking in the attention from both of them.

I looked over at Baba, wondering—not for the first time—what she was making of all this.

She met my gaze and nodded, a twinkle in her catlike dark brown eyes.

After the cake and coffee were gone, Gabby pulled up another oversized designer purse—yellow this time—and dropped it on the table with a *thunk*.

"OK, time to get this show on the road," she said.

"Do you want me to shut off the power?" I asked.

"No need," she said cheerily. "At least, not yet. First we find out if there are any of the little suckers. And where they're hiding."

She opened her handbag and pulled out something that looked like a walkie-talkie with a cord attached.

"This thing is top-of-the-line—it'll sing out if you've got microphones or cameras," she said, pressing a couple of buttons on the device. "OK, sugar, we're good to go."

For the next half hour, Gabby walked each room twice, first around the walls, then doubling back to check features in the room itself—overhead lights, smoke detectors, electrical equipment, and even the air vents.

"Can't be too careful, sugar," she said, by way of explanation.

The rest of us followed her in a little cluster. Watching and waiting.

"What's that smell?" Gabby asked me quietly when I stepped up to help her move the barstools in front of the breakfast bar.

"Goulash," I said softly. "The whole bug thing has Baba a little upset."

"Gotcha."

When she got to the kitchen counter—and my tea box—she ran it over the thing twice. She pressed a button on her little machine, and it emitted a loud, fast electronic beep.

"He didn't," I said, exasperated.

"He didn't," Gabby said, winking. "Your brother's idea of a joke."

"Not funny, Nick," I said.

"Hey, I was laughing."

"You nearly had another Boston Tea Party on your hands," I said. "Only instead of a harbor in Massachusetts, it would have been a condo pool in Miami."

"Might kill that bleach smell," Trip said softly to no one in particular.

Finally, after we'd circled back, she checked the hall bathroom. Then Gabby shut off her handheld gizmo and tucked it carefully into her purse.

"Clean as a whistle, guys," she said happily. "Whatever else that little gremlin did up here, she didn't plant any bugs."

CHAPTER 66

The next morning I got up early. After a long walk with Lucy, a stop at the doughnut shop, and two cups of coffee to strengthen my resolve, I was finally ready to call Ian.

My younger brother had demonstrated—once again—what class looked like. I wanted to follow his example. While it was fresh in my mind.

I didn't have to look up the number. I still knew it by heart.

"Cotswolds Inn, Ian Sterling speaking."

My heart did that little fluttery thing. Uh-oh.

Ian's Victorian inn had a landline on the desk. An old-fashioned model, no caller ID.

Even though he took reservations on an electronic tablet, it disappeared discreetly under the antique desk when not in use. So as not to spoil the ambiance.

"Hi, Ian, it's Alex."

"Alex, how are you—and how's Miami?" He sounded genuinely delighted. Then again, he could just be happy that I wasn't a bill collector.

"The family's great. Miami's great. Sunny and hot."

Sheeesh, ten seconds in, and I'd already devolved into

talking about the weather. "So how are you guys?" I added quickly.

"Fantastic," he said. "Dad and Daisy are house hunting. I know they want a little space of their own, but I confess I'm really going to miss having them here."

"With any luck, they'll find something nearby. Have they checked out Mr. Rasmussen's place?"

"Yes, I think my father was rather taken with that one. He keeps using the phrase 'move-in ready.' And Daisy favors the garden."

I pictured Lucy and Alistair romping back and forth between my backyard and the one behind it.

"They'd be my neighbors, too," I said. "That would be so cool."

He went quiet and, for a few beats, neither of us said anything.

Suddenly there was a strange noise. As if someone sat on a goose. And the goose was none too pleased.

"What's that sound?" I asked.

"We're hosting a wedding later today. The bride is from Glasgow. The groom is from Mobile. They had their hearts set on having a piper at the wedding, and Daisy was able to procure a musician. I must say, you haven't lived until you've heard 'Sweet Home Alabama' on the bagpipes."

I giggled. And I could picture the scene. The piper. The inn. The wedding. And him.

"I wanted to thank you for the present," I said. "It's lovely. And I can't wait to try it."

And maybe someday I'll tell you the story of how Nick guarded it with his life during a twenty-hour train ride.

"I'm so glad you like it," he said warmly. "Things haven't quite been the same around here since you left. You and your family," he added quickly. "So is your grandmother enjoying South Beach?"

"She is—but she worries about all of us, no matter where

she is," I said, noticing that the goulash was still simmering gently on the back of Annie's state-of-the-art stove. My sister was going to need an industrial cleaning crew to get the smell out of the walls once we left. Baba's goulash had a half-life.

"Well, give Alistair a hug for me," I said, as Lucy turned and gazed up into my face. As if she could see into my soul.

"Please give my best to everyone," Ian said. "And have a safe trip home. I'll look forward to seeing you around the neighborhood."

"You too," I said. And, at that moment, I realized just how much I truly meant it.

CHAPTER 67

"Oh man, doughnuts," Nick said. "And I don't even have to make them."

"Not itching to get back to the bakery, then?" I asked, as I topped off my coffee and poured a cup for him.

"Actually, I am. But just the bakery. I'm still not ready to dive into the renovation thing. You OK with taking a break from it for a little while longer? I just want to focus on the baking side of things."

"I'd be OK with taking a break from it forever, if you want. We'll do the kitchen when you're ready. Or when Ian marries Lydia and finally throws you out of the inn for good. Whichever comes first."

"You called him, didn't you?"

"First thing this morning."

"Annnnd?"

"And nothing. I said 'thank you.' He said 'you're welcome.' No biggie."

"No biggie, but you're smiling."

"It's the doughnuts. Sugar and caffeine make me happy."

"Whatever. You know I think this whole tiff between you and Ian is crazy, right?"

"Yes, I believe you've said as much. Although you never used the word crazy."

"It was implied."

"So you'd have been OK if he'd planted a mike in your room, too?"

"The guy is no Leslie McQueen. He wasn't doing it to make money or dig up dirt. Or take over some crappy condo board job that no one in their right mind would want."

"I know, right?"

"Truth," he said, slapping my palm.

"Ian's father was in danger," he continued. "Real mortal danger. Harkins had a hired gun breathing down his neck, a secret family in hiding, and a whack-job billionaire who would have killed them all. I mean, if planting a few bugs helps Ian protect his dad? I say bring on the biggest, baddest, buggety bugs you can find."

I smiled and brought the cup to my chin.

"Come on, what if it was our dad?" he said. "What if we could have him back? And all you had to do was plant one of those things at Ian's place. Would you do it?"

I sighed. "Yeah."

"To be clear, I'm not saying you should date the guy. Just don't be hacked at him for going to the wall for his family. That's pretty much what we do around here, too."

This coming from the man who'd taken a pretty big hit for the team yesterday himself.

"Are you OK?" I asked. "Seeing Gabby and all?"

"Yeah, I actually am. Look, I like her. And I'm *always* gonna like her. But I don't want to get back together. I'm good."

"Excellent," I said. "Now all we have to do is figure out how to get rid of that goulash and make it look like an accident."

CHAPTER 68

Later that morning, after a long walk on the beach, Baba, Annie, and I were stretched out on chaises by the pool. Each of us had oversized sunglasses, a big sun hat, and a tall, cold glass of juice on the rocks. But that's where the similarity ended.

Annie was wearing a sun hat, shorts, and a T-shirt with flip-flops. Baba matched her own straw hat with turquoise clam-diggers and another multicolored shirt—this time in sea tones. And I had covered as much of my skin as was humanly possible.

"Turns out, Leslie did have a cleaning lady," Annie said, as she reached for her drink. "How did you find that out?" I asked.

"Marilyn and Ethel told me last night. It seems Kelsey has already hired her. She's going to be at Kelsey's place this afternoon. And Kelsey's making noises about buying Leslie's condo, too."

"You mean, once the police are finished with it?"

"I know, it's a little ghoulish, right?"

"Not exactly the behavior you expect from a BFF," I

said. "You think Kelsey suspects some of the money is stashed there? Or the blackmail goodies?"

"I read it more as her attempt to step into Leslie's designer pumps, but I could be wrong," Annie said.

"Heaven help us if there's a baby HOA president in the making," I said.

"Well, there is good and bad news on that score," she said. "Dennis and Geoffrey have hired another management company. And they've both resigned from the board."

"So there's another election in Oceanside's future?"

"Possibly."

"Did you know that Dennis minored in electrical engineering?" I asked.

"Gracie did tell me he changed his major after they started dating. Something about pleasing her father. That, and he hated his old major."

"Annie, he's got the know-how to rig that elevator. So does Geoffrey, by the way. His dad is in the business, and he's some kind of electrical whiz himself."

"You're afraid we covered up for a murderer?"

"Kinda, yeah. You hear anything from your friend Logan?"

"Well, he did call last night," she said, twirling a lock of hair. "Just wanted to let me know that Ethel was on her way home. With Mrs. Pickles. You know, so we wouldn't worry."

"He didn't ask about Lucy, did he? Because if Mrs. Pickles is really off the hook, they're gonna start looking at other dogs."

"Of course, he didn't. And I think they're dropping the dog angle. Since the bite didn't happen at the time of death, they think it's probably incidental to the murder. Right now, they're trying to crack her computer."

Baba reached into her straw bag and pulled out a bottle

of the sunblock she'd gotten from Annie. She checked the cap and gave the bottle a good shake.

"Alex, why don't you just use the sunblock I gave you?" my sister asked, taking in my mix-and-match combination of hat, multiple scarves and long-sleeved shirt. "It's good stuff."

"Strong," Baba said, holding up the bottle as she added another coat of the lotion on her arms.

"I have—it just doesn't work for me," I confessed. "I don't know what the deal is. I've been using it since I got here, and all I do is burn and peel."

Part of the reason for my cover-up was to hide from the sun. The other part was to hide. I'd seen Muppets with better skin.

"I didn't give you that stuff until yesterday," Annie said. "Did you bring a bottle with you? Because I've never seen it outside Miami."

"No, I found some in the guest bathroom when I arrived," I said, pulling the bottle out of my purse. "And I put it on right away. But it just doesn't help."

"Let me see that," my sister demanded.

I handed it to her. She looked at the label, then she took off the cap and sniffed it.

"Alex, this isn't the bottle I gave you," she said.

"No, that one's still in the gift bag. But this is the same stuff. It was in the linen cabinet in my bathroom."

"Alex, this is all my fault," she said sheepishly. "Welcome to the dark side of modeling."

"What do you mean?"

"This isn't sunblock. It's mayonnaise and cooking oil. Probably with a little Tabasco and vodka thrown in."

"What? I've been rubbing that stuff on my skin since I got here! I look like a boiled lobster."

"I'm so sorry," Annie said. "It's an old trick in modeling. And a nasty one, to boot. You're all staying in a house together. And you're all competing for the same gigs. Or space in the same show or magazine layout. So some of the . . . well, more malicious girls switch a competitor's shampoo for dish detergent. Or hair conditioner for furniture cream. Or, in your case, sub out sunblock for something that will do pretty much the opposite. Before we arrived, I let this place out to a bunch of girls from another agency. A friend of mine is a director there, and they were in a bind. After they left, I had a service tidy up and change all the linens. But I forgot to go through the cabinets.

"And this," she said, holding up the offending bottle, "is definitely not sunblock."

CHAPTER 69

"On the bright side, at least now we know you're not allergic to the sun," Trip said, as we rode the elevator down to the fifth floor.

"No, I'm just allergic to mean models," I said. "And possibly mayonnaise."

"So what's our best move here?"

"I'm hoping Kelsey won't be home. High-powered junior executive that she is. But if I'm wrong, you keep her busy while I excuse myself to use the bathroom and chat with the cleaning lady."

"Sounds like a plan," he said, as we exited the elevator on the fifth floor.

"She's down here," I said, leading the way. I was still wearing the same jeans and long-sleeved T-shirt I'd worn to the pool. But I'd lost the hat and scarves. And added a lot more concealer. At this rate, I figured, my face was more makeup than skin.

We'd packed a couple of leftover doughnuts into a little gift bag with some wax paper. It wasn't a condolence dish, but I figured it would at least get us through the door.

As we approached, I could hear what sounded like a

vacuum cleaner inside. I pasted a smile on my face, as Trip rapped on the door.

The vacuum cleaner quit. Silence.

Trip knocked again. The smile was beginning to hurt. Or maybe it was the sunburn.

I saw a shadow behind the peephole. Then the bolts turned, and the door opened slowly.

A petite middle-aged woman looked up at us. She wore a gray and white uniform dress with heavy stockings and spotless white nurse's shoes. Her black hair was pulled back into a low, practical bun.

"Lady not here now," she said slowly in heavily accented English. Then she looked at the floor.

Trip held up the gift bag with the doughnuts.

"We just wanted to drop this off," I said, pointing. "Can we come in?"

"The lady is not here now," she repeated.

"Should we warn her about the murderer?" I asked Trip. "You know, so she can look out for herself?"

Her eyes widened in alarm. Then she looked down again.

I handed her the bag. "Doughnuts. And they're not for Kelsey, they're for you. Let's go inside, I'll make us some coffee, and we can chat."

"I'm Alex Vlodnachek, by the way. And this is Trip Cabot. We're visiting my sister Annie, upstairs."

"Mia," she said simply.

"So how come you pretend not to speak English?" I said, once we'd clustered in Kelsey's kitchen. Unfortunately, her coffeemaker had more buttons and levers on it than Annie's.

"Let me do that," Mia said, with no trace of an accent. "It's what people expect. It's what they want. Half the time, they think I'm illegal."

"But you're not, clearly," I said. She spoke English better than I did.

"Hell no, my people are from California originally. Family's been here longer than most of the folks I work for. Look, is there really a murderer running around?"

"'Fraid so," I said. "But unless you were helping Leslie McQueen with her blackmail business, I doubt you're in any danger."

"Blackmail? So that was it," Mia said. "Knew she was into something shady. Just didn't know what."

"What was the tip-off?" Trip asked.

"She was so secretive. I mean, everyone is, to a certain extent. I understand it's a little unnerving to have someone come into your house and sift through your stuff, even when it's a pro you invited. It feels unnatural. Especially for new money. Old money, they're used to it. But with McQueen? Not a scrap of paper. Password protected everything. Big heavy cabinets with double locks. Lock boxes in strange places. The weird thing is, she was the same way with the other two places. And they weren't even hers."

"What other places?" I asked.

"She had a couple of other units in this building that she was selling for clients. You know, as an agent. Sometimes, if I finished her place early, she'd have me hightail it down there and give one of them a little TLC. Light dusting, vacuum, shine up the stainless in the kitchen—that sort of thing. Didn't take fifteen minutes, and she'd throw me some extra cash."

"Which units?"

"Well, there was one on the fourth floor. But she sold that to a young guy. That was just a month or so ago. The other place is on seven. Still for sale, as far as I know. Number 7112. Why?"

"I have a friend who's looking for a place," I said. True

enough. But I doubted Harkins and Daisy would relish high-rise condo life. No garden.

"So how did you meet Leslie McQueen?" Trip asked.

"My main gig. The woman there inherited a second home when some local relative died. Needed to sell it. So she called McQueen. One day, I'm there cleaning the kitchen and she passes me a note. In Spanish. With a fifty. Do I take side jobs and would I be interested in cleaning her place once a week?"

"I didn't know Leslie spoke Spanish," I said. Even dead, the woman was full of surprises.

"She didn't," Mia said, grinning. "Used some online translation thing. The note was a mess. But I got the gist. And the job. She paid good money, I'll give her that. Her little friend here? Not so much. First thing she tried to do was cut my fee. Not doing that."

"So why tell them you're illegal?" Trip asked.

"I never actually tell them anything," Mia said. "But when I got my first cleaning job, I sussed out it was what the woman wanted, so I just didn't correct her. When people hire a maid, they want a clean house, but they don't want anyone who's going to learn their secrets or gossip about them. At least, not to people they know. They'd hire a deaf-mute, if they could find one. I'm the next best thing. So, you know, give the people what they want."

"Do you have a lot of clients?" I asked. I was thinking my sister might need a new cleaning service. Or at least someone to clear out that linen closet.

"My main gig's a big house off Collins Avenue. She's nice. And I've been doing that one for over fifteen years. I just pick up a few extra jobs for spending money."

"Seems to be a hard way to make a living," I said, as she set up three cups and pulled out a plate for the doughnuts. "Why do you do it? Just between us."

"When I started this, I was a divorced single mom with two very bright little girls. And Collins Avenue? Great school system."

"So you could work and send your kids to a good school?"

Mia nodded. "Every morning, I'd get there before sunrise, and see them to the school bus. And every afternoon, they'd get off the bus and hang out with me until it was time to go home. They'd play in the yard or do their homework in one of the unused rooms. And there are a lot of unused rooms. Plus, when people don't think you speak English, they don't hesitate to talk business in front of you. And they don't mind if you dust their desk and happen to see their mail—especially those investment account statements."

"How does that help?" I asked.

"I see what does well and put my money there. Plus, her nibs is on the front end of every fashion trend that comes down the pike. She gives me and the kids the leftovers and the rest goes to charity. I've got the two best-dressed scholars on the East Coast and a collection of Prada bags I could retire on."

"We won't say a word," Trip promised.

"Doesn't matter. They're in college now. University of Maryland and Columbia. God help me, they both want to be journalists."

CHAPTER 70

"Let me guess, our next stop is the seventh floor?" Trip asked, as he pushed the elevator button.

"No, we're having dinner with the fam, then you're going back to your hotel."

"Used and dumped. The story of my life. But at least you're buying me dinner first. Just for the record, why am I being excluded?"

"You have a real job to worry about. I got myself into this mess, and I'm going to get myself out."

"No offense, Red, but you can use all the help you can get. And I'm not just talking sunscreen."

I shook my head. "If I get caught, I might be able to talk my way out of it. I'm a freelancer—no one cares. But you're an editor at a major metro daily. It'll be a scandal. We can't risk it. Besides, if I go down in flames, I'm gonna need someplace to live. And Nick's already developed a taste for life in Georgetown."

"Did he really say that?" Trip sounded genuinely touched.

"Loved the townhouse. Hated the commute."

"Oddly, I'm planning a tattoo using that exact phrase. You think the cops have been into the unit on seven yet?"

"That depends on how many people know about it. I'm guessing not many."

"OK, but if you see crime scene tape . . ."

"We give up and come home. Yes, Mom."

A few hours later, I met up with Gabby on the seventh floor.

"You got the gloves, sugar?" she drawled.

"Yup," I said, pulling them out of my purse. "Have you got the silver thingamabobbies?"

"You know it."

I closed the door behind us and turned the privacy lock. The living room was empty. Just a wide expanse of windows and gleaming espresso hardwood floors. I couldn't tell if the owner had moved out or if the place had never been occupied.

"It sure is clean," Gabby said with admiration.

"Leslie was repping it. And I'm hoping she might have been keeping a few things here, too."

"You think it's bugged?" she asked, mouthing the last word.

"Hope not," I whispered. "But maybe we get in and out quick, just to be on the safe side."

I walked into the kitchen. Not so much as a coffee-maker. I opened the refrigerator and freezer. Nothing.

I pulled open the cabinet drawers. I found some extra lightbulbs. And a roll of painter's tape.

In a lower cabinet, there was also a partially used can of paint.

"Find anything?" I called.

Gabby popped into the kitchen. "There's a queen-size bed in the master bedroom. Sheets, frilly little duvet and everything. And there's a big flat-screen on a little cabinet, with a little DVD player. But no DVDs. You think she used this for a crash pad? Or a love nest?"

"Or it could just be an attempt at staging. You know, to show you how big the room is."

"Weirdest thing I've ever seen. It's the only furniture in the whole place."

"Let's check the bathrooms," I said. "I'll take this one, you take the other one. Maybe there's something in there that might help."

Two minutes later, we met in the hallway.

"I didn't find a thing," I whispered.

"Me either."

I looked at the bed again. For some reason, it reminded me of Lucy. Then it dawned on me: the eyelet fabric of the coverlet resembled the dressy little collar she'd worn as the ring bearer at Daisy and Harkins's wedding. And her collar had had a little hidden pocket to conceal the rings.

I grabbed the coverlet, yanked it off the bed and started crawling around on it—running my hands over the outside seams. Then I worked my way toward the center, searching for anything inside the fabric. At one point, I looked up, and Gabby was staring at me gape-mouthed.

"It's not like she's going to yell at us for getting it dirty," I said softly. "And there could be something hidden in this. You want to give me a hand?"

But it took us only a few minutes of working together to determine that Leslie's duvet was just a duvet.

"What about between the mattress and the bedspring, sugar? That's a popular spot, too."

"OK, if we can tilt the mattress, I can hold it up while you look underneath."

Easier said than done. We struggled and, between the two of us, barely got the mattress at a forty-five-degree angle.

I was beginning to wish I'd taken Trip up on his offer. We could use a little more muscle right now.

"See anything?" I grunted, as I strained to keep it from falling on Gabby.

"Oh yeah, sugar," she whispered, waving two DVD cases in front of my face. "I think we hit the motherlode."

CHAPTER 71

"Well?" Trip demanded as we came through the door. "Pop the popcorn and pass out the candy, because we've got movies to watch," I crowed.

"I can't believe you found anything," he said.

"Actually, I didn't. Gabby did."

Gabby beamed. "There are certain places people hide stuff," she explained. "And under the mattress is a classic."

"It worked for me as a teenager," Nick said, ducking into the kitchen to grab a treat for Lucy, who was circling his legs.

"So where's Annie?" I asked. "And does anyone know how to work her DVD player? Or if she has a DVD player?"

"I do, and she does," Nick said. "But Annie's gone. The cops took her away."

"What!" I exclaimed.

"Relax, Red," Trip said, patting me on the back. "It was one detective, and he brought flowers. They just went down the street for coffee."

"Let me guess. Logan Alvarez?"

Nick nodded, grinning. "So what's tonight's feature?"

"More like a double feature," I said. "And I'm hoping it's called *Who Killed Leslie McQueen* and *Who Killed Leslie McQueen, Part Two*."

"The sequel is never as good as the original," Trip said.

"Word," Nick responded, as they slapped palms.

"So who's on it?" Nick asked. "Or do we have to guess?"

"No idea," I said. "We were kind of in a hurry to get out of there."

"Yeah, sugar, that place was creepy," Gabby agreed.

I pried open the case. The DVD was unmarked. Definitely a home-burn job. I flipped it over and saw *#3517* written on the back in heavy black pen.

Oh geez.

"This one is Geoffrey," I said, handing it off to Nick, who slipped it into the machine. "Of him or about him—I'm not sure. That's Leslie's system. She uses the unit numbers instead of names."

"Don't have to look too far for the psychology behind that one," Trip said.

"Behold, the master of technology!" Nick announced, hitting a button on the remote as Lucy planted herself in front of the screen.

Nothing happened.

"The master should have gotten a doctorate," I said. "The screen is blank. OK, now you're getting an error message."

"That's weird," he said. "Hang on, let me see what's wrong."

"Snack break!" I called. "Seriously, I wonder if Annie has any popcorn in that kitchen of hers."

"Movie popcorn with melted butter? Sugar, I could go for some of that."

Baba nodded as she appeared from the hallway, and the three of us headed out to the kitchen to see what we could scavenge.

That's when I heard a key, and Annie came bouncing through the door.

In a cool blue sundress and flats, with her long blond hair loose, she looked about eighteen. And she was smiling from ear to ear.

"Nick said you were hauled away by the cops," I said.

"Coffee with Logan. It was nice."

"Are you gonna see him again, sugar?" Gabby asked.

"He mentioned maybe catching a movie. But we might have to wait until he wraps up the whole Leslie McQueen thing. So, what have you guys been up to tonight?" she asked, alighting on a stool at the breakfast bar as we foraged through her kitchen for snack food.

"Alex broke into another condo and found more blackmail stuff," Nick called from the living room. "We were getting ready to watch the DVD, but this old-timey machine of yours isn't cooperating."

"Oh geez, what did you find?" Annie said, looking at me.

"No idea. The one DVD has Geoffrey's unit number on it. The other one, we haven't even opened yet."

"What if that had been playing when Logan brought me home? What if I'd let him come in?"

"Did he ask to come in?" Nick asked.

"They always ask to come in," I said. "Even if they tell you they just need to use the bathroom. Trust me, they don't need to use the bathroom."

I looked over at Baba. I was afraid she might be shocked. Instead, she nodded.

"But what if that thing had been playing?" Annie asked. "Whatever it is?"

"That, as Geoffrey says, would be bad," I said. "Very bad."

"OK, I think I've figured out what our problem is," Nick

shouted. "This is probably some kind of computer program. We need to put it into a computer."

"I have a DVD drive in my laptop," I hollered back.

"We have no way of knowing what's on there, Red," Trip warned. "What if it's a virus or some other little nasty?"

I looked over at Baba. She crossed herself.

"Gabby and I knocked ourselves out finding this thing. OK, Gabby found it, but I nearly gave myself a hernia holding up that mattress. I want to see what's on it."

I snatched two large bags of potato chips from the pantry and headed back to the living room. Gabby followed me with a jug of orange juice and a box of paper cups. Baba, with a stack of napkins, brought up the rear.

"You sure?" Nick asked.

I nodded.

He grabbed my laptop off the table, slipped the disc into the drive and hit a button.

This time, the screen jumped to life.

"*Shtow eta?*" Baba asked, leaning forward to get a better view of the screen.

"Two files," I said. "One is in a format I don't recognize. The other looks like an app. Something called Fun-Money."

Trip leaned over the screen and tilted his head. "I recognize this file extension. It's something programmers use."

"Translation for the rest of us mere mortals?" Annie asked.

"Think fashion sketch and finished garment," I said. "Only for an app."

"Nice," Annie said.

"Never heard of FunMoney," Nick said. "I wonder if your friend Geoffrey created it?"

"He's an accountant," Annie said. "Could it be an accounting app?"

"Only one way to find out," I said, pressing a few buttons. "Here goes nothing."

After about thirty seconds, a new icon popped up on my screen. I clicked on it.

A display in shades of blue, green, and turquoise filled the screen.

"Oh, sugar, that's pretty," Gabby said.

"The man does have a nice eye for design," Trip remarked.

I paged through a few screens. It had sections for checking, savings, credit cards, and budgeting. All in shades of blue and green, with little pops of pink, orange, and yellow. The colors of South Beach.

The way Geoffrey had it laid out, even I could navigate it. It really did look like fun.

"This is really cool," Nick said. "I wonder if he's going to market it."

"I wonder what the heck Leslie McQueen was doing with it?" I asked.

"The same thing she was doing with everything else," Annie said grimly. "She stole it."

"She put a keylogger in his computer," I said. "I remember the notation in her book."

"If that's the case, Red, she branched out from blackmail to industrial espionage," Trip said. "Would he kill to get it back?"

"It's possible he didn't even know she had it," I said. "If she swiped it and realized what she had, she might have decided to sell it. This was in her special, super-secret stash, after all."

"If it was a copy, he wouldn't have even known it was gone," Annie said.

"But if he discovered it, that might be a motive," Trip countered.

"Man, that board president of yours was some piece of work," Nick said. "So can we look at the other one?"

"Knock yourself out," I said, opening the case. "And the winner is . . . number 9002. Annie, that's your friend Quinn Whitmore."

"Computer or DVD player?" Nick asked.

"No idea. Try the DVD player first. Somehow, I don't see Quinn designing an app."

He popped the disc in the player.

Leslie and Quinn appeared on the screen, relaxing in deck chairs on a balcony. Leslie's. I recognized it—and the view—from the night of the party.

Both he and she cradled drinks in their hands—what looked like tumblers of scotch. Quinn was smoking a cigar.

"Wow, an action flick in living black and white," Nick said.

"That almost looks like infrared film," Trip said, squinting at the screen.

"Shhhh! I can't hear it!" I complained.

"Turn it up," Annie said, reaching for the remote.

"So how much did you take them for this time?" Leslie asked.

Quinn chuckled. *"A little over fifteen grand. Chump change."*

"They wouldn't think that if they knew how you did it," she teased.

"You ran the table," he said lightly.

"Good thing I didn't win. And you're so skilled, I had no idea what you were doing until tonight. That takes brains. And talent."

"Eh, you pick up a few tricks over the years," he said modestly.

"I could never keep it all straight," Leslie said.

"It's all I can do to concentrate on the cards in my hand."

"Takes practice," Quinn said, puffing on the stogie. "You add one element at a time, until you master it. Then you add something else. First you pick up how to count cards. Then you learn to deal the right way. Throw the right cards to the right people. Now you're actually controlling the game. Then you add a little UV ink, and you're off to the races."

"Well, I think it's brilliant," she gushed.

"Most important part is picking the right players. Smart enough that they've got some cash to burn. Not smart enough to question why they don't win more."

"See? That's why you're so good at this."

"Have to lose once in a while, too," he said. "They're not the brightest bulbs on the tree, but even this bunch would get suspicious if I won all the time. You play the game, but you can't get greedy. That's the real secret. Poker is all about knowing your opponent. Reading people."

The clip cut off. We all sat there in stunned silence.

"Looks like there's at least one person old Quinn didn't read as well as he thought," I said. "Leslie bugged her own balcony and got him on tape admitting to cheating at cards."

"Yeah, but would he really kill over that?" Nick asked.

"Depends on who he took at that table," I countered.

"That one is bad," Baba said, crossing her arms over her chest. "Bad man."

"I don't remember Quinn's name on our electrical experts list," Trip said.

"It wasn't," I said. "And he's one of the few. He actually owned a very successful advertising firm. From what I gather, they sold everything from ketchup to political candidates."

"The man's got the morals of an alley cat," Annie fumed. "But I can't see him getting his hands dirty rewiring an elevator."

"Yeah, unfortunately I'm with you on that one," I said.

"He's a puppet master," Nick said, miming dancing marionette strings.

"Exactly!" I agreed.

"OK, kids, so what do we do now?" Trip asked, stretching and stifling a yawn. "Two more good candidates. And we can't exactly take this lead to the police. Considering how we got it."

"I say we follow Nick's advice and sleep on it," I said.

"That, Red, is the best idea I've heard all day."

CHAPTER 72

The next morning, I woke up at three a.m.. Try as I might, I couldn't go back to sleep.

Not even with Annie snoring softly beside me.

Yes, even supermodels snore. At least, they do if they're Vlodnacheks.

The three-sided puzzle of Leslie, Geoffrey, and Quinn was nagging at the back of my brain. And I knew the only way to solve it was to usher it to the front of my brain. And serve it plenty of coffee.

I padded out to Annie's kitchen. Luckily, I'd watched my sister use her complicated. coffee contraption often enough that I'd actually learned how to work it. Sort of.

Take that, Nick.

As I sat there, waiting for my caffeine infusion, I pondered the facts. But the only conclusion I reached was that I needed chocolate in my coffee.

A quick search of Annie's cupboards revealed a box of Ghirardelli cocoa. I ripped open one of the little envelopes and poured the contents into my mug. Followed by a second one. I added steaming hot coffee, a little cold milk, and took a long, happy sip.

Standing there, looking out at the cloudless moonlit sky and the ocean beyond, I had an idea. I considered the personalities involved, drained my cup, and fixed a second one. As I drank it, I could feel the chocolate and caffeine kick in. I reviewed the details again, turning it over in my brain, looking at the question—and my solution—from different angles.

Bottom line: I'd need a little more information.

And a lot of help.

CHAPTER 73

When Nick stumbled out to the kitchen a few hours later—with Lucy bouncing at his heels—I was dressed, brushed, combed, and ready to go. I was even wearing makeup.

"Is this one of the signs of the Apocalypse?" he asked, looking first at me, then at the pot of coffee.

"I'll take Lucy for her walk this morning," I said. "I figured I'd make a doughnut run, too."

"Knock yourself out," he said, scratching his head. "I'd go back to bed, but I think I must still be dreaming. In case I'm not, I'd like a couple of those chocolate crullers."

After a caffeine-fueled walk, and a stop at the doughnut shop, I had one more errand to run: a visit to the pool deck.

When Lucy and I strolled in, I spotted Ernie and Stan by the pool.

"Hey, how's the little pup this morning?" Stan asked.

"She loves this place," I said, as Lucy busily sniffed Stan's knees, and allowed him to scratch behind her ear.

"How's Ethel doing?" I asked, putting one of the boxes

of doughnuts on the table and popping the lid. "Fresh out of the oven."

"Nice," Ernie said, reaching to take one. "She's actually doing pretty good. I think she's shared more a' the details with Marilyn. But it seems like the cops believe her."

Stan nodded, smiling as Lucy licked his hand. "And they can't pin anything on Mrs. Pickles. So she won't have a record, either."

That, I was very glad to hear. Especially since both Lucy and I knew who the real culprit was.

"Cops don't seem to be any closer to solving it, though," Ernie said.

I felt a stab of guilt. They probably would have, if I hadn't been running around shredding evidence. But maybe I could make it up to them. Karmically speaking.

I finally asked the question I'd come to ask.

Ernie's bushy eyebrows went up. "Why d'ya wanna know that?" he challenged, scooping a second doughnut out of the box.

"Just curious. Trip asked me the other day. I had no idea, but I told him I knew who would."

"Yeah, right," Ernie said, smiling. "I look like a mushroom to you?"

"Even trade. You tell me now. And I give you a front row seat in a couple hours when this whole thing comes together."

"I'd kinda like to see that," Stan said. "Can I bring a date?"

"The more the merrier."

Ernie looked skeptical. But he answered my question. And the next two that followed it.

"OK, gentlemen, that's everything I need," I said, grabbing Lucy's leash and giving them a little salute. "Let's meet back here at noon."

I prayed I hadn't just shot myself in the foot.

CHAPTER 74

I presented my plan—in all its gory detail—to the rest of the crew over doughnuts and coffee that morning.

"It sounds good now," Nick said. "But what do you do if you're wrong?"

"Same thing I always do. Punt."

"That would give your face time to heal," he said. "Although it looks a lot better this morning. Almost human."

Thanks to some home-brewed concoction of Annie's, I'd gone from bright red to pleasantly pink. And the peeling was easing up, too.

I looked over at Baba. She nodded. "*Da*, I come," she said simply.

I was already seeing signs that she might be missing Baltimore. To compensate for the air-conditioning, she'd topped off today's South Beach ensemble with a heavy black cardigan and added calf-high sweat socks under her pastel blue clam-diggers.

Classic Baba.

Trip nodded, dropping a doughnut onto his plate and licking the icing from his fingers. "I think it's a rather elegant solution. Let the punishment fit the crime."

"Annie, it's your home and you have to live here after we leave. What do you think?"

She paused to swallow a mouthful of cinnamon doughnut. "Definitely," she said. "Somehow, it just feels right."

Good thing I'd stocked up on doughnuts.

CHAPTER 75

I checked the peephole before I opened the door. I'd learned my lesson.

Geoffrey blinked repeatedly. As if it was the first time he'd seen the sun in a while. And looking at his pale but perfect complexion, I could believe it.

Luckily, he didn't have someone spiking his sunblock with mayo.

"Come on in," I said. "We've got doughnuts and coffee. And there are a few people here you haven't met."

As I introduced him, he gave a nervous wave and grimaced. Or it could have been a smile. It was hard to tell.

Nick handed him a cup of black coffee. "Cream and sugar on the table in front of you. And the chocolate doughnuts are first-rate."

Geoffrey lurched forward, considered the box carefully and finally selected a plain cake doughnut.

He held it in his hand, studying it as if it was a diamond. "Did you know that the acceptable number of rodent droppings in a pound of industrial flour is four?"

"Good to know," Nick said.

"Tell us about FunMoney," I said, finally.

He dropped the doughnut and seemed to fold in on himself. "You know that I did it," he whispered.

Wait, what?

So much for my gut instinct. I struggled to keep my poker face. "We do," I said, nodding encouragingly.

"I didn't mean to," he said softly. "It was an accident. She was so angry. So angry."

"So tell me," I said.

He shook his head.

"We've all seen the app," I coaxed. "It's beautiful. I'm lousy with numbers, but it actually made me want to draft a budget. It was fun."

He smiled and seemed to perk up a bit. "That's the idea. Anybody can design a budgeting program that's complicated. It's a complicated subject. But I wanted to invent one that made it easy. For people just starting out. For older people who aren't really good with computers. And for people who are too busy to learn another spreadsheet program."

"I was really impressed with the design, too," Annie said. "You created something really gorgeous."

Geoffrey's pasty cheeks went pink. As a redhead, I could empathize.

"I wanted it to be useful and beautiful," he said. "That would make it special."

"It must have taken you forever to design it," I said.

He nodded. "Since college. But I liked working on it. It was my hobby. I'd get an idea, and it would go into the program. It's not really ready yet. But I wanted to beta test it."

"So what happened with Leslie?"

"She's in business. She sells real estate. Sold real estate. So I told her all about it. I asked her if she wanted to try it. But she said she wasn't much of a computer person. I tried to explain that was the whole point of FunMoney. A computer program for people who hate computer programs. Or numbers. But she said no."

"So you got angry?" Nick asked.

"Oh no," Geoffrey said, looking startled. "That's what everyone says. People say no to me a lot."

"It's a visual thing," I said. "You have to see the app to really get it."

"Exactly," he said, nodding.

"But then Leslie got her hands on the program," I said.

"She stole it," he said, looking like a kid who'd just dropped his ice cream cone. "Took it right out of my computer. And she wiped my hard drive."

"You didn't have a backup?" Trip asked. "A cloud account?"

"The cloud's not secure," Geoffrey said. "It's just another server. Well, lots of servers. No, I had a disc. I kept it next to my computer. She took it."

"How did you know it was Leslie?" I asked, holding my breath.

"She told me," he said, as though it were the most obvious thing in the world.

"And that's how she got your vote for her little experiment—firing the management association and everything?" I asked.

"No," he said. "I thought that was a good idea. We were paying them. The management company. She was going to do it for free. Free is better."

In mathematical theory, free was better. In the real world, free usually cost more.

"So why did she tell you she stole it?" I asked him gently.

"She wanted something," he said, blanching. "Something bad. I didn't know it was bad. But it was."

"What did she want?"

The room was silent. Not a sound. Not so much as the rustle of the wax paper in the doughnut box.

Even Lucy, settled on the floor next to Nick, seemed riveted.

"She wanted to know how to work the elevator."

Now we were getting somewhere. But unpacking Geoffrey was like defusing a bomb. Slow and steady, no sudden movements.

"To do what exactly?" Trip said quietly.

Geoffrey looked at him and blinked. But I could tell that his mind—his memory—was somewhere else. "I didn't know it then. I know now. She wanted to hurt someone."

"Who?" I asked.

He shook his head vigorously. "Don't know. Never found out."

This was excruciating. I felt like I was torturing a puppy.

Annie reached out and patted his hand, the way a mother might. Not our mother, mind you.

"It's OK," she said in a soothing voice. "Everybody in this room is on your side. Just tell us how it happened."

Geoffrey nodded and swallowed. More like a gulping motion. If I didn't know he hadn't touched that doughnut, I'd have sworn it was riding his Adam's apple.

He sighed. "One evening, I went to play around with FunMoney and it was gone. Just all gone. And the disc. I thought I'd lost it. Or accidentally deleted it. And that was it. All that work. Gone. But a couple of days later, Leslie saw me at the mailboxes. She told me she'd erased it. And she had my disc. I didn't believe her. But she showed it to me. And she said she'd give it back if I just did her a favor. But if I didn't, she'd erase the disc, too."

I nodded and looked at Annie. She smiled at Geoffrey.

He took a deep breath. "I said I'd help her," he said quietly. "She asked me to stop by that night. After her party. Really late. When I did, she told me she wanted to send the elevator car away. To the top floor – and make it stay there. But if someone pressed the button, the doors would still open like normal. Even though the car wasn't there. She'd read about it."

"Did she say why?" I asked.

"She wanted to go inside the shaft. And climb on the rungs up the wall. And take a selfie. I told her that only the technicians can go in there. It's dangerous."

"Not what she wanted to hear, was it?" Annie said.

Geoffrey shook his head. "'It's the price of your little game, Geoffrey,'" he said, doing an eerie impression of Leslie McQueen's voice. "'It's the price of your little game.'"

"I told her it's not a game, it's an app. Anyway, I wanted it back. So she let me into the elevator closet. And I did it. The closet's on the top floor. That's where all the machinery has to be. After, we walked down to the ninth floor, just to check. And it was exactly like she wanted. She pushed the button, the door opened. But the car wasn't there. The car stayed up on ten. She didn't know it, but I'd locked all the other doors. Everything except nine. So they wouldn't open. So no one would get hurt."

"So what happened with Leslie?" I asked.

"She was really excited. And happy. She was jumping up and down and clapping. I thought she'd want to climb in and take her selfie. So I told her I wanted my disc. But she said we weren't done yet. There was one more thing. Now that I'd proven I could do it, she wanted me to show her how. So she could do it herself."

He shook his head. "That's when I knew. She didn't want to take a picture or climb the ladder. She wanted to hurt someone. I said no."

Geoffrey sighed. He looked like he was close to tears.

"She grabbed my wrist and twisted it. I just needed to get away . . ."

Annie patted his shoulder. "It's OK, baby. It's OK."

"She started hitting me," he said, so softly I had to lean in just to hear him. "With her fists. She wouldn't stop. And yelling. With her face this close," he said, holding his fingers about two inches apart. "It was bad. She just wouldn't stop. So I put my fingers in my ears and dropped to the ground."

What?

"Stop, drop, and roll," Geoffrey said, looking vaguely relieved. "It's supposed to be for fires. But it works for other things, too."

"Then what happened?" I asked.

"I took off," he said sheepishly. "I know you're supposed to stand up to bullies. Everyone says that. But it doesn't work. Not really. So I left. But when I got home, I remembered the elevator. I didn't want anyone getting hurt. I had to fix it. So I went back to the tenth floor. The closet was still unlocked. And I reset it. Then I locked it up and went home."

"So Leslie was alive when you left the ninth floor," I confirmed.

"Alive and angry," he said. "Not good."

"The police didn't find any fingerprints on the elevator closet," Annie said.

"Of course not," Geoffrey said, as though we were children. "With electricity, you have to wear gloves."

"So why did you say you killed her?" I asked him, as we all digested the new information.

"She fell because of me," Geoffrey said simply. "Because I opened the door. I didn't stand up to her. I ran away. I caused the accident."

"You didn't cause it," I said. "She didn't fall. And I think you can help me prove it. But, first things first. Here's FunMoney."

I handed him the disc. And I swear his face lit up like a kid's on Christmas morning.

CHAPTER 76

True to their word, Ernie, Stan, and the gang were sitting around the pool at high noon. Stan had, indeed, brought a date. And, as I suspected, it was Ethel.

Everyone had a cocktail and they seemed to be in high spirits. Literally.

"How's Mrs. Pickles?" I asked.

"Oh, honey, she's her happy, smiley little self. But it's way too hot out here for her today. So I left her upstairs watching the soaps."

We did the same thing with Lucy. Minus the soaps. The pup was more of a Discovery Channel fan.

"Alex, over here," Trip called from a table across the patio.

"Gotta go," I whispered. "Wish me luck."

Ethel held up both hands with her fingers crossed.

"Everything ready?" I asked Trip, approaching the table.

"All systems go," he said. "And Gabby, Nick, Baba, and I will be right behind you at the next table. Just in case."

"Anyone hear from Annie?" I asked.

"Yup, all set on that end," Nick said.

I pulled out my laptop and typed in a familiar URL, then flipped through a few pages until I found what I needed.

"You might want this, sugar," Gabby said, leaning over as she handed me the cord.

"And here comes the guest of honor, right on time," Trip said under his breath.

"I don't know whether to hope he's been drinking or hope he hasn't," I confessed.

"Either way, I'm betting five bucks someone goes in that pool," Nick said.

"If this heat keeps up, it's gonna be me," I said.

Baba, I noticed, had lost the black sweater. But the sweat socks remained. And she was packing the black leather bag. Battle-ready Baba.

"Mr. Whitmore," I said, standing as he strolled over. "Thanks for meeting me on such short notice."

"Call me Quinn," he said genially. "One of the advantages of being retired. Less formality. So what was it you wanted to talk about?"

"Leslie McQueen," I said, settling in my seat. "I know you two were friends. So this whole thing can't have been easy. And now that the police are about to arrest her murderer, I thought you might want to hear the news from a friendly face."

"Well, that is something," he said. "Had no idea. About damned time, though."

I nodded. "It took a bit of doing. To piece together what happened the night she was killed. Leslie was a top real estate agent. But what most people don't know is that she was starting a second career in blackmail."

"I don't follow," he said flatly. "But I'd be very careful if I were you."

"Oh, that's OK. I know you weren't in on it. The day she died, Leslie was testing a little theory. She'd heard it was possible to rig an elevator so the doors opened even if the car wasn't there. And I admit, I don't know exactly why this little factoid was important to her. But I do know that Leslie liked to plan ahead. Maybe she was thinking of faking her own death. Maybe she felt threatened and wanted to have this in her back pocket. Who knows? But the bottom line is, she needed to do a dry run. Now, you might not know this, but the elevator controls are on the tenth floor. So Leslie goes up there, does her bit—and wants to see if it works. She walks down a flight of stairs and rings for the elevator. And—presto—the doors open, but there's nothing there. Her plan is a success.

Quinn Whitmore pushed away from the table and crossed his legs. I was afraid he was going to leave. So I amped up my smile and just kept talking.

"Now this is the good part. While she's up there on the ninth floor, who should open his door, but her old friend and poker buddy. Were you still up, or did you hear all the commotion in the hallway?"

"I would be very careful about where you're going next, young lady," he said evenly. "I may be a retired old duffer. But I'm a retired old duffer with money and some very good lawyers."

"So you walk in on the perfect scene. Leslie's there. The elevator door is open. The car is missing. And with one little shove, your troubles are over. Done and dusted, as a friend of mine likes to say."

"What is this, a shakedown?" he growled.

He stood suddenly, looming over me. His face was red. And it wasn't from the sun. "Are you trying to blackmail me, you little pisher?"

Simultaneously, I caught movement, out of the corner of my eye. Nick. Gearing up for combat. I shook my head, ever so slightly.

"No, just the opposite," I said conversationally. "Black-mailers charge money. I'm doing this for free. And black-mailers keep secrets. I say, 'tell the world.'"

I pressed the button on my laptop. And crossed my fingers.

The big screen in the bar came to life. As did a giant fifty-inch we'd set up on the other side of the pool. The video was identical. Two figures in the moonlight. Recognizable even on infrared film.

As the clip played, Quinn Whitmore seemed to deflate. Until he was sitting in his chair again, all but doubled over.

"As a special bonus, I had someone email it to the local police department and upload it onto YouTube," I said, turning the screen so he could see it. "And, hey, look at this: You've already gotten ten thousand likes."

Thanks to Geoffrey's computer magic, both the email and the upload were also anonymous.

"You have no idea what you've done," Whitmore rasped. "Not a damned clue."

"You mean I don't know that a couple of the guys in your regular poker game have more than a few connections on the wrong side of the law? And that they're not going to take too kindly to Leslie's little video tape? That's called motive, by the way."

"Go to hell," Whitmore snarled, rising from the table. Then, as he turned, he froze.

I looked across the deck, and one of the retirees was giving him the big wave.

"Who's that?" I leaned over and whispered to Trip.

"One of the poker buddies," my best friend hissed. "I think Ernie did a little crowd salting of his own."

Quinn Whitmore sank back into his chair.

"First you killed Leslie McQueen," I continued. "Then you sat back, smiled, and waited for the police to dismiss it as an accident. Or a suicide. Or, failing that, to blame someone else. Now, I'll let you in on a little secret. There's a detective in the lobby. His name is Logan Alvarez. And if you tell him what you did, he might be willing to protect you. You know, in a nice safe prison cell."

Whitmore stared at me with pure contempt. Then he rose out of his seat and walked across the pool deck with the look of a man going to his own execution.

But, to be fair, I don't have his people-reading skills.

As he marched through the door toward the lobby, everyone broke into wild applause. Over the hooting and hollering, I looked over and saw Ethel Plunkett pumping her fist.

CHAPTER 77

The next morning, Nick and I raced around the penthouse like a couple of crazy people stoked on caffeine. Which we were.

"Three booties," Nick said. "I'm looking at three booties. And I'm not leaving here until I have all four."

"Hey, a set of booties is a lot less expensive than another ticket if you miss the train. But if you happen to find a white T-shirt with a chocolate stain, let me know."

"Don't you have several of those already?" Nick said, checking behind the couch cushions. "Complete with the chocolate stains?"

"Yes, but this one's my favorite."

Meanwhile, Baba was sitting on the sofa next to her suitcase. She had on her normal black sweater/ankle-skirt traveling combo. But in a nod to South Beach, she'd paired it with one of the rainbow-colored Lilly Pulitzer blouses and a straw hat. And she was packing two purses: one light straw, one black leather.

Ready-for-anything Baba.

"Hey, where's Lucy?" I asked, suddenly realizing the

pup was missing again. I pictured another stop at Diamond Jack's to collect her before we left town.

"Gabby took her for one last run on the beach," Nick said. "They're on their way. Where's Trip?"

"Probably at the train station, wondering where the heck we are. He had to turn in his rental car."

"Hey, sugar, look who the cat dragged in," Gabby drawled, strolling through the front door with Trip and Lucy.

"I thought you were meeting us at the station?" I asked.

"I overslept," Trip said. "I think your friend Marilyn spiked the punch."

"Yeah, that was some party."

"Is Annie coming with us?" my best friend asked.

"Got it!" Nick yelled, holding up a little blue bootie. "She hid it under the sofa. Hey, is this your T-shirt? And what are the Doggles doing under here?"

Lucy looked up innocently at Gabby, who rubbed the pup's velvety red flanks. "I know, sweetie, it's a stress thing. You're absolutely fine."

Annie walked into the living room, and I detected a decided absence of luggage. But then, with homes all over the globe, she tended to travel light.

"Are you ready?" I asked.

She smiled broadly. "I think I'm going to follow along in a couple of days. I have a couple of things to catch up on here."

"Is one of them named Logan Alvarez?" I teased.

"Maybe," she said lightly. "It's kind of scary, but I like him. Really like him."

"I know the feeling," I said. "Sort of like you're at the top of a roller coaster, looking straight down."

"Exactly," she agreed.

Baba, standing next to us, nodded seriously. She reached up, took Annie's face in her two strong hands, and kissed her on the tip of the nose. "You are good girl," she proclaimed. "So good."

Annie wrapped her in a hug, and I piled on.

"I hate to break up the love, girls, but that train won't wait," Trip said. "By the way, who's driving to the station?"

"I hope I am," a deep voice behind us said politely.

I turned, and Logan Alvarez was standing in the doorway.

This time, instead of the suit, he was wearing jeans and a dark blue dress shirt. "I might be able to hit the speed limit, but I can't use the siren."

He looked at Annie, and she looked at him. The rest of us might as well have been invisible.

I turned to say goodbye to Gabby, but she'd vanished. I noticed she tended to do that whenever the police showed up.

Hopefully, I'd see her again soon.

A few minutes later, we were packed into Logan's sedan, making haste for the train station. And the guy wasn't kidding about his driving skills. He hit the top of the speed limit for every stretch of road, without ever going over. But, presented with the opportunity of finally getting some time alone with Annie, I'm guessing he was pretty motivated, too.

"That's Lucy's favorite dog beach," I said, frantically pointing to a turn-off sign ahead. "I need a quick photo for my travel story."

"Ten-four," Logan said. "But it's gonna have to be fast. I haven't got the juice to flag down a train."

He made a neat turn, cruised straight through the parking lot, and stopped just short of the sand.

Everybody piled out of the car and ran toward the water.

"OK, line up and squeeze together," I said, holding up my phone.

"Hang on," Nick said, as he pulled the Doggles out of his pocket and put them on Lucy. He moved her out front and knelt beside her. She cocked her head and grinned.

"May I?" Logan asked, pointing to my phone.

"That would be great," I said, handing it off.

I crouched down on the other side of Lucy. Trip stood behind me. Beside him, Baba had one hand on her hat, as she stared up at Annie in wonder. And my sister was incandescent, beaming into the camera. Or, more accurately, the guy behind it.

Wouldn't you know, that was the photo that made the front page of the travel section a week later. Under the headline "Lucy's Summer Vacation."

ACKNOWLEDGMENTS

A very big thank you to my editor, Alicia Condon. You truly "get" the Vlodnacheks. I also need to thank the rest of the wonderful team at Kensington Books. A big thank you to editorial assistant Elizabeth Trout, and special shout-outs to copy editor Victoria Groshong, production editor Rebecca Cremonese, and art director Lou Malcangi. You guys made this into a real book! Also, a grateful thank you to cover artist Michelle Grant—you always make Alex look good! Many thanks to publicist Larissa Ackerman. Last, but definitely not least: a big hug to my agent, Erin Niumata, of Folio Literary Management, who first noticed, read, and believed in *Confessions of a Red Herring*. You helped unleash the Vlodnacheks on the world!

Read on for a preview of
FLAME RED
the next Alex Vlodnachek adventure.

Alex Vlodnachek is in the hot seat again. This time, she has a century-old mystery, a reclusive billionaire, a secret tunnel, and a dead body to thank. But when a photojournalist flame hits town—and checks in to the neighborhood B&B—that really turns up the heat . . .

I was fine until they discovered the body.

After a couple of months of icy silence, Ian Sterling and I had recently reached a neighborly detente. By phone.

Fresh off a Miami vacation—that turned out to be anything but relaxing—I hadn't yet visited his B&B. To be fair, he hadn't shown up at my house either.

Frankly, I think each of us was waiting for the other to make the first move. So neither one of us did.

Nick thought we were both nuts. But my brother wasn't the one who found a bug planted in his bedroom. Long story.

Imagine my surprise when I heard a gentle knock on the door one afternoon, glanced through the peephole, and spotted Ian on the front porch.

I looked down at Lucy. The pup looked up at me. "What do you think?" I whispered.

She appeared perplexed.

I debated not answering the door. But my car was in the driveway. And, more important, my brother was baking peach pies in Ian's kitchen. If something had happened to Nick, I needed to know.

On the bright side, my sunburn was pretty much gone, and my face had stopped peeling. So at least I looked fairly normal.

I opened the door a sliver. Lucy stuck her snout through the crack and sniffed the air.

"Hullo," he said, in his clipped British accent. Spotting Lucy, his face relaxed into a smile. "I was wondering if I might speak with you a moment. It's a bit of a ticklish situation."

"Is Nick all right?"

Ian looked puzzled. Clearly, whatever it was didn't involve my brother. "He's fine. No worries there."

He hesitated.

I pulled Lucy back by the collar. The house was a wreck. And no, I still hadn't quite forgiven him for planting that bug.

Call me crazy, but I'd pictured our first outing taking place on neutral ground. Somewhere with nice lighting. And me wearing something besides worn jeans and my last semi-clean T-shirt. A restaurant. A coffee shop. The post office.

My own home? Especially when it looked like an army had just marched through? No dice.

But Lucy had her own plans. She wanted to go out and play.

"Could we sit on the porch?" he asked. "I have to tell you something, and there's no good way to say it."

"Is everyone OK? Alistair? Daisy? Harkins?" I loved Ian's family like my own. And my tiff with him didn't involve the rest of the clan. Even at the height of our cold war, I'd watched baby Alistair when Daisy and Harkins needed a sitter.

"Everyone's very well, thank you. Shipshape, in fact."

I gestured at the plastic lawn chairs and stepped outside,

as Lucy trampled my feet racing ahead. Then I closed the door firmly behind me. If Ian was expecting a tea party today, he'd come to the wrong house.

Lucy tore around the lamppost at top speed, like a young filly. Now in her canine adolescence, her legs were growing longer and stronger. And she was getting faster. She raced around the side of the house.

I expected she'd be gone for a few minutes. The pup liked her privacy.

Ian settled into one of the faded yellow chairs. "As you may or may not know, I'm having some renovations done at the inn. Nothing that impacts the guests or the kitchen. But I'd wanted to finish out some of the basement areas, so that we could make use of the space for storage."

Nick had told me as much. But I wasn't going to sell him out to Ian. I said nothing.

"While they were examining one of the walls, the workmen discovered a tunnel."

My eyebrows shot up, and Ian paused. Nick had said nothing about a tunnel.

"We found it just this morning, in fact," Ian added. "We were exploring it, to see how far and where it went. And, I'm afraid, that's when we found it." He stopped.

"It?" I asked.

"A body," he said. "Almost at the end of the tunnel. Very near a door of some kind."

"Ian, that's awful!" I blurted. "Is it . . . ?"

He shook his head quickly.

What neither of us said aloud: Three particularly nasty characters had disappeared from the B&B about two months ago. None had ever been seen again. I knew at least two of them were dead. I'd found their bodies. Before they disappeared again.

Ian had sworn he didn't know their final resting place. But I had my doubts.

It was part of the reason I still didn't quite trust him.

Out in the yard, Lucy reappeared, refreshed. She bounded up the steps and threw herself at Ian's feet. He grinned and scratched her left ear. She thumped her tail in bliss and rolled over, exposing her fluffy white belly.

I struggled not to smile.

Ian looked at me. Willing my face blank, I waited for him to continue.

He folded his hands in his lap. "This appears to be a woman," he said slowly. "From the clothing. The rest is . . . well, bones."

This news would ricochet around our small-town-slash-D.C.-bedroom-community like a bullet. I wondered what kind of reaction he'd get from our patrician, pain-in-the-association neighbor, Lydia Stewart. She had at least ten years on (and a serious case of the hots for) Mr. Ian Sterling. As head of the neighborhood homeowners group, she was also a stickler for community rules and regs. And a dead body probably wouldn't help property values.

Still, when love-sick Lydia heard about the corpse, my money was on her showing up with a shovel and a can-do attitude.

"The builders actually stumbled upon it," Ian continued. "Almost literally. I'll alert the proper authorities, of course. But I felt it was only cricket to tell you first. A bit of a heads-up, so to speak."

That phone call would bring a swarm of cop cars, a crime scene van or two, and—last but not least—a hearse from the coroner's office. Along with a few news crews. And every neighbor within walking distance. The town gossip mill would ratchet into overdrive.

Not exactly a good ad for his pricey B&B.

Still, with Nick operating—temporarily—out of the inn's kitchen, it was genuinely kind of the guy to let me know. At least I wouldn't see the ruckus and assume the worst.

"Well, thanks for cluing me in," I said, standing. "I'd love to hear what the police discover."

Oddly, Ian didn't budge from his seat. "You need to sit down," he said softly.

I started to protest. The look on his face stopped me. His blue eyes were dark. But his expression wasn't anger. It was concern. I sank back into the chair, tendrils of dread wrapping around my stomach.

"The tunnel?" Ian started. "It leads to your house. Living room or kitchen would be my best guess. The body is on your property."